Yearning

The Dennamore Scrolls: Book One

What Reviewers Say About Gun Brooke's Work

Treason

"The adventure was edge-of-your-seat levels of gripping and exciting…I really enjoyed this final addition to the Exodus series and particularly liked the ending. As always it was a very well written book."—Melina Bickard, Librarian, Waterloo Library (UK)

Insult to Injury

"This novel tugged at my heart all the way, much the same way as *Coffee Sonata*. It's a story of new beginnings, of rediscovering oneself, of trusting again (both others and oneself)."—*Jude in the Stars*

"If you love a good, slow-burn romantic novel, then grab this book."—*Rainbow Reflections*

"[A] light romance that left me with just the right amount of 'aw shucks' at the end."—*C-Spot Reviews*

"I was glad to see a disabled lead for a change, and I enjoyed the author's style—the book was written in the first person alternating between the main characters and I felt that gave me more insight into each character and their motivations."—Melina Bickard, Librarian, Waterloo Library (UK)

Wayworn Lovers

"*Wayworn Lovers* is a super dramatic, angsty read, very much in line with Brooke's other contemporary romances. …I'm definitely in the 'love them' camp."—*Lesbian Review*

Thorns of the Past

"What I really liked from the offset is that Brooke steered clear of the typical butch PI with femme damsel in distress trope. Both main characters are what I would call ordinary women—they both wear suits for work, they both dress down in sweatpants and sweatshirts in the evening. As a result, I instantly found it a lot easier to relate, and connect with both. Each of their pasts hold dreadful memories and pain, and the passages where they opened up to each other about those events were very moving."—*Rainbow Reviews*

"I loved the romance between Darcy and Sabrina and the story really carried it well, with each of them learning that they have a safe haven with the other."—*Lesbian Review*

Escape: Exodus Book Three

"I've been a keen follower of the Exodus series for a while now and I was looking forward to the latest installment. It didn't disappoint. The action was edge-of-your-seat thrilling, especially towards the end, with several threats facing the Exodus mission. Some very intriguing subplots were introduced, and I look forward to reading more about these in the next book."—Melina Bickard, Librarian, Waterloo Library, London (UK)

Pathfinder

"I love Gun Brooke. She has successfully merged two of my reading loves: lesfic and sci-fi."—*Inked Rainbow Reads*

Soul Unique

"This is the first book that Gun Brooke has written in a first person perspective, and that was 100% the correct choice. She avoids the pitfalls of trying to tell a story about living with an autism spectrum disorder that she's never experienced, instead making it the story of someone who falls in love with a person living with Asperger's. ...*Soul Unique* is her best. It was an ambitious project that turned out beautifully. I highly recommend it."—*Lesbian Review*

"Yet another success from Gun Brooke. The premise is interesting, the leads are likeable and the supporting characters are well-developed. The first person narrative works well, and I really enjoyed reading about a character with Asperger's."—Melina Bickard, Librarian, Waterloo Library (London)

Advance: Exodus Book One

"*Advance* is an exciting space adventure, hopeful even through times of darkness. The romance and action are balanced perfectly, interesting the audience as much in the fleet's mission as in Dael and Spinner's romance. I'm looking forward to the next book in the series!"—*All Our Worlds: Diverse Fantastic Fiction*

The Blush Factor

"Gun Brooke captures very well the two different 'worlds' the two main characters live in and folds this setting neatly into the story. So, if you are looking for a well-edited, multi-layered romance with engaging characters this is a great read and maybe a re-read for those days when comfort food is a must."—*Lesbians on the Loose*

"That was fantastic. It's so sweet and romantic. Both women had their own 'demons' and they didn't let anyone be close to them. But from the moment they met each other everything felt so natural between them. Their love became so strong in a short time. Addie's thoughts threatened her relationship with Ellie but with her sister's help she managed to avoid a real catastrophe..." —*Nana's Book Reviews*

The Supreme Constellations Series

"*Protector of the Realm* has it all; sabotage, corruption, erotic love and exhilarating space fights. Gun Brooke's second novel is forceful with a winning combination of solid characters and a brilliant plot. The book exemplifies her growth as inventive storyteller and is sure to garner multiple awards in the coming year."—*Just About Write*

"[*Protector of the Realm*] is first and foremost a romance, and whilst it has action and adventure, it is the romance that drives it. The book moves along at a cracking pace, and there is much happening throughout to make it a good page-turner. The action sequences are very well done, and make for an adrenaline rush."—*Lesbian Review*

"Brooke is an amazing author. Never have I read a book where I started at the top of the page and don't know what will happen two paragraphs later. She keeps the excitement going, and the pages turning."—*Family and Friends Magazine*

Fierce Overture

"Gun Brooke creates memorable characters, and Noelle and Helena are no exception. Each woman is 'more than meets the eye' as each exhibits depth, fears, and longings. And the sexual tension between them is real, hot, and raw."—*Just About Write*

September Canvas

"In this character-driven story, trust is earned and secrets are uncovered. Deanna and Faythe are fully fleshed out and prove to the reader each has much depth, talent, wit and problem-solving abilities. *September Canvas* is a good read with a thoroughly satisfying conclusion."—*Just About Write*

Sheridan's Fate—*Lambda Literary Award Finalist*

"Sheridan's fire and Lark's warm embers are enough to make this book sizzle. Brooke, however, has gone beyond the wonderful emotional explorations of these characters to tell the story of those who, for various reasons, become differently-abled. Whether it is a bullet, an illness, or a problem at birth, many women and men find themselves in Sheridan's situation. Her courage and Lark's gentleness and determination send this romance into a 'must read.'"—*Just About Write*

Coffee Sonata

"In *Coffee Sonata*, the lives of these four women become intertwined. In forming friendships and love, closets and disabilities are discussed, along with differences in age and backgrounds. Love and friendship are areas filled with complexity and nuances. Brooke takes her time to savor the complexities while her main characters savor their excellent cups of coffee. If you enjoy a good love story, a great setting, and wonderful characters, look for Coffee Sonata at your favorite gay and lesbian bookstore." —*Family & Friends Magazine*

"Each of these characters is intriguing, attractive and likeable, but they are heartbreaking, too, as the reader soon learns when their pasts and their deeply buried secrets are slowly and methodically revealed. Brooke does not give the reader predictable plot points, but builds a fascinating set of subplots and surprises around the romances."—*L-word.com Literature*

Course of Action

"Brooke's words capture the intensity of their growing relationship. Her prose throughout the book is breathtaking and heart-stopping.

Where have you been hiding, Gun Brooke? I, for one, would like to see more romances from this author."—*Independent Gay Writer*

"The setting created by Brooke is a glimpse into that fantasy world of celebrity and high rollers, escapist to be sure, but witnessing the relationship develop between Carolyn and Annelie is well worth the trip. As the reader progresses, the trappings become secondary to the characters' desire to reach goals both professional and personal."—*Midwest Book Review*

Visit us at www.boldstrokesbooks.com

By the Author

Romances:

Course of Action

Coffee Sonata

Sheridan's Fate

September Canvas

Fierce Overture

Speed Demons

The Blush Factor

Soul Unique

A Reluctant Enterprise

Piece of Cake

Thorns of the Past

Wayworn Lovers

Insult to Injury

Ice Queen

Science Fiction

Supreme Constellations series:

Protector of the Realm

Rebel's Quest

Warrior's Valor

Pirate's Fortune

Exodus series:

Advance

Pathfinder

Escape

Arrival

Treason

The Dennamore Scrolls:

Yearning

Lunar Eclipse

Renegade's War

Novella Anthology:

Change Horizons

Yearning

The Dennamore Scrolls: Book One

by

Gun Brooke

2021

YEARNING

ISBN 13: 978-1-63555-757-2

This Trade Paperback Original Is Published By
Bold Strokes Books, Inc.
P.O. Box 249
Valley Falls, NY 12185

First Edition: July 2021

Credits
Editor: Shelley Thrasher
Production Design: Susan Ramundo
Cover Design By Gun Brooke

Acknowledgments

The premise of this science fiction trilogy was the last one I had the joy to run by Elon before he died. He, who loved science fiction—everything from the cheesy old films with sputtering rocket ships of the fifties, to the advanced stories of later years—told me this premise felt original and interesting—which was high praise. *smile*

My son, Henrik, who has seen a TON of science fiction movies, agreed from his POV, which helped seal the deal. I'm grateful my son is here to be a sounding board for the story when I need it.

I also want to thank my daughter, Malin, and her family for their unwavering love and encouragement. The fact that they take such pride in me and my writing makes me very happy. My brother and family always show their support for each book. I'm delighted to be represented on their bookshelves.

My friends Birgitta, Kamilla, and Soli, and my art class friends, your cheering on and support mean so much. My online friends, especially my first readers, Annika and Sami, thank you for your patience and for taking time out of your busy lives to read.

My publisher, Len Barot at Bold Strokes Books, provider of my literary home and family, I am so happy that I get to continue working with you. Dr. Shelley Thrasher, my editor, what would I do without you? Our working relationship and our friendship mean so much to me. Sandy Lowe, senior editor at BSB, is always ready to help and advise, for which I'm utterly grateful. Carsen Taite, Ruth Sternglantz, Stacia Seaman, Victoria Villasenor, Cindy Cresap, Toni Whitaker, and all the others at BSB that work so hard at making our stories the best they can be—you are amazing. The way you work to make us feel part of the BSB family during these crazy times when it is so easy to feel adrift from friends, coworkers, and family is immensely appreciated.

Lastly, I want to thank everyone who has kindly checked in on me during this last eighteen months after I lost Elon. You know who you are, and I also want you to know how much that means to me.

Dedication

For Elon

You loved the idea of this trilogy.

Chapter One

It wasn't the first time Darian Tennen literally ran into someone, but the last time it happened, she was chasing a criminal scumbag, and it had been more of a full body slam than an accidental collision caused by rounding a corner too fast.

"Oh!" a husky female voice called out just before Darian was knocked over and ended up on her ass on the flagstone floor.

"Shit!" Darian could feel the ache from her tailbone sing through her spine all the way to the base of her skull. Around her, she saw droves of loose printed pages. Dazed, she looked over at the person she had collided with, and what little breath she had left whooshed from her lungs. A woman with strawberry-blond hair and bright-green eyes sat on the floor in front of her. Dressed in a pistachio skirt suit, she was perfectly poised, as if she were taking part in a Sunday picnic. Except for the fact that her hair hung in tousled locks around her shoulders, nobody would have guessed she had just taken a tumble.

"Damn it," Darian muttered. "Are you all right?"

"I'm fine, despite your best efforts to kill us both," the woman said, her throaty voice sending shivers through Darian—until her words registered.

"Hey. I wasn't the one carrying such a heap of documents that I couldn't see where I was going." Darian groaned and began to get up on her knees. "I was in a hurry, though," she confessed grudgingly. "Sorry."

Moving lithely into a crouch, the elegant woman began gathering the scattered documents. "Apology accepted."

Ah. Ms. Strawberry-Blonde wasn't going to offer an apology in return.

"Let me help you." Darian could hear her grandmother Camilla's voice in her head. "Four things, Darian. Never assume. Be a gentlewoman. When someone shows you their true colors—believe them. And don't take any crap from anyone."

"What brings you to the town hall? You're not from around here." Ms. Strawberry-Blonde had moved farther away and bent on all four to coax some papers out from behind an old-fashioned radiator.

Darian blinked. How could she know this? "My name's Darian Tennen. I came to visit the library. My grandmother was born here. We just moved back, and we need copies of the blueprints of her house. As far as I understand, the library also handles the town hall archives."

"You understand correctly." Turning around in a graceful pirouette, which was quite the feat since she was crouching on four-inch heels, Ms. Strawberry-Blonde extended her hand. "I'm Samantha Pike, head librarian. It's me you want for that research."

Nearly choking at Samantha's revelation, Darian managed to turn it into a cough. "Nice to meet you. Well, now that we both survived."

Samantha gave a quick smile. "Oh, I assure you, Ms. Tennen, that it takes a lot more than this to injure me." She paused for a few moments, frowning. "However, you seemed to take a worse tumble. I think I should be asking *you* if you're all right."

"Never better," Darian lied. Her ass was smarting, and her tailbone had now gone numb. Great. "I hope you can help me with the blueprints though. My gran's house is in decent condition, considering how old it is, but it needs renovating, and I want to make sure I don't run into trouble since I'll be doing the work. And it's Detective Tennen."

"You're a police officer." Samantha looked surprised. "Are you joining Chief Billings's office?"

"I'm on an extended leave of absence from LAPD, so no. I'm just helping Gran until her house is in good shape and she settles in and reconnects to her hometown."

Gathering the last of the papers, Samantha stood. Darian did her best to stand up without groaning in pain.

"I was just going to have a cup of coffee. You're welcome to join me. I can take some notes about the house in the meantime." Samantha pointed at the corridor she'd just come from. "I need to print these again anyway."

Darian winced. "Sorry again."

"No matter. So?"

Drawing a blank first, Darian then nodded. "I'd love some coffee. I spent most of the morning in the slightly creepy basement of Gran's house."

Motioning for Darian to follow her, Samantha walked with long strides that made her hips move discreetly, but oh, God, this woman was sexy in an understated way. Perhaps Dennamore had more to offer than she'd thought at first glance.

When she had driven up to the parking lot of the impressive building, she'd thought the town hall looked like something out of an old Frankenstein movie. Made from dark, chiseled stones, it sat at the far end of the square. Small shops framed the square on the other three sides, much like any American small town had looked in the 1950s. Darian had pointed it out to her grandmother the first time she saw it, and Camilla had merely shrugged and said something about the people of Dennamore being particular about traditions. For a female, gay cop, that mindset didn't sound entirely promising.

"When was this built?" Darian gestured to the building surrounding them as they walked toward the library's double doors.

"In 1788-1790. It took them a while to transport the stones from the closest quarry. Before then, a large log structure sat where the library is now." Samantha dropped the papers into a large bin next to the reception desk. A young man sat in front of a laptop at one of the tables in the wide center aisle, and the sound made him jump.

"Oh, goodness, Carl. Didn't think it'd be that loud." Samantha placed a hand on Carl's shoulder. "Wi-fi working all right today?"

"Yes. Ms. Pike. I can even listen to music, for once." Carl grinned and looked over at Darian. "Hello."

"Carl, this is Darian Tennen. Detective Tennen, this is Carl. He's a senior in high school."

"Hence the frantic way I'm trying to force knowledge into my brain at the last minute." Carl rolled his eyes dramatically. "Not sure if it's going to work." He studied Darian carefully. "You a returnee?" he asked.

"Excuse me?" Darian frowned. "A returnee? What's that?"

"Don't be nosy, Carl." Samantha pointed at his screen. "Keep at it."

"Yes, Ms. Pike," Carl said, looking good-naturedly chastised.

"My office is over here." Samantha pointed to an open oak door to the far-right side. As they walked between the tall shelves, all made from the same wood as the door and walls, Darian felt dwarfed. Each bookshelf had a sliding ladder to reach the top shelves. This didn't look like any library she had ever visited.

Samantha's office consisted of a desk and cabinets from the same darkened oak wood as the rest of the interior. A leather desk chair looked almost as old as the rest of the furniture, its tall backrest making it resemble an ornate throne. Samantha sat down and pointed to the visitors' chair, also made from oak and leather, but not as impressive. Darian sat down, wincing again at the stinging sensation from her tailbone.

After waking up her computer, Samantha tapped in a few commands. "All right, Detective Tennen—"

"Darian, please." Cringing at any formality, Darian hoped Samantha wasn't a stickler for such things. She looked like she might be, especially surrounded by this centuries-old interior.

"Then please call me Samantha." Samantha nodded and managed to look regal as well as friendly.

"Not Sam?" Darian had her hopes up.

"No."

All right then. "Got it."

"Address of your grandmother's house?" Samantha kept typing as she spoke.

"Brynden 4. It's belonged to the Wells family for more than two hundred years, Gran says, and..."

Samantha stopped typing and stared at Darian. "Brynden 4. You're sure?"

Taken aback, Darian nodded. "Of course, I'm sure. I had my coffee in the old kitchen this morning."

"I apologize. It's just...that house has been sitting empty for more than fifty years." Tapping at her keyboard again, Samantha now looked completely interested. "Here we are. Brynden 4. Owner, Camilla Tennen. Good. I have a code for where the blueprints are stored in our archives." She paused and leaned back in her chair. "I know the firm that's been taking care of the maintenance of the house and yard. They do that for several of the original homes that are still waiting for the owners, or their heirs, to return."

Return. Returnee? The word the boy, Carl, had mentioned popped up in Darian's mind. "I never understood why Gran didn't just sell it after fifty years in LA. Well, until she started talking about how she had to return here. That was five years ago."

"Ah. Yes. A common thing for someone born in this town. Either we stay, or we come back." A shadow passed across Samantha's face. "What took your grandmother so long, if her desire to move back began only five years ago?"

"I have no idea. No matter what, she talked so much about Dennamore, I started feeling the same way, and I've never set foot here. For some reason, I was suddenly curious to see her hometown. Experience it, you know." And it had not been a case of mere curiosity, Darian admitted to herself. Half a year ago, almost from one day to the next, Darian knew she had to help her grandmother move home and that she had to go with her, at least for a while. The fact that her father hadn't lived long enough to see his mother's home was part of her urge too. Nobody but Darian had a reason to inherit Gran's house in Dennamore.

"I've heard that from other people as well. Only a month ago, someone returned who was a third-generation Dennamore resident. He was almost ninety." Samantha scribbled something on a piece of paper. "Why don't we head down to the basement together? It's not open to the public, but since I'm going down there anyway, you're welcome to join me." She stepped over to a mirror that hung just inside the door and deftly put her hair up in a low twist. "Better," she said after smoothing it.

Darian wasn't so sure. Yes, the updo was elegant and suited Samantha, but the loose hair around her shoulders had looked fantastic. "Sounds interesting. This place is growing on me, despite it being so far from civilization."

"We are quite self-contained here," Samantha said as they walked through the library and out into the hallway. Her heels made a slightly eerie echoing sound against the flagstone floor. "Which is a blessing, as you may have noticed there's only one way in and out of here."

"Yes. It's like being in a bowl, surrounded by mountains." Darian noticed that they were the same height, but she probably had well over fifteen pounds on the slender woman next to her. Loving to work out and go for a run at all hours, Darian had also taken martial-arts classes of different kinds. Samantha might look more delicate, but Darian hadn't forgotten how agile the woman had proved to be when she, completely unfazed, rose from the floor earlier.

Samantha stopped by the stairwell behind the front desk. "It's down this way." She walked ahead of Darian down the worn steps, also made from flagstones, their steps echoing between the now stone-clad walls. Darian noticed how the wall sconces looked like torches from ancient times. Was this part of the aesthetic? They reinforced the gothic feel of the structure, and the only other place that had ever given Darian such a vibe was a theme park she'd visited as a child.

Samantha led her down two sets of stairs, which made Darian wonder how deep the basement of the town hall actually went. Wasn't the building resting on bedrock? How the hell had people managed to dig, or blast, space for a basement in the late 1700s?

Stopping in front of a massive oak—again—door, Samantha produced an impressive key and turned it in an ancient-looking lock. She also punched in a six-digit code before opening it. The smell indicated old books and papers, not moldy, but dusty. Samantha pulled at a thin chain hanging to the left of the door opening, and fluorescent lights flickered before they stabilized and lit up the room.

Darian gaped. If the fact that this old structure had a two-story basement within the bedrock had baffled her a minute ago, the size of this room rendered her speechless. It seemed to go on forever and was filled with cabinets, shelves, desks, and a tall ceiling that explained why they had to walk down so far.

"Holy crap." Darian turned to Samantha. "Is this for real? This…how can this even exist here?"

Samantha smiled indulgently. "I know. The first time I came down here with my great-aunt Tara—I think I was ten years old—I decided to become a librarian just so I could help research these materials."

"These materials" didn't fully cover the items she saw—the large rolls of paper, the books, and whatever lurked in the back of this room. No, hall. Somehow, someone had chiseled, or blasted, an enormous hall under the structure that looked impressive from the outside but was nothing compared to these archives.

"How can you find anything in here?" Darian felt stupid for asking, but to her it seemed impossible to even know where to begin.

"My great-aunt Tara, who was the previous librarian, started digitizing the catalogues of everything here in the eighties on a very simple computer, and when she retired, I took over and kept going. I've completed most of the ledgers, but the papers and objects in the far back will keep me busy for years to come. Fortunately, the blueprints and historical documents regarding houses and structures in Dennamore have been fully digitized for years. Over here, please." Flicking her fingers for Darian to follow her, Samantha showed the way to a more modern part of the large hall. Here, two stationary computers sat, each with their own twenty-six-inch screen, and to the right of them stood a large A3 laser printer.

"Let me pull up the file." Samantha sat down and began typing.

"Why couldn't you do this from upstairs?" Darian sat on the other chair next to Samantha.

"Oh, that. These computers aren't linked. We are quite careful with our historical items and records. These two computers hold all the information, but there's no access via any intranet or internet."

This sparked even more interest. "Why is that?"

Samantha sent Darian a look through narrowed eyes. "It's in our local rules and regulations."

"Ah. I see." Darian really didn't but kept quiet and merely observed how Samantha pulled up the information she needed. After she tapped in a few commands, the quite impressive printer whirred and began producing the documents. To Darian's surprise, the blueprints of her grandmother's house were not done in a style she'd seen before. Instead, the printer created what looked like an amazing old artwork. In full color, she saw the floor plan, the exteriors from all angles, even from above, done in the style of some Leonardo da Vinci facsimiles she had seen at an exhibition when she was a kid.

"Wow," Darian said, carefully pulling the floor-plan document closer by pinching the corner. "I…I didn't expect this. It's fantastic." She glanced up at Samantha, who was switching off the screen. "I assume you scanned some really old document?"

"We did. The originals are kept in a secure area where the temperature is set to keep mold away and help them not age." Samantha came over and examined the printed copies. "These turned out all right." She tapped the sheet showing the front exterior. "I have always dreamed of seeing one more of the original homes of Dennamore. It's a beautiful house."

To Darian, her grandmother's home looked mostly like a lot of hard work on her part, getting it in working order. "I suppose. I'm afraid to turn on a light in there. The wiring is ancient."

"The house has been maintained, but nothing's been altered," Samantha said and began rolling the prints up. She took a cardboard tube from a box behind the printer, and after carefully inserting the documents into the tube, she placed a lid in each end. "Compliments of the library. Here you are."

"Thank you." Darian's fingers accidentally grazed Samantha's as she accepted the tube, which was a mistake. The way her fingertips tingled made Darian want to groan out loud. She had no time for any sort of flirtation, let alone some fling. She eventually would return to LA and her job as a homicide detective.

"My pleasure." Motioning for the door, Samantha walked Darian out of the amazing hall, causing a surprising sense of disappointment. What she wouldn't have given to be allowed to explore some of the documents. Darian had always wanted to know more of her father's family, but even if her grandmother had raised her, she knew only the basics. Orphaned at age eight, she remembered some things of her parents, but it was like the memories were still images in black and white. Gran had been both mom and dad to her these last twenty-one years, and Darian adored her.

As they reached the foyer where the security guard now was in place behind the desk, and men and women milled back and forth between the office wing and the entrance, Darian impulsively turned to Samantha. "You said you were curious about Gran's house. Would you like to come and have a tour before we start renovating? We're not planning to do anything crazy, just make it safe and so on, but still." Darian fired off a smile that usually worked on the ladies.

Samantha raised her eyebrows. "Really? Would Ms. Tennen agree to that?"

"Are you kidding? Gran thrives on meeting new people. She'd love to have you over." Perhaps she was losing her touch, as it seemed that Samantha appeared more eager to see the house than about the invitation per se.

"Well, if you're sure?"

"You free tonight? We're ordering in food as the stove looks like it might explode if we try to switch it on," Darian said.

"That's very generous. Thank you." Samantha laced her hands in front of her.

"Seven? That okay?"

"Seven is perfect." Samantha nodded and then pulled a card from her jacket pocket. "Here's my card if something comes up."

"Thanks. And here's mine."

"Thank you."

After walking out of the town-hall building, Darian couldn't stop thinking about the huge archive in the basement. Something about it thrilled her, and she kept trying to come up with reasons why Samantha needed to let her in there again.

Also, Samantha Pike had to be the most stunning woman Darian had ever met. It wasn't just her classic features, but the way she spoke and carried herself. Where the hell did some women learn to walk like that—as if they floated on air in those impossible heels. Darian looked down at her sneakers. She was a casual dresser unless she was working. As a detective, she could wear a leather jacket, black slacks, and black loafers. Some of her peers preferred suits, but secretly, Darian referred to them as FBI wannabes. If, on top of everything else, they wore black pilot sunglasses, it was definitely a fitting description.

Getting into her car, Darian placed the tube on the passenger seat. She was excited about showing its contents to Gran. It had to be hard to return after fifty years and try to find something, and someone, to reconnect with. Gran had slept a lot since they arrived in Dennamore. Darian had driven them across the country from LA since Gran hated flying, and it was little wonder that Gran was still exhausted. As soon as she was ready to go for walks or drives, surely, they'd run into someone she used to know. If nothing else, they could probably ask Samantha about people of Gran's generation tonight.

Pulling out into the modest traffic, Darian glanced at the tube holding the prints. "Great. I'm going to be working my ass off these upcoming months." Strangely, when she said it aloud, it didn't seem like such a chore. She was doing this for Gran, and she might just have a chance at a peek at that library and the archive, if she was lucky.

Smiling now, Darian drove along beautiful Main Street on her way home to Gran. She couldn't wait to tell her about Samantha.

CHAPTER TWO

True to her nature, Samantha didn't bother much with the full-length mirror, as she always dressed in a similar way. After merely a quick glance to make sure her lipstick hadn't smeared and that her hair, now in a loose twist, looked all right, she stepped out of her small house at the edge of the forest covering the western part of the mountain chain. Her childhood home, a small house originally built in the 1920s, had been added to several times, making it unique. Samantha loved her home. Every piece of furniture and most of the items within its walls held so much history and so many memories for her. She did possess a flat-screen television and a computer, but those were the only items belonging to the twenty-first century. Even the kitchen range and washing machine were older than that. This was not unheard of in Dennamore. Skilled handymen and craftsmen, or women, kept the traditional homes in good shape. The newer homes, of course, had all the equipment young people normally demanded.

It was a lovely summer evening, and Samantha had already decided to walk to Brynden 4, the Tennen residence. It had been very generous of Darian to invite her to her grandmother's home of local fame. Samantha hoped it would sit well with Camilla Tennen to have a surprise guest for dinner. At the same time, Samantha was honest enough with herself to know that she would never have been able to decline the invitation since she'd wanted to explore the house for years.

As she made her way down the road toward the outskirts of Dennamore, Samantha pulled off her light-yellow cardigan and draped it on her arm. It was quite humid this evening, and she didn't want to arrive all sweaty and rumpled. Her white, short-sleeve blouse was flattering with its lace collar, and the tan slacks went with most tops in her closet. Giving in to comfort, Samantha wore two-inch-heel white pumps. The open toe made them comfortable in the warm weather. It continually baffled tourists in this area how Dennamore always held an even temperature, albeit on par with the current season. In summer, the average daytime temperature stayed around 78 F. The other seasons were also remarkably even. Scientists explained that the phenomenon was caused by Denna Lake toward the south. The same scientists had long tried to gain access to the lake by petitioning the Elder Council but had always been denied. As curious as Samantha was about every secretive detail of her hometown, she was glad no small submarine would disturb the ecosystem.

Samantha nodded at an older man coming to a halt next to her on the sidewalk. "Good evening, Chief Walker. Heading out to get those last rays of the sun in the west, I see?" She indicated his camera, which looked almost as old as Geoff Walker himself, former chief of police turned avid amateur photographer.

"Aye, Ms. Pike. And in a week from now, I'll be all set up to catch the lake lights."

Samantha smiled. She looked forward to the festival next week. The Lake Light Festival drew big crowds, the Dennamore inhabitants joined by the neighboring towns and villages, and even people from out of state, for the two nights this time of year when the lake would sparkle. Its beauty was enough to make a person cry.

"I'll be there too." Samantha always took every opportunity to promote the library and to talk to the oldest population in Dennamore, who might not normally be out and about in a casual way.

"Where are you off to this fine evening?" Chief Walker hoisted the case holding his tripod.

"I'm having dinner with some returnees." Samantha could see this comment sparked his interest.

"Yes? Who's come back this time?" He took a step closer, lowering his voice. "Anyone we've heard of?"

"I'd say so. Tennen. Brynden 4." If Walker hadn't been the much-loved chief of police for thirty years, Samantha wouldn't have volunteered any information.

"I'll be dammed. Camilla has returned?" Walker rubbed his goatee. "I knew the day would come, and to be truthful, I had hoped it would come much sooner." He shrugged, his eyes suddenly holding a distant expression. "Better late than never, I suppose."

"Do you know Ms. Tennen?" Curious, Samantha wished she'd have more time to talk to Walker.

"I knew her as Camilla Wells. She's five years older than me, but, oh yes, I knew her. She was friends with my older sister, and I, along with every other boy in Dennamore, had a crush on her."

Samantha thought of Darian, wiry and strong, and with a face that was more handsome than pretty—which made her enigmatically beautiful. Hearing Chief Walker speak about Camilla Tennen with such longing in this tone, Samantha was even more interested in learning about the newest returnees. "Well, I won't keep you and make you miss the sunset, Chief." Samantha patted his arm. "Don't forget to show me the best ones, as usual."

"Don't worry. I'm just happy anyone is interested in my photos at all." Walker saluted Samantha. "Give Camilla my best."

"I will."

Samantha walked the last blocks and then found herself unable to move for a moment as she took in the sight of Brynden 4. Someone, a gardener no doubt, had removed some of the ivy clinging to the log walls. The deep-set windows sparkled in the last sun rays, and the carefully pruned fruit trees framed the house. A simple flagstone path led to the double front door. The house looked small from the street, but Samantha knew it stretched far into the backyard, which was one of the biggest in Dennamore.

Opening the gate, she noticed that the fence had received a fresh coat of white paint, and the upkeep made her smile. Whenever a returnee came back, it was a lovely sight when they began restoring their family homes.

The right half of the double door opened, and Darian stepped out onto the small porch. The roof cast a shadow across her, but Samantha could still make out her broad smile. As she came closer, she saw the smile reflected in Darian's cognac-colored eyes. Some might simply call them brown, but that would be too easy. They had a different, special hue that gave them a liquid appearance.

"Welcome. Glad you could make it," Darian said and motioned for Samantha to step inside. "Please be careful around the cables and ladders. I'm trying to find out how many layers of wallpaper there are, and what shape they're in, but it's driving me a little crazy."

"My pleasure. Truly." Samantha looked around the foyer. A perfect square, it had one door on each wall. In one corner, she saw a coatrack and hung her cardigan there. Another corner boasted a full-length mirror, but the rest of it was indeed littered with cables, work lights, and two ladders. It had a tall ceiling, at least twenty feet, and a winding cast-iron staircase led to a mezzanine on the far wall.

"It's amazing." Samantha did a slow pivot to take it all in. "Thank you for having me, Darian."'

"Ah, so this is the lovely Samantha," a clear voice said from the left, and Samantha turned to greet her hostess. Tall, willowy, with glowing white hair piled on top of her head in the most elaborate of hairdos, a stunningly beautiful woman gazed keenly at her. "I'm Camilla Tennen. Welcome to Brynden." Camilla extended her hand, and the gesture was so regal, Samantha envisioned some knight in armor kneeling to kiss it. She took it firmly, but also with care, because the swollen joints suggested that Camilla Tennen suffered from some form of arthritis.

"I'm so pleased to meet you, Ms. Tennen—"

"Camilla." Camilla's blue eyes glittered.

"Thank you. Camilla. And yes, I'm Samantha." How old was Camilla? Walker said she was five years older than him, and he was at least seventy. Camilla looked sixty, if that.

"Join us in the parlor. We have a lot to do there, but it's clean and fresh at least. I mean, the people in charge of the maintenance while I was gone have done a great job, but when a house isn't lived in, things happen."

"Yes. That's true." Samantha followed Camilla into the parlor and could tell that it needed some upgrades, but the old furniture was still beautiful. Framed in wood, they were carved by a master carpenter, so ornate and perfect, you'd think they were made in a modern CNC wood carving machine. The fabric on top of the upholstery was worn and faded though.

"We're keeping the furniture. Just need some new fabrics and more…um…padding." Darian sat down and grimaced. "They're a little hard for my taste."

"Because your old couch in LA was more like a padded hammock," Camilla said and chuckled. "But I agree. We need to modernize them very carefully."

Bookshelves lined the room and were filled. "Does this room serve as a library too?" Samantha asked, tipping her head back to see the top shelves.

"Nah, not quite," Darian said and shook her head. "I thought so too when I first got here. But the real library is upstairs, to the left. This is the surplus, you could say."

"Are they catalogued?" Samantha's fingers were itching.

"No idea." Darian looked at her grandmother. "Are they?"

"Some of the shelves upstairs are. I remember that much. The books down here…I doubt it." Returning her focus to Samantha, Camilla tilted her head. "You're a librarian. Would you be interested in taking a look one day? I'll pay you for your trouble, of course."

"I wouldn't dream of taking your money for the privilege." Samantha was shocked. "If you let me peruse your shelves and create a small catalogue, that would be payment in itself."

Darian glowed. "Told you, Gran."

Samantha raised her eyebrows. "Excuse me?"

"Darian, using her detective skills no doubt, was certain you'd jump at the chance to browse through our books." Camilla gave Darian a mock scowl. "And she's insufferable when she's right."

"Well, she is in this instance." Samantha leaned back into her chair. "I've dreamed of being allowed into this building for as long as I can remember. I used to sneak into the garden as a child and look in the windows," she confessed. "My parents were horrified. They acted as if I were being blasphemous. I meant no harm, naturally."

"Oh, my goodness." Camilla laughed, a perfectly contagious sound, like silver bells. "You are welcome any time, my dear. Just call ahead so I'm not indisposed. I sometimes am." She frowned down at her hands.

"Of course." Samantha couldn't believe her luck. Sending Darian a glance, she hoped Camilla's generous invitation didn't cause her problems. "If that's all right with you, Darian. You live here too."

Darian merely grinned. "Are you kidding? I barely know a soul here." She stood. "Why don't I give you the grand tour? There's a wall in the basement that puzzles me."

A puzzling wall? Intrigued, Samantha got up. "I'd love to."

"In the meantime, I'll go into the kitchen to make sure Brandon thinks the food that was delivered is up to par," Camilla told Darian.

"You okay, Gran?" Darian hesitated when Camilla moved even slower than before.

"I'm fine, Dar. I'll just grab an extra pill. The weather is going to change. Mark my words." Camilla walked toward a door at the opposite end of the parlor. "Run along now."

"Run along," Darian muttered when Camilla left the room. She sounded worried.

"She's in pain," Samantha said.

"She is. Every day. But when the weather changes, she feels worse than normal.

"Arthritis?"

"Yup." Darian took a deep breath and then straightened her back. "Let's do the grand tour. It's quite a cool house, actually."

Samantha followed Darian out into the foyer and into the room across from it. It was empty of furniture, except for a large, equally ornate desk made from oak.

"This will be Gran's study. She still writes. I'm going to buy her the best work chair I can get my hands on, so she'll be comfortable. She'll enjoy the view of the street, I think."

"I agree. I'm mostly working in the windowless part of Town Hall, and sometimes I wish I had a beautiful view from my desk." Samantha looked straight at Darian when she spoke, and her cheeks warmed. Oddly, Darian also colored faintly. *Goodness*. Unable to maintain eye contact, she looked around the room. "That is some thick wallpaper," she said, feeling breathless. The wallpaper had peeled in the corners, and it looked like you could simply pull it off.

"At least eight layers, if not more. I'm going to enjoy pulling it down. We might hire a firm to do some of it, but I'm not half bad at hanging wallpaper unless it has a crazy pattern going on."

"Wine red," Samantha murmured. "If I lived here, that's what I'd choose for this room." Shocked at her audacity, she turned back to Darian. "I'm sorry. I'm overstepping."

Darian gaped at her. "Are you psychic, Samantha?"

"What?" Samantha frowned, but then had to smile. "What do you mean?"

"Camilla and I were talking about that yesterday. Wallpaper, fabric texture, with wine red as the dominant color." Darian placed her hands on her hips. "So. Psychic."

A new kind of warmth spread within Samantha. "Hardly, but it's a nice thought."

Darian waved her along and showed her the rest of the house that consisted of two parlors, the study, four bedrooms, a kitchen, a vestibule, and two bathrooms—all in various need of upgrades. And then there was the library, but Darian shook her head no.

"If I let you up there now, I won't get to pick your brain about the basement. You'll be stuck in the library and abandon me for all those musty old books." Darian pointed to a narrow door in the mudroom. "There's the staircase."

Darian was right. Despite being intrigued earlier when thinking of the books, Samantha wasn't all that keen to investigate a basement that might be dirty and spooky. As Darian led the way down the stairs, Samantha followed and tried to hide her reluctance. When they reached the end of the stairs, she was relieved to see that it was well lit by construction lamps and, if a bit dusty, not gross or spooky.

Wooden shelves held tools, baskets, crates, metal boxes, and so on. A furnace that looked antique sat against the center wall. Next to it, someone had spread a new tarp and then a blanket.

Pointing to the old furnace, Darian said, "That monstrosity will be exchanged for a new one next week."

"Probably safer that way." Samantha stepped closer to the tarp. "This the wall?"

"Yes. Look here." Darian waved her along. "I have the relevant part of the blueprint here. I mean, I managed to copy part of the one I got from you and blow it up on my laptop. I printed this part of the basement, and the measurement doesn't make sense. This wall shouldn't be so massive." She pointed at it. "It's more than three feet deep. And what the hell is it made of? It looks like it was carved out in one big block of bedrock, and the surface is super even. Or am I missing something?"

Kneeling carefully on the blanket, Samantha ran her fingertips along the smooth wall. Darian was right. It was not just one block. It was also glasslike smooth, more so, even, than the modern granite counters that were all the rage. "I don't get this either." Glancing down at the A4 paper Darian handed her, she held it closer to the light. On the blueprint, the wall should be aligned with the furnace. This was an old document, that was true, but if it was accurate regarding the rest of Brynden 4…?

"What's on the other side?" Samantha looked up at Darian.

"I think it used to be a pantry or something. Want to see?"

Fascinated now, Samantha followed Darian through another doorway and into a smaller room with empty shelves lining the walls. "I agree. It looks like a pantry." In here, the walls were made of thick planks. Samantha placed a hand between two shelves against the wall that was behind the furnace but yanked it back.

"What is it?" Darian stepped closer, placing a hand at the small of Samantha's back.

"Is the furnace on? I mean, are you running it?" Samantha carefully touched the wall again. Darian did the same, placing her hand next to Samantha's. She jerked also.

"It's warm. Not just warmer than the surrounding rock. It's *warm.*"

"You haven't felt it before?" Samantha took a step back and examined the wall.

"I've only tapped it with the hammer to try to determine if it's hollow. The wood is so thick, I couldn't judge."

"This is a mystery," Samantha said. "Are you going to take down part of the wall?"

"I hadn't exactly planned to do it before I've gotten the upstairs in good working order, but now…I'm damn curious."

"Me too." Samantha carefully felt the wall again. This time she moved her hand horizontally. "If I'm not imagining things, it is cooler toward the outer wall. I suppose that makes sense." She shook her head. "What am I saying. None of this makes sense."

"Well, I for one am going to get a stronger circular saw and cut some of this down. Have you seen the size of these planks?" She pointed at the end wood. "At least eight by ten, or so. More logs than planks, really. How the hell can heat permeate that barrier?"

Thrilled at the complete mystery, Samantha pulled up her cell phone. "May I take some photos?"

Darian nodded. "Sure. I'm going to do the same. I love a mystery." She produced her own cell phone and tapped the screen a few times.

"I'd think that loving mysteries is a requisite for being in law enforcement." Samantha took several pictures of the shelves, the end wood, and walked around the corner to photograph the old furnace and the amazing wall next to it. When she was done, she placed her hand on the smooth surface and leaned into it. A faint hum against her palm made her take several steps back, right into Darian.

"Whoa. Easy there." Darian placed a hand against Samantha's back again. "You all right?"

"Not sure." Samantha pushed her shoulders back and felt the wall once more, annoyed at being so skittish. And why the hell could she still feel Darian's hand through her shirt? Touching the wall again, she clearly felt the hum. "Touch this. Press hard." Samantha tapped her perfectly rounded and painted nail against it.

"What? Oh, okay." Darian stepped closer and mimicked Samantha's movements. She yanked her hand back. "What the fuck?"

"Exactly. What did it feel like to you?"

Darian grimaced as she tucked her phone back into her pocket. This time she pressed both palms against the wall, leaning in with her entire weight. "Like someone trapped a massive hive of bees.

Buzzing, rather than vibrating. I didn't feel that on the other side. Then again, I didn't press this hard." Darian let go and hurried around to the pantry side of whatever was making the sound. She repeated the maneuver and closed her eyes. Her hair lay in soft waves around her shoulders, and for a brief moment, Samantha forgot about anything else but how stunning she found this woman. "It's not as clear, but I don't think I'm imagining it." Darian surprised Samantha by taking her hand and placing it under her own, pressing it against the wooden wall. "You feel it?"

It was hard to say at first, since Samantha's heartbeat was so fast all of a sudden. She forced herself to calm down and, like Darian, closed her eyes. And yes, there it was. A very fine, but unmistakable, hum.

"This is crazy," Samantha said and opened her eyes. "I'm glad you're going to take down part of the wall. I hope Camilla won't mind."

"Are you kidding? I'll have to restrain her to keep her from getting her hands on an ax." Darian grinned and let go of Samantha's hand, quickly, as if she just realized she was trapping it. "Sorry."

Samantha dismissed the apology with a flick of her fingertips. "I would love to be in the loop with how it goes. If you'll agree to that, I can in turn share a few interesting discrepancies that I've found in old Town Hall records." She gazed hopefully at Darian, praying that the lure of more mystery would be enough.

Darian didn't disappoint her. "That'd be cool. I mean, I love being here with Gran, but my brain will need more than being the unofficial contractor for restoring this house. Gran realizes this and has been after me to check in with the local law enforcement to see if they have an opening. I still might, but first I'm going to get to the bottom, or should I say, behind, this thing." She motioned toward the log wall.

"I won't interject myself into your quest uninvited—"

"Whoa. Please do. I don't want to do this alone." Darian touched Samantha's arm. "I mean, where's the fun in that?"

Samantha knew her cheeks reddened again as they warmed. She cursed inwardly and could only hope that the construction lights didn't show her reaction. "I appreciate it. I'll extend the same courtesy, of course. It'll be a welcome change to have someone actually interested in my research. Normally the people around here don't care or downright discourage me." Feeling awkward for sharing too much information, because it was a touchy subject with her, Samantha smoothed down her hair and tucked her cell phone back into her pocket.

"Ah. Well, screw them. I'll read through your stuff, and though I'm no scholar, I have a good nose for when something doesn't add up. And this," Darian pointed at the wall again, "is beyond not adding up. Now, how about a peek at the library before we have dinner?"

"Sounds great." Relaxing again, Samantha followed Darian as they made their way up the stairs.

Darian knew she would never forget the look on Samantha's face when she saw the library upstairs. She propped her hip against the doorframe and pushed her hands into her back pockets. It was fascinating to watch how reverently Samantha placed a gentle index finger along the spine of a book every now and then.

"These are…treasures," Samantha said, sounding breathless, which in turn sent shivers through Darian. "I think some, and perhaps more than some, might complement our older books at the library. I have only skimmed through two shelves so far, and I see so many books that I'm dying to peruse." Turning to look at Darian, Samantha smiled broadly. "Not to mention catalogue."

"You're welcome here anytime, as Gran said." Darian tried to not sound too eager. The idea of having Samantha as a frequent visitor made her prolonged stay in Dennamore more promising. "I can be your secretary when I'm not overseeing the contractors."

"Now there's a tempting offer." Samantha walked slowly among the shelves, stopping every now and then to tilt her head sideways to read the spines of the books. The loose tresses around her face that had escaped the soft twist caressed her cheeks and neck, which made

Darian's stomach clench. Samantha moved with an innate grace and as if she had no idea how effortlessly elegant she came across. How old could she be? Thirty? Thirty-five? Her demeanor could add to her years, as it was more stylish than youthful, but these days it was impossible to judge a person's age.

"Oh, wow," Samantha gushed, pulling Darian out of her reverie.

"What?" Pushing off the doorframe, Darian joined Samantha, who had climbed up on one of the small ladders to check out the top shelf by the window. "Careful. I can't swear these steps aren't centuries old." She wanted to place her hand on Samantha's hip to steady the clearly excited woman but thought better of it.

"Never mind that. May I pull this one out?" Samantha tapped a fingernail against the spine of a large leather-bound book.

"Of course. Hand it to me. It looks heavy, and I'd rather you didn't break your neck stepping down."

"All right." Samantha carefully coaxed the book out. "Oh, good. I was afraid that it might have gotten stuck against the other books or the shelf." She handed the large volume to Darian and descended the ladder.

Darian placed the book on the desk in the center of the room. "There you go."

"Oh, this is absolutely astonishing. I wish I had cotton gloves…I should have brought some." Samantha sat down on the leather-clad desk chair. "I could have used the sleeves of my cardigan, but I left it downstairs."

"Take my shirt." Without really considering the appropriateness of taking off her long-sleeve shirt and ending up in just a tank top, Darian pulled the garment over her head.

"Oh. Eh…thank you." Samantha blinked and gazed up at Darian for a prolonged moment. "It might get a bit dusty."

"The ancient washing machine works remarkably well." Darian grinned and went to stand just behind Samantha as she pushed her hand into one of the sleeves of her shirt to use as a makeshift glove.

"Let's see." Pulling gently at the hard cover, Samantha moved it as if she were handling a broken limb, gently setting it down in an open position. The first page was sepia colored and blank. Expertly, Samantha turned it, stopping when they heard a soft creak. "I don't think it'll break," she murmured, and Darian was about to answer something, when she realized that Samantha was probably talking to herself. The idea of this stunning woman spending hours among musty books in a strange basement at Town Hall, talking to herself, made Darian wonder if Samantha felt lonely having this type of job.

After moving the page with so much patience that Darian almost cried out twice in frustration, Samantha revealed another sepia-colored page. However, this page wasn't blank. The entire spread was filled with letters and...Darian squinted. Symbols?

"What is that?" Darian asked and pulled up a wooden stool. Sitting down close to Samantha's right side to not be in the way of her turning any pages, she absentmindedly registered Samantha's perfume, a vanilla-bergamot scent, mixed with something fresh... lemongrass?

"Let me see." Samantha bent over the pages. "I've seen this before. I mean, this lettering. It's not cursive, nor is it block letters. See?" She pointed to the precise lines. "And the lines are entirely straight even if they're not lined. Such perfection." Giving a sigh that conveyed admiration, Samantha let the nail of her index finger follow the first line without touching the page and began to read.

"Within these pages I will commit treason, and though I may forfeit my life because of it, I cannot let the truth remain in the hands of those who seek to hide it. This, my journal, will be kept well away from the eyes of my fellow travelers. My intention is to pass this information on to my children, should..."

Samantha frowned and leaned in closer to the book. "What does that say? *G-a-i* apostrophe *u-s-t-o*?"

Moving her head in next to Samantha's, Darian followed the perfect, pink-varnished nail as Samantha pointed to the word—or name. "Gai'usto? A name?"

"It's written in such an intricate way, it's hard to make out... but, as the rest is in English, albeit quite formal, it's puzzling how it could be a name. From which country could they be? Sounds almost Slavic." Samantha leaned forward again.

"Should Gai'usto and I be awarded sons or daughters. This land is rich with resources, and once we have gathered enough information to blend in with our neighbors, I have hope we can co-exist until we one day might return to our distant home."

She looked up at Darian. "They must have traveled far to get to the US. Do you see a date?"

Darian scanned the margins. "I see some symbols, but that has to be an alphabet from their old country, because I can't make it out at all."

Samantha nodded. "It reminds me of the Cyrillic letters, but not quite. I'll have to look into that." She kept reading. "'Rei'tien'—another name?"

"Rei'tien is our only true confidante. It is thanks to her that we manage to assimilate the tongue with which the inhabitants of this world speak so quickly."

"Now, that's damn weird." Darian straightened. "Assimilate the tongue? Inhabitants of this world? North America was called the New World, of course."

"True." Slowly pivoting on her seat to face Darian, Samantha looked at her with eyes wide enough to show the white all the way around them. "This…I have come across similar writings, as I said, but only in scattered documents with no obvious connection between them. This…this book." She swallowed and shook her head. "I have no words. It's been my obsession, you could say, to find something that might shine a light on the discrepancies in our town's past." Samantha spoke quietly, as if she'd forgotten where she was.

"Discrepancies? You mentioned that before." Darian frowned. "What do you mean?"

"Oh. Right." Squaring her shoulders, Samantha cast a longing look at the old journal. "Of course, I can't know that this book is the document I've hoped to find for years, or if very much is written beyond this first spread, but—what are you doing?"

Darian, who wasn't much for waiting to find things out, or as reverent about old books as the woman next to her, had just put her finger in between the pages and now pushed about ten of them open. The book obediently flipped open, sending some dust whirling. "That should answer that. More writing and—a date!"

"You could have broken it." Samantha growled but leaned over the book again. "Don't do that again."

"All right." Darian scooted closer. "Some of the strange symbols, and then...January the twenty-eighth, in the year 1776." She gaped. "Holy shit.""

"God." Samantha covered her mouth, her hand unsteady. "1776."

"Pretty old. I'll be more careful." Feeling guilty at how she'd flipped the pages, she kept her hands well away from the book.

"The Elder Council has introduced a new law that forbids us to dress in uniform, or any of our old garments. I can see the reason for these rules but do not agree with the severity of the punishment for the ones who wish to live according to our old ways in the privacy of their homes."

Samantha leaned back in the chair, making it squeak. "Uniforms?" She rubbed her temples. "This is so much new information at once, my brain's overheating." She smiled faintly. "This book, combined with your mystery in the basement, is staggering."

Darian nodded. "It sure is. So, you've been researching Dennamore's history, and this is the first time you've found anything this detailed?"

"Exactly." Samantha gripped Darian's hand and squeezed it. "Will you help me? I mean, with the journal. You did offer to be my secretary." She looked hopefully at Darian.

Darian returned the squeeze gently. "Absolutely. This is like catnip to a detective, you know." She grinned.

"Girls!" Gran's surprisingly strong voice carried from the hallway downstairs. "Dinner's ready."

"Coming, Gran!" Darian looked at the book. "Something important though. We can't keep anything from Gran. If there's anything I know about Camilla Tennen, it is the futility of trying to be sneaky. I learned that the hard way as a teenager. And, after all, it's her book."

"It is." Samantha nodded solemnly. "And another thing that may sound odd to you. We shouldn't be too obvious about it with anyone but your grandmother. One reason I've found it difficult to do my research is that some on the Elder Council are not exactly keen on it. I wouldn't be surprised if they keep old documents or journals out of the public record."

"Like this one?" Darian tilted her head. "It sounded like on that first page that this person, whatever their name is, had good reason way back when to keep it on the down-low as well. Interesting."

"It sure is. Mind if I use your shirt to cover the book until next time?" Samantha held up the rather dusty shirt.

"Go ahead. I'll just pop into my room and get another one. Don't think Gran will appreciate me being quite this informal at the dinner table when we have a guest." Grinning, Darian enjoyed how Samantha's cheeks briefly turned a faint pink.

Darian dashed over to her room and pulled on another long-sleeve shirt, this one cobalt blue, and then joined Samantha in the hallway. As they walked to the dining room where the ornate oak table was set with a crisp white linen tablecloth and matching napkins, Darian could tell that Samantha was preoccupied, and who could blame her. The strange discovery in the basement together with the ancient journal were almost too much to take in. When Darian took her seat next to her grandmother and across from Samantha, she realized that right this instant she felt more alive than she ever had chasing criminals in LA.

CHAPTER THREE

Samantha thought Camilla Tennen looked every bit the matriarch, as well as the Hollywood-conditioned glam queen, where she presided at the head of the dining table. It didn't matter that the table was old, and quite sturdy, or that the rug had seen better days. The charismatic woman managed to give the impression that she sat on a throne, benevolently regarding her subjects. If it hadn't been for the fact that Camilla exuded warmth and brilliance, the woman could have been considered arrogant.

"A journal, you say?" Camilla asked as she forked a piece of asparagus on her plate with some difficulty. "I was hardly in that room as a young girl, because it smelled of moldy old books. Who knew I'd become a writer myself?" She shrugged.

"Not moldy," Samantha said after swallowing the excellently prepared salmon. "Musty, perhaps."

"Either way, I loathed the smell." Camilla crinkled her nose. "What's so special about this journal? Who kept it?"

"We don't know that yet," Darian said. "They wrote about wanting to form a family with their Gai'usto."

"Gai'usto?" Camilla raised her eyebrows. "What sort of name is that?"

"No idea." Samantha sipped her chardonnay. "Slavic, maybe? Or Mediterranean?"

"I never knew we had any Slavic ancestors, but I can't say the topic came up much when I was young." Looking absentminded,

Camilla put down her fork and rubbed her knuckles. "My parents' names were British enough—Richard and Alison Wells." She smiled faintly. "I took my husband's last name when we got married."

"I'm psyched about delving into the mystery." Darian grinned and waved her fork in a circle. "Considering the wall in the basement, we have a proper mystery on our hands. Or a mystery combined with some riddles, as half the journal seemed to consist of these strange symbols. Perhaps our ancestors were heavily into cyphers? Or code!"

"In the seventeen-hundreds? I imagine they were more heavily into surviving," Samantha said, unable to hide her smile. Something about Darian was disarming, even if she could be a flirt and a heartbreaker.

"Hey. Once darkness fell and they barricaded the doors to keep bears and wolves out, who knows? I can just picture them sitting in their log cabins, making up puzzles to keep from going insane." Darian chuckled.

Camilla took the linen napkin from her lap and delicately dabbed her lips. "As much as I can envision your vivid description, Darian, I want to know what you meant by the wall in the basement."

"Oh, right." Darian used her napkin as well, though with more efficiency than delicacy. "We were so excited about the journal, we forgot to tell you." She recounted the oddities in the basement to her grandmother. "Once I've had the carpenter make sure the stairs are safe, because right now they're a bit on the creaky side, I'll help you downstairs, Gran. You'll get a kick out of the old furnace. Looks like something from one of your scary movies. Good thing I don't frighten easily."

"A very good thing." Camilla smiled, but Samantha thought she saw something sad in the tension around her blue eyes. "And I appreciate you being cautious with me, but don't overdo it." She flicked her napkin toward Darian before putting it down.

Darian merely smiled at Camilla. "Are you kidding me? I know who's the queen around here."

This comment erased whatever sadness Samantha thought she might have picked up in Camilla's eyes. Laughing, she leaned back in her chair. "I don't know about you girls, but I'm ready for some dessert and coffee, or perhaps Samantha prefers tea? Why don't we return to the parlor? No, no," she said to Darian, shaking her head. "Before you object to the old furniture, Brandon placed extra cushions on them, just for you." She winked at Samantha, who quickly bit her lip to hide yet another smile.

"Oh, great." Darian muttered, but she got up from her chair to assist Camilla, who waved her away.

"I'm doing much better." A barely-there frown showed up between Camilla's eyebrows, but that seemed to be all it took for Darian to stop hovering.

They returned to the parlor, where Samantha's gaze kept being drawn between the abundant bookshelves that Darian had called "the surplus" earlier and Darian's lithe body as she helped a bald, burly man pull in a delicate brass cart from the kitchen area. Samantha had briefly said hello to the man, not quite sure if he was merely the cook, or also a butler, and a chauffeur, and perhaps a bodyguard as well, for Camilla. His voice was remarkably soft and low, but it was obvious that his bulk consisted of all muscle and little fat. It was impossible to judge his age or his ethnicity. Models would kill for his smooth, clear complexion. A few wrinkles around the eyes suggested he did smile on occasion. He was younger than Camilla, but by how much? Fifteen, twenty years? Samantha chastised herself for always being so prone to compartmentalize people when it came to their statistics. She wasn't being judgmental—she knew herself well enough to realize that fact—but she did want to make the world easier to understand. Everything in its place and so on. Her tendency could take ridiculous turns; of this she was well aware.

"Thank you, Brandon. You're off duty now," Camilla said, her voice holding something close to tenderness. "You're working far too many hours as it is."

"Hardly, Camilla." Brandon smiled quickly, showing off perfect white teeth. "Even so, good night, all. Nice to make your acquaintance, Ms. Pike."

"Samantha. Please."

"Thank you, Samantha. I'm Brandon Reyes but call me Brandon."

"Thank you. So much easier to be on a first-name basis," Samantha said.

He made a small bow and returned toward the kitchen area.

"Now, where were we?" Darian asked as she poured their hot beverages.

"The basement. Or in the journal." Camilla locked her gaze on Samantha. "As fascinating as all that is, I want to hear about Samantha. Are you a born-and-bred Dennamore girl?"

Put on the spot, Samantha held her mug tight. "I am. I left only for the years it took me to earn my master's degree in library and information. Once I had that in the bag, I returned here. I suppose my yearning came even before I left."

"Excuse me? Your yearning?" Darian put her coffee mug down.

"Oh. Right." Willing herself to relax, now that they were perhaps moving to more general topics rather than her life, Samantha nodded. "It's probably nothing more than a coincidence, but according to popular belief, especially among the older generations, Dennamore has a pull on the people who move away. I don't know if that theory is even quantifiable, but most people who move away for college, work, or for any other reason, really, return at one point. Like you, Camilla. There are even records of it in Old papers in the town hall basement contain references to it, calling it the yearning."

"Wait. That kid at the library. The young guy. He wondered if I was a returnee. Is that the same thing?" Darian looked back and forth between Samantha and Camilla.

"Carl. Yes. It's related. A returnee is what you become when you've heeded the yearning and returned to Dennamore." Samantha enjoyed the surprised look on the others' faces a little too much. Pulling herself together, she shook her head. "A self-fulfilled prophecy. You have a longing for home. That's not uncommon. You know from your early age about the yearning, so when you miss your family and friends, you can easily interpret it a little too easily as the much-talked-about yearning."

"My yearning started eight years ago, right about when I turned sixty-seven. At first, I thought it was because I was nearing retirement age. But now that you mention the yearning, I remember people talking about it in the sixties, when I was a teenager. It's quite a phenomenon if it still goes on."

"Hey, hold on, hold on." Darian raised both her hands, palms forward. "If you'd forgotten about the yearning, and you still experienced it when you were sixty-seven and onward...how can it be a self-fulfilling prophecy? And even if you might have remembered on some subconscious level, I felt the damn overpowering urge to come with you, to see where we come from—and I've never been here!"

"But you love your grandmother, and it's natural to take an interest in one's background. That's what I love to research, so I know that feeling well." Samantha tried to keep Darian from reading too much into things.

"True." Darian didn't seem entirely convinced. "And if I hadn't just come across the freaking wall, seen the enormous basement under the library at Town Hall, and found a journal from the seventeen hundreds, I might have been able to brush it off." Darian tapped her chin. "The thing is, I just made detective a year ago, and it has always been my dream. Then nine months ago, three months after I got my detective badge, I get what can only be described as a damn yearning to go with Gran to Dennamore, which you can barely see on the map."

Samantha didn't know how to respond to that statement. When Darian put it like that, it sounded compelling to her as well.

"What I know," Camilla said and fumbled a bit with her dessert fork before placing a piece of the cheesecake in her mouth. After swallowing, she hummed and then continued talking. "Is that the two of you look like you're dying to figure out more about our ancestry in this town, as well as what's going on in our basement... and whatever Darian found odd about the basement in the town hall."

Samantha had to concede. "So true. I'm grateful to have Darian join in. She'll look at it from a completely different viewpoint...Oh!

I forgot. I had a greeting for you, Camilla. I ran into Geoff Walker on my way over to your house. He remembers you fondly and told me to say hello from him."

"Geoff Walker?" Camilla frowned for a moment but then lit up. "Young Geoff. Yes. Yes! I remember him well. He and I went to school together. What is he up to these days?"

"He's the former chief of police. Some of us still think of him that way, even if Chief Billings has held the job for a few years." Samantha placed her tea mug on the side table. "Nowadays, Chief Walker enjoys photography more than anything else. He reminded me that the Lake Light Festival is taking place soon. It's only a week from now. I hope you both can attend. It's quite something."

Camilla brightened. "I remember those from when I was young. They're beautiful, and they always happen on the same days, every year."

"Oh, God. Is that another mystery I need to factor in?" Darian groaned, but she winked at Samantha.

"Not at all," Samantha said and smiled. "Just a natural phenomenon that occurs this time every year. It brings in tourists and much-needed revenue before the skiing season begins. We're not Aspen, thank God, but we get our fair share of skiers around the holidays and onward. That's when you see the Airbnbs pop up. There's also a log-cabin retreat on the opposite side of the lake. It's no gold mine, but it does all right."

"I have a lot to explore," Darian said. "There's a lot more to Dennamore than I thought possible. I knew very little about it until Gran started getting homesick."

"I'm glad you returned," Samantha said, looking over at Camilla. "I hope you'll be able to reconnect with old friends."

"So do I." Camilla shifted on the couch, a faint grimace betraying her discomfort. "Darian, I'm sorry, but I can't seem to get comfortable. I think I need to lie down."

"Let me help you," Darian said and stood.

"No, thank you, dear. I'm fine. Just give me a hand to get up from the couch. The sooner it's reupholstered, the better."

"I hear you, Gran." Darian assisted her grandmother. "Careful."

"Yes, yes." Camilla turned to Samantha, who also stood. "It was so lovely to meet you, Samantha. Please don't be a stranger. Come peruse our books as often as you like. I look forward to discussing all the details with you and Darian."

"Thank you. I look forward to finally making some headway in my research about Dennamore. I hit a roadblock several years ago, and this opportunity means more than I can say. That, and getting to know you and Darian, it's truly my pleasure." Knowing she sounded her usual formal self, Samantha hoped the other two women could still tell how heartfelt her words were.

"I'll retire to my recliner and my TV," Camilla said after squeezing Samantha's hand between her own trembling ones. "I believe some of my favorite shows are on."

"They are," Darian said after checking the time.

"I should let you both continue with your evening," Samantha said, thinking Darian might need to tend to Camilla. "I'll be back soon enough."

"Oh, no, don't leave earlier on my account," Camilla said as she slowly made her way to the hallway. "Darian will be disappointed."

Samantha cast a glance at Darian, who groaned.

"Thanks, Gran. Now I know you're okay." Darian looked toward the ceiling."

"You're welcome, dear." Camilla nodded and left them alone.

"You really don't have to go yet," Darian said, pushing her hands into the pockets of her jeans.

"I don't want to. I'd rather stay here and discuss our projects and learn more of your life before Dennamore, but Chief Walker reminded me of the Lake Light Festival, and I have to go over the plans for Town Hall." Samantha checked the time. "It'll get dark very soon."

"At least let me walk you home." Darian didn't wait for a response but hurried out into the hallway and returned moments later, holding Samantha's cardigan and wearing a leather jacket.

Samantha had thought to object, as there really was no need for Darian's gallant gesture. Samantha was used to walking around her hometown at all hours, and she'd never been in danger or felt unsafe. But she really wanted Darian's company for a few more precious moments, and the revelation was mindboggling. She didn't know this woman, not really, and already their upcoming days and weeks, perhaps even months, were enmeshed because of their series of inexplicable finds. Samantha told herself she felt so eager about their research because of her interest in Dennamore's history. Another voice, one that rarely spoke up at all, insisted that there was more to it. The mere idea that Samantha would find Darian interesting on a personal level was disconcerting and equally mystifying. She shrugged on her cardigan and quieted the voice.

"All set?" Darian smiled, and the room seemed brighter than before.

"I am, yes, thank you." Samantha stepped past Darian and out the front door. As she walked down the garden path, she turned her head and looked back at the house. The sun's last rays framed it from behind, giving it a golden hue that made her think of storybooks she'd read as a child.

"It's pretty," Darian said quietly.

"It is." Samantha kept walking, and soon they were shoulder to shoulder on the sidewalk. "It's been an interesting day, to say the least. If I were prone to believing in fate, I'd say such forces were at large."

"I'm not much for fate, horoscopes, and so on." Darian shrugged. "I have to agree though. As soon as I ran into you—literally—one thing after another has slipped into place. I mean, like into a prefabricated slot, like a perfect fit."

Amazed at Darian's words, because they described how she felt in several ways, Samantha knew she had to be careful. She couldn't be tempted into reading too much into what Darian was saying. Darian was talking about the basement and the journals, nothing else. That was fortunate because a worldly person like Darian, born and bred in Los Angeles, a tough woman who had made detective in such a city this early in life, would not be a good fit for a small-town librarian. Looking over at Darian to confirm her own thoughts, of course the setting sun ignited highlights in Darian's hair and made her brown eyes sparkle. At this moment, Darian Tennen was the most attractive woman Samantha had ever seen.

Groaning inwardly, she knew she was in trouble.

Chapter Four

Darian pulled the car up to the lake's crowded parking lot. Thanks to Camilla's new disability tag she found parking for them. Then she helped Camilla into the lightweight wheelchair she used when the walking distances were too long for her grandmother to handle. A stroll around the lake in the evening was far too much, especially at this late hour.

"Need the blanket, Gran?" Darian asked.

"I might as well. It's not cold, but it can change as the night moves on. I don't want you to have to go home any sooner than you want to because I'm vain about blankets." Camilla pursed her lips. "At least we brought the cashmere one so I can ride in style."

Darian chuckled as she spread the blanket across Camilla's lap. "So true."

They made their way through the crowd. A wooden path enabled visitors maneuvering wheelchairs and baby carriages to walk around the calm lake, a forest on three sides and a field on the fourth. Captured in an indentation in one of the mountains, it reflected the full moon and the stars like a mirror. Darian had tried to look up which river supplied Lake Dennamore with water, but the town's website stated only that the water came from within the mountain towering above it. The outlet created a small river that ran between two mountains in the chain surrounding them.

"Perhaps we'll run into Samantha." Camilla's words startled Darian. "Pity that she became so busy after her visit. I know the two of you were ready to go at it."

Darian agreed but didn't respond. A week had passed since she walked Samantha home, and after that, Samantha had been busy with the festival. The Elder Council had given her extra assignments, and Darian had heard the frustration in Samantha's voice when she called to explain. Darian would have been even more disappointed at their delayed plans if she hadn't had her own unforeseen chores. Camilla had needed help getting to the local doctor's office. Then Camilla's medical files had disappeared, and Darian had spent almost an entire day on the phone before they were relocated. It was one thing after another, and now it was Saturday, a little more than a week later. The Lake Light Festival had begun this morning, and now Darian and Camilla gathered around the lake with most of the Dennamore population and enough tourists to boost the town's economy for the upcoming months.

"I'm so glad I found you." Samantha's voice made Darian pivot so fast, she nearly toppled over. "I managed to shake the Elder Council's chairman and went looking for you. I've been at his beck and call for a week. Enough is enough."

Darian took in the vision that was Samantha. Dressed in tan chinos, a white turtleneck, and a navy-blue down vest, she managed to look outdoorsy and elegant at the same time. She kept her hair in a twist, but the faint breeze had tugged a few tresses free that caressed her cheeks.

"Finally," Camilla said and waved Samantha down to her level to place a kiss on her cheek. "We've missed you."

"And I've missed you." Samantha looked a little amazed at her own words, but the sparkle in her eyes warmed Darian.

"Let's hope the elders don't monopolize you this way again until next year," Darian said. "Are we at a good spot to watch the lights?" She peered into the lake. "That's not it, right? The moon's reflection?"

"No, not at all." Samantha chuckled. "Trust me, when they start, you'll know."

"I can't understand how I've never thought of the lake lights until now. I mean, for all those years away from here, it's like I completely forgot them. When you mentioned the event last week, Samantha, it was like a pinprick to my brain—and then I remembered all our family outings to the lake and how we always came here to watch the lights. So strange."

Darian agreed. Camilla had never mentioned any light phenomena in her hometown.

"Oh, look!" a female to their left exclaimed. "It's starting!"

Curious, Darian leaned against the railing. Small tendrils of light seemed to flicker deep in the black water. Not only did the lake resemble glass, but it gave Darian the impression that she would be able to walk on the surface. It was a silly thought, but she had never seen such a still surface—and despite the gentle breeze. Gazing around the lakeshore, she saw the huge crowd completely focus on the water. Normally, some kids would be throwing rocks, but it was as if the lights had everyone enthralled.

"Good evening, ladies. I see I'm just in time." A soft baritone sounded behind them, and Darian turned her head and saw a handsome older man carrying a camera attached to a tripod. "Mind if I join you?"

Considering the dense crowd around the lake, Darian was surprised this man had managed to push through. Then again, he possessed a certain authority that perhaps made people defer to him.

"Chief Walker." Samantha smiled broadly. "Please, take my spot."

"No need, Ms. Pike." Chief Walker shook his head. "I'll just set this thing up real quick and work it remotely." He gazed down at Camilla, who had pulled herself up by the railing. "Need a hand, Ms. Tennen?"

"I'm so sorry." Samantha made quick introductions.

"Oh, I'd recognize young Geoff anywhere," Camilla said. "And no need for assistance for the moment. Please, call me Camilla." She placed her frail hand in his and shook it.

"Thank you. And Geoff, or just Walker, is fine. I'm not the chief anymore." Walker took her hand between his in a gentle gesture. After shaking hands with Darian, he deftly placed his camera on the other side of the railing and directed it to the lake. "Last year, I shot from the woods, and the year before, from farther up the mountain. It's been a while since I was this close."

They returned their focus on the lake, and Darian saw how the tendrils had become long, broad streaks of colors going from bright yellow to dark blue. They looked oddly like flames, which only added to the mystery. Moving slowly, as if waves shifted them, even if the lake was entirely still, they almost danced under the surface.

"Amazing." Camilla breathed the words and clutched the railing. As if on cue, both Samantha and Darian placed a hand gently against the small of Camilla's back. She merely smiled but didn't take her eyes off the water. "How could I have forgotten this? I came here every year, like most of the townspeople and an increasing number of tourists, but after I left…I kind of forgot." She shook her head slowly.

"If it's any consolation, I never thought of the lake lights when I was away at college," Samantha said. "I was singularly focused on my studies, and then when I returned, I went back to what I call Dennamore mode. This place is magical once you let it under your skin." She shot Darian a glance as she spoke.

Not sure what to say, Darian merely nodded. "I can feel it. And I think there's a lot here to discover." She didn't want to reveal what they'd found at Camilla's house among all these people, or Walker.

"There sure is." Samantha looked back at the lake. "It's time."

Time for what? Darian scanned the surface, and then the lights shifted again. Trembling and growing in size, they seemed to be trying to ignite everything under the surface. After a while, Darian couldn't tell how long, perhaps a minute, they began to fade. At the same time, they swelled, and the bigger they grew, the more they appeared to dilute in the water. Eventually, all Darian saw was the perfect, still reflection of the moon. When she automatically checked her smart watch, she saw the lake lights had actually lasted for forty-five minutes.

"What the fu—" Darian turned to Camilla. "What time do you have, Gran?"

Camilla sat down in her wheelchair and pulled up her cell phone. "Eight twenty. We've been here a while."

"Feels shorter, doesn't it?" Walker said after returning from retrieving his tripod. Darian saw it was an interesting contraption, able to hold two cameras. "One for still and one to film the event." Walker disassembled his equipment and placed it in a backpack. "May I invite you to my humble abode for tea, or coffee? I've made a carrot cake."

Camilla laughed, and people passing them turned their heads and smiled. "Who can pass up carrot cake at any hour of the day? What do you say, girls?"

Darian was immediately eager to pick Walker's brain about the lights and Dennamore in general. "Sounds great. I'm in."

Samantha seemed to hesitate but then accepted. "It would be lovely. Your baked goods are legendary for a reason."

"See you at the house then. You know the way." He directed the last comment to Samantha and then strode through the throng of people who, just like Darian had noticed earlier, parted as if on cue to let him through.

"He's quite something," Camilla said as they began making their way toward the parking area. "Authority without even trying."

"So true. I miss him being our chief of police," Samantha said. "The current one is all right, and comparing him to Walker is really unfair, but I doubt there'll ever be another Chief Walker."

After helping Camilla into the car, Darian waited to back out until she saw Samantha pull up in a small blue car. She followed Samantha through the streets and found that Walker lived near a wooded area. He too resided in a log house that seemed to originate from the time Dennamore was founded. It stretched halfway into the woods to the west, and on the other side of the house sat a large conservatory. It was lit by a multitude of fairy lights that made the house look magical.

"I remember this house very well." Camilla steadied herself against the car. "Look at the roof, Darian."

Darian lifted her gaze and gaped. "Is that grass?"

"It is. Grass. Wildflowers when they're in season. Our house used to have a roof like this, but my grandfather changed it into shingles at one point. The Walkers never did. I think it's the last roof of its kind in Dennamore."

"It's beautiful."

"And surprisingly low maintenance," Walker said from the walkway. "May I offer you my arm now, Ms. Camilla?" His dark eyes sparkled.

"This time I'll take you up on that." Camilla gracefully accepted his proffered arm and walked as if she had never known pain in her life. Darian knew the effort that took and hoped Camilla wouldn't pay too dearly for their outing the next day.

Samantha walked next to Darian as they made their way to the house. "I just want you to know that if we can trust anyone to keep a secret, it's Geoff Walker," she said quietly. "Besides, I can tell you're dying to ask him questions, and he's no fool. He'll know you have specific reasons for asking."

Darian paused, but she knew, somehow, that Samantha was right. "Okay. Good to know. I trust you to have your neighbors pegged since you work in such a central capacity at Town Hall."

"True." Samantha surprised Darian by snorting softly. "Sometimes I learn more than I care to know, judging by the books they check out."

Darian chuckled. "Please don't tell me about how old little Ms. Smith reads nothing but bodice rippers in the wee hours."

Samantha laughed out loud. "Oh, God. If you only knew."

The interior of Walker's home resembled Camilla's when it came to the layout. But someone had obviously lived in this house, while Camilla's had sat empty for decades. Here, modern furniture was mixed with antiques, technology upgraded to a degree.

"I thought we'd sit in the conservatory." Walker showed them into a room that made Darian gasp. If it had looked pretty from the outside, the inside was magical. The small lights were woven among a multitude of plants. Palms, grass, succulents, small fruit trees, and climbing greenery all surrounded a rustic dining-room set, able to seat ten people.

"Geoff." Camilla covered her mouth with her free hand. "This is stunning."

"My wife's doing." A trace of sorrow laced Walker's voice. "She made this room happen, and after she passed, I vowed to keep it going even if I know zero about plants."

"You must have learned fast." Darian pivoted slowly. "I would've killed off half of these in a month or two, despite my best intentions."

Walker grinned. "I won't ask you to house-sit when I go on my next hike then."

Darian gave a thumbs-up. "Good thinking, Chief."

"I told you, no need for formalities." Walker raised his hand as if warding off the title.

"Force of habit with this one," Camilla said and sat down on one of the chairs. "Thank you, unnamed deities, for a proper cushion." She patted Darian's hand when she helped push the chair closer to the table. "My granddaughter is an LA detective."

Wanting to groan at Camilla's rare bout of bragging, Darian pushed her hands into her jacket pockets.

"Ah." Walker didn't comment further but gave Darian an appreciative glance. "Please take a seat while I fetch the tray."

"I can help," Darian offered.

Walker hesitated only for a second but then nodded. "Thank you."

The kitchen looked exactly like Camilla's, with the same appliances that appeared to be ancient and identical cabinets. On the counter, two thermoses sat next to a tray holding plates, forks, mugs, and an impressive carrot cake.

"You can carry the thermoses and—damn it, I forgot to ask if anyone takes milk or sugar. I drink my coffee black, and it always slips my mind."

"Just some milk for Camilla. I take it black too, and I think Samantha uses milk as well."

Walker poured some milk into a small jug and placed it on the big wooden tray. "There. I think we're all set." He stopped in mid-motion. "Unless you want to tell, or ask, me anything?" He leaned against the counter. At least six foot four, he could have easily towered over Darian if he wanted to. Instead, he kept a respectful distance.

"That obvious, huh?" Darian grabbed the thermoses. "I just want you to know that Camilla isn't well. Her arthritis takes a toll on her, and as much as she'd hate for me to tell anyone about her frailty, she's blossoming after returning to Dennamore. Seeing you, even more so. That said, she needs her breaks. Other than that, she's entirely her own person, with a mind of her own. She doesn't need me to speak for her."

"She does because you see her when she pays the price for exerting herself and others normally don't." Walker sighed, but it was an empathic sound. "My wife was the same way, albeit for a different reason. I was the only one who saw her struggles to keep up."

Darian relaxed. If she had had any doubts about Walker, his obvious love for his wife was evident in his voice and demeanor. "I'm sorry your wife suffered." Holding the thermoses close, Darian then smiled. "Actually, I do need to say something else. If you try to be too protective or pity Camilla, she'll kick your ass."

Walker threw his head back and laughed. "Now, that sounds like the Camilla I had a crush on from afar. I was fourteen, and she was unapproachable. Much like the lights tonight."

Darian could see Walker meant what he said. "We better take them the coffee before Camilla comes out to get us."

"I hear you." Picking up the tray, Walker motioned to the doorway with his head. "After you."

The carrot cake tasted like a piece of heaven. Having been to quite a few coffee shops and famous bakeries in LA in her day, Darian considered herself something of a connoisseur, and Walker's cake was right up there with the best. After the oohs and ahs around the table had died down, Darian decided to get to the point. This was an opportunity to begin their research. The delayed start, as Darian hadn't even wanted to chip away at the planks in her basement without Samantha helping to document potential finds, had made her more impatient than usual. She waited until Walker put down his mug. "Is your house as old as Camilla's?"

"I think so," Walker answered calmly. "I've never been inside Camilla's house, not even back in the day, so I can't say how similar it is—but the exterior suggests it's one of the first log houses. Originally, I think there were a dozen of them, but now only five remain. I suppose fires can have taken a few of the others."

"One was demolished despite the Elder Council's objections." Samantha took another bite of her cake. "The Normans' house was inherited by a relative who wanted to build a modern cookie-cutter kind of house. The Elder Council couldn't stop the demolition, but the relative ended up with an empty lot afterward, as they could, and did, stop them from building the new house. The heir sold the lot to, was it the oldest Baker daughter?"

"Yes." Walker nodded. "I remember this situation well. It was the last year I served as chief of police. We had to enforce crowd-control measures because the demolition outraged so many people."

"Is the lot still empty?" Camilla asked.

"No. The Bakers all pitched in and built another log house on top of what was left of the old foundation. Fortunately, the heir hadn't gotten as far as actually digging that out." Walker smiled sadly. "It's not the same, of course, but it helped settle the uproar. We don't have much crime here, normally, but that time, I thought the pitchforks would come out."

Darian could tell Walker was only half joking.

"I asked," she said, picking up the last bite of her cake with the fork, "because we've come across some anomalies, and some interesting documents. Would you be interested in comparing your house to Camilla's—especially when it comes to the basement."

"The basement?" Walker's full eyebrows went up as he turned to Camilla. "What's in your basement?"'

"I haven't ventured down due to a less-than-reliable staircase, but apparently a strange, warm wall." Camilla gestured at Samantha and Darian. "These two were down there for quite a while a week ago and came up all excited. Then they found an old journal that even I'm quite taken with."

"My basement is the way it's always been. An ancient furnace that I should exchange, but never get around to. Some storage. To be honest, I'm rarely down there." Walker rubbed his chin. "If you want to have a look, it's all right with me."

"Truly?" Samantha sounded hesitant. "We wouldn't want to impose—or invade your privacy."

Walker laughed again, like he had in the kitchen. "It really is okay, Samantha. I have no hidden secrets in the basement. Just cobwebs and old stuff I should go through and recycle."

"Will you be all right if we head down for a quick look now, Gran?" Darian tried to judge if Camilla was reaching her breaking point. To her relief, Camilla moved her arm easily as she flicked her fingers in their direction.

"Don't be silly—of course I'll be fine. I'm going to have young Geoff here pour me another cup of coffee before the three of you go and then just enjoy the beauty of this room in private."

"You have your phone." Darian knew she was pushing it when Camilla's brow furrowed. "I know, I know. I'm hovering." She stood and waited for Samantha to do the same and for Walker to pour more coffee before joining them.

The door to the basement was located in the same area as it was at Brynden 4. But here the staircase leading down was well kept and completely free from cobwebs. Fluorescent lights lit up the entire basement.

Walker said, "Watch your step. It turns a sharp—"

"Right at the bottom. Same as ours," Darian said. She glanced back at Samantha. "Feels very familiar."

"It does." Samantha was right behind Darian and put her hand on Darian's shoulder. "Look where you're going. You have a habit of running into things, remember?" She managed to look almost serious.

"That's not fair. Once isn't a habit." Darian almost stuck her tongue out but thought better of it before she made a fool of herself.

The furnace was the same type but looked better kept as well. Samantha stepped closer and pressed her hands against the wall.

"Oh, my God." Samantha let go and pivoted. "Feel this."

Darian slid her hand along the black surface. She had half expected it, but it was still something of a shock. "I can't believe it." She snapped her head around. "Have you never wondered about this rock?" she asked Walker.

"What do you mean? The wall?" Walker scratched his head. "It's always been there. Why would I wonder about the wall?"

"Did you grow up here?" Darian asked, feeling the warmth of the wall against her palm.

"Yes, of course. This is my childhood home. It's been in the family since forever." Walker frowned. "Are you saying something's wrong with my basement?"

"No. But this wall is made from one single block. And it's warm. Feel it." Darian stepped back, and so did Samantha. She watched as Walker pressed a hand against the rock and let it slide along it in both directions. "What the—" He swept with his other hand and then both, as if trying to make snow angels. "Wait." Walking over to the other wall, he opened a drawer in an old desk, pulled out a flashlight, and quickly checked the light beam against the palm of his hand. "Let's see." As he pressed his cheek against the wall, he slowly let the beam travel along the surface. Then he jerked his head away from the wall and switched it off. "I must be…I mean, I thought I heard something. And it is definitely warm, and one huge piece of perfectly carved-out block of…whatever it is."

For Walker to sound so uncertain, Darian knew he had to be rattled. "What did it sound like?"

"A hum? Or a vibration." Walker rubbed his neck with his free hand.

"What's on the other side?" Samantha stepped back and peered into the corridor that was around the corner.

"Just storage." Walker's eyes narrowed. "Are you saying something strange is in there too?"

"At Brynden 4, there's a pantry. The wall is made of huge boards, and they're warm. We're going to tear them down asap." Darian pointed. "May we look?"

"Sure." Walker motioned for them to go ahead of him. Darian wasn't sure if it was due to the light, but she thought he looked pale.

The storage room was packed with things, but enough of the wall on the other side was exposed, and it was also covered with boards. Samantha pressed her hands against them.

"It's not as obvious, but to me they feel warmer." Leaning in, she aligned her head with the closest log. "Ow. I'm going to get splinters on my face." This comment didn't stop her from pressing her index finger against her lips though. "Shh."

They stood in silence for a good fifteen seconds, but then Darian's impatience made her tap Samantha's shoulder. "And?"

Samantha pushed herself off the wall and angled her body enough to free herself from the rough shelves. "The warmth is there, though not as easy to feel as in your basement. But the hum, or vibration, is undeniable."

"What the hell's going on?" Walker felt the log behind the shelves. "Can't say I feel any hum, but they're warm."

Samantha stood silent for a moment, and Darian, recognizing the way Samantha squinted slightly and pressed her lips together, waited for her to gather her thoughts.

"We need to be methodical instead of going at this haphazardly with axes and so on," Samantha said slowly, turning to Darian and Walker. "You both have mysterious walls in your basements. I have access to the library and Camilla's private library as well. We can ask Camilla if she's up for some reading."

"Up for it? Are you kidding? Try keeping her out of there." Darian snorted. "Remember, she's a writer."

"I take your word for it, but it's still polite to ask." Sounding absent-minded, Samantha tapped her lower lip with an index finger. "And we might need more people later, depending on our finds. Right now, we must keep this to ourselves. The rumor mill in this town is alive and well on a normal, uneventful day, and if we talk about this too openly, we'll spend more time trying to explain things to people than getting any work done."

"I agree completely." Walker put the flashlight back into its drawer. "Our current Elder Council members are quite nosy, and after the debacle with the house that got torn down, they sometimes… overcompensate."

Samantha nodded. "True."

"If we're done here for tonight, I have to get up to Camilla," Darian said. "I'll fill her in on the way home, if that's okay?"

"It absolutely is. I was just going to suggest that." Samantha walked up the stairs behind Darian. "I know she said I could come by any time, but please reassure her that I'll always call ahead first. That way if she's not feeling up to it, Brandon can let me know."

Darian's heart clenched at Samantha's warm tone. "I'll tell her." She turned to look at Samantha and missed a step on the stairs. She swayed, trying to regain her balance as Samantha wrapped an arm around her, steadying her.

"Careful," Samantha said. "I hate to say it, but 'I told you so.'"

"Damn it. Seems I'm hellbent on knocking us over." Darian groaned. She had to pay better attention and be her usual coordinated self.

Camilla was looking a great deal more tired when they joined her in the conservatory. Darian quickly promised to tell her everything about Walker's basement, and she immediately called it a night, which was a clear sign. Before they said good night to the other two, Camilla stood on her toes and placed a gentle kiss on Walker's reddening cheek. She murmured something to him, which didn't exactly lessen the hue on his cheekbones.

"Come visit me soon, Geoff." Camilla accepted Darian's arm as support when they walked out onto the porch.

"Oh, I can promise you that." Walker bowed slightly, his right hand on his chest.

Samantha walked out with them and hugged Camilla by the cars. "It was lovely to see the lights with you."

"Likewise, my dear." Camilla gave a tired smile after getting into the passenger seat. "Get home safely."

"You, too." Turning to Darian, Samantha hesitated but then gave her a quick hug, which Darian was completely unprepared for. She barely had time to reciprocate before Samantha pulled away. "Good night."

Darian merely stood there, mouth half open, for long enough to make Camilla chuckle. "Damn it, girl. Close your mouth and drive me home." Her gentle voice showed she had an inkling how much the quick hug had stunned Darian.

She slipped in behind the wheel. It was a hit-and-run kind of hug, but one that had made her feel more than she had in a long time.

CHAPTER FIVE

Samantha moved through the narrow aisles at the far end of the basement of Town Hall, and the echoing clatter of the heels of her pumps against the flagstone floor made her wince. She had battled a persistent headache ever since lunch, and the reverberating onslaught against her eardrums wasn't doing her any favors.

She hoisted a small yet heavy box she was carrying from the library and descended the stairs into the bowels of the building she normally loved. Now she felt as if the basement went farther into the bedrock of the surrounding mountains than normal, which was of course ridiculous.

Trying to cheer herself up, she thought about her plan to explore Camilla's library in general, and the journal in particular, this evening. She hoped she'd be able to kick her headache before then and reminded herself to take yet another acetaminophen extra-strength and force down some food. Lunch had been a power bar and a cup of coffee, which was not the right way to ward off a headache.

Turning a corner, she reached the narrowest of all the aisles. If Phileas Beresford, one of Dennamore's most revered scholars, hadn't asked for these documents a month ago, Samantha wouldn't be down here now, putting them back where they belonged. Only Beresford enjoyed the privilege of checking out priceless historic documents from the library and Town Hall archive. Anyone else would have looked them over at one of the library stations and been meticulously supervised, but Beresford was special. He carried out his enigmatic research with the Elder Council's approval.

At the end of the aisle, the closest light fixture was dim, and Samantha shoved the box onto her hip and plucked a small flashlight from her pocket. Finding the code lock, she slid her card through it and punched in her code. The lock clicked, and she pulled the old oak door open. Feeling inside to the right, she found the light switch, relieved when the inner part of the archive storage stopped being a black cave and instead clearly showed off its old wooden shelves.

She checked her notes on her cell phone, murmured, "H41D. Okay," found the shelf halfway into the room, and located the empty slot where the box lived. Relieved to let go of it, she rolled her shoulders and carefully tilted her head from side to side. God, her head was doing a number on her today. How disappointing. She wanted to make a good impression on Camilla and, even more so, be at her best when she spoke to Darian, who always seemed to have more energy than an entire police squad.

Not sure why, Samantha strolled among the shelves. In the beginning, when she was new at her job, she had diligently walked every single aisle of this place, trying to memorize where everything was, until she realized it housed too many documents, books, ledgers, and even artifacts. Now she ran her fingers along the old spines, much like she had at Camilla's, and eventually she reached the back wall of the room. Stopping, she frowned, trying to remember if she had ever been this far into the oldest section of the basement. Surely, she had to have. Still, it didn't look familiar at all.

The wall rose at least eight feet straight up, and it was amazingly smooth-looking, if not as smooth as the rock in Camilla's and Walker's basements. However, it wasn't the wall that sparked Samantha's curiosity, but the strange shelves lining it. Looking ancient, they were obviously untouched, judging from the undisturbed dust. She stepped closer, curious about what could be stored on the shelves, which were slanted at a forty-five-degree angle toward her.

Samantha cleared off some dust with her fingertips, expecting documents, or perhaps books, but found neither. Instead, she saw some flat metal boxes. The lids were dirty, but the metal was very dark underneath the grime, and she used both hands to lift one very carefully. It was heavier than she expected, but she managed to hold on to it and take it to an empty shelf that she could use as a table. Placing it there, she felt for an opening mechanism but couldn't find any, no matter how she pressed and pulled. Samantha's efforts made her increasingly dirty and the box cleaner. It was made of a gunmetal-gray material, and the ornaments, or was it writing, were sharply chiseled.

"What is this?" Samantha murmured. Returning to the shelf, she walked slowly along the shelves that were all filled with the boxes, quickly counting seventy-six of them. Why didn't she know about these boxes? Granted, she hadn't explored these parts as much as some of the others, but surely, she ought to remember seeing an entire collection of some odd-looking containers?

Returning to the one on the table, Samantha stood motionless for a moment. The box wasn't a perfect rectangle. The left end had a cylindrical shape that suggested it might hold an object. A bottle? Secret potions? Snorting at herself, Samantha made a spur-of-the-moment decision. Yet another mysterious find—too much of a mystery. She grabbed the metal case and walked rapidly toward the exit before she started second-guessing herself. She was elated at the idea of showing this discovery to Darian and Camilla. She hadn't seen them for two days but had talked on the phone with both of them last night. Darian had spent yesterday getting her own power tools so she could have a go at the logs in the basement. Camilla had used the day to rest up, eager to make herself useful when it came to the documents. This box would enthrall them.

Halfway to the door leading to the outer archive, Samantha stopped, realizing she was about to carry a Dennamore artifact from the premises. This move could get her fired, as she wasn't Phileas Beresford with special privileges. She looked around, trying to think of a way to disguise the heavy case, and spotted some old maps kept in a barrel-like basket. The barrel looked about the same size as the box, so she hurried over and pushed the rolled-up maps to the side. As they were obviously old and potentially frail, she tried to be careful when she slipped the box in among them. The map holder had a metal handle, and she lifted it cautiously, making sure it would hold the added weight.

Making her way out the door, careful to close and set the alarm behind her, Samantha strode through the outer archive and entered the corridor leading to the stairs. Just as she stepped into the large foyer, she feared her luck had run out. Four members of the Elder Council walked in from the bright summer's day right in front of her.

"Ms. Pike," the oldest of them, the Elder Council chairman, Desmond Miller, said jovially.

"Good afternoon, Mr. Miller." Samantha nodded politely to the man and what she considered his entourage.

"Hard at work, as always. What would we do without you?"

"We'd be lost," Nonnie Wu, the youngest among the council members said, sounding sincere. "I wouldn't be able to do my job without Ms. Pike showing me the right direction when it comes to our documents." Wu was a bright woman in her late fifties, which was considered record young to be on the council. Most people in Dennamore found this age issue normal, but Samantha didn't. She could only imagine what Darian would say about it. Tradition? Pffft.

"What's all this?" Miller said, gesturing at the maps. "Are these from our artifact archive."

Nothing slipped by this man. He might cultivate his amicable mask, but Samantha knew from experience that Desmond Miller ruled the council with a firm hand. He wasn't stupid.

"You're correct," Samantha said calmly, even if her heart began to race. "They're maps from the inner archive. I promised Mr. Beresford I'd scan them for him. Even he understands they can't leave the premises."

"Rightly so, rightly so," Miller said, beaming again. Beresford was perhaps the only one he considered a peer. "Well, we won't keep you, Ms. Pike. Carry on."

Snorting inwardly at Miller's pompous way of dismissing her, when he really wasn't her employer, per se, Samantha bid them good afternoon again and walked toward the library entrance. After making it to her office, she put the map holder on her chair and checked that she was alone before she pulled out the maps. The strange box just fit into her tote bag, which made her smile. As she was about to put the maps back into their holder, she stopped in midmotion. These could be useful later. She had told Miller she was going to copy them, and now she decided that was a brilliant idea. Making two copies of each, she rolled the originals up carefully and placed them in the corner of her office. She would put them back in the basement tomorrow.

Inserting the copies into cardboard tubes, she sealed them with lids in each end. Then, after she checked the time, relief streamed through her when she saw she could close up shop and go home. Opening the top drawer to get her acetaminophen, she hesitated and smiled. She had been so wrapped up in what she was doing, she hadn't even noticed that the headache had disappeared.

Darian gripped her brand-new circular saw and checked the depth setting of the blade. After putting on a visor and ear protection, she was ready to cut along the line she had drawn vertically two feet into the heavy boards after she'd removed the old shelf units.

"Here goes," she muttered and started the battery-operated saw. Carefully, she let the circular blade dig into the boards at shoulder level. Letting the saw do the work, not forcing it, she was pleased to see the nice, deep cut. If she had calculated the depth correctly, the saw would leave an eighth of an inch so she could easily pull away the boards with a crowbar.

It took Darian about fifteen minutes to cut through them. Her shoulders ached from holding the powerful tool, but she was pleased to see the boards loosen. They appeared to be attached to each other with wooden nails, or plugs, as the blade never encountered any metal.

Setting the saw down and removing the ear protection, Darian grabbed the crowbar and was just about to start the next part of the demolition, when Camilla called her name from above.

"Yes, Gran?" Darian walked over to the stairs.

"Just wanted to say that Samantha's pulling up. Want me to send her down before she buries herself in the library?"

"Yes. That'd be great. I'll work some more on the wall, and then we'll join you and Brandon in the library." Darian's chest seemed to swell and then cave in at the thought of Samantha. Pleased that they were finally trying to solve the Dennamore mysteries, Darian couldn't deny that she was jittery around Samantha. Something about her kept pulling Darian in, though the reason was anybody's guess, as Samantha was not anything like Darian's former types. She had so far never gone for the stylish or elegant.

After she returned to her wall, Darian began to chip away at what was left of the boards. As she cleared some of the bigger parts, she heard soft footsteps on the stairs. So, no heels today? Looking around the corner, Darian saw the vision that was a leisurely dressed Samantha approach. Wearing gray chinos, a white button-down shirt, and white sneakers, Samantha wore her hair loose around her shoulders, held back from her face by a broad headband.

"You're hard at work, I see." Samantha stepped over a log. "Good to see you again."

"Same." Darian had to actually keep her jaw from dropping. "You look amazing." Groaning inwardly, she now wished she had engaged her brain to command her vocal cords as well.

"Thank you." Tilting her head, Samantha let her gaze linger on Darian's work clothes and then her messy ponytail, before she shifted her focus to the wall. "You have a good start."

"Yeah. Just need to get that thin layer off, and then we should be able to see if there's more of the smooth wall. Step back just a bit in case some splinters fly your way."

Samantha took two steps back. "Be careful."

"I will." Darian firmly gripped the crowbar and began to chip away at the wood. After removing the upper half, she thought she'd have more control if she stepped farther to the left. Shifting, she raised her arms to give what remained of the boards a good whack, but she stopped when Samantha, who had moved to the same angle, called out.

"Wait! What's that?" Samantha pointed to the area Darian had cut with the circular saw.

"What? What do you see?" Lowering her arms, Darian walked up to the wall and ran her fingertips along the exposed part of the wall. She yanked them back just as fast. "Damn. It's hotter."

"Did you get burned?" Samantha grabbed Darian by the wrist, looking concerned.

"No, not that hot, but definitely too hot to keep your fingers against it for long." Darian felt an entirely different heat from Samantha's grip, not to mention the warmth of being on the receiving end of Samantha's concern. "I'm fine though."

"Good." Samantha took another step to the left, aligning her sight with the wall from the side. "What I saw…wait." She squinted. "There's a glow."

"A glow? You sure?" Darian pushed her face next to Samantha's without thinking about how close they ended up being. "Where?"

"Here. Look here." Pulling her even closer, Samantha guided Darian's head by cupping her cheek. "In there."

Darian saw it immediately. A faint greenish glow came from behind the boards. "What the hell's that?"

"Another mystery to add to our list." Samantha spoke weakly. "I'm losing track."

Something in Samantha's tone made Darian glance at her again. "Something else happen?"

"I found something in the library that I brought with me. I actually smuggled it past Mr. Miller."

"Miller? Is that the Elder Council dude? The head honcho?"

"That's the one." Samantha shook her head. "I must be out of my mind. I could lose my job."

"I'm still glad you brought it." Darian wanted to put her hand on Samantha's shoulder as reassurance but thought better of it, as she was quite dirty and Samantha so…crisp and clean.

"I did. It's up in the library. Camilla and Brandon brought it up. They were going to start going over some of the maps." Sounding absentminded, Samantha extended her hand. "Do you think you'll be able to chisel more of the wood away?"

"Yeah. I just need a mallet." Darian plucked one from her toolbox and then pushed the chiseled end of the crowbar along the edge between the wood and the rock. Wiggling it in between, she pushed. "Stay back a little bit." Using the mallet in short, precise strokes, she slowly uncovered more of the rock. After an additional ten minutes, what had been a faint glow was now growing increasingly brighter.

"Is it just me, or is that glow flickering?" Samantha sounded breathless.

Taking a step back, Darian squinted at the light. "No, it's definitely flickering. Can it be something in the old furnace?"

"You mean, if the furnace is set deep enough in the rock to shine through it?" Samantha peered around the corner. "I can't see how that can be. The rock wall is at least a foot deep."

Darian stretched and rolled her right shoulder, which had taken the brunt of the work she had done with the mallet. "I need to take a break and talk to Camilla. Why don't we go upstairs? We can ask Brandon to make us all some tea."

"Good idea. I'm so curious about what I brought from the archives." Samantha stepped around the tools and walked ahead of Darian up the stairs. Reaching the hallway, they ran into Brandon, who must have read Darian's mind, as he was carrying a tray loaded with mugs, a thermos, and a plate of Gran's favorite oatmeal cookies. Darian had many times teased Camilla about her less sophisticated taste in cookies, but after all the physical labor in the basement, she was ready for one of them right now.

"Good timing, Darian," Brandon said.

"Yeah. What's in the thermoses?" Darian walked up the stairs to the mezzanine after Brandon and Samantha.

"Tea and hot chocolate, but that's not what I meant." Brandon huffed. "I was thinking of Camilla blowing a fuse from pure excitement over the maps Samantha brought."

"I heard that." Camilla's voice came from the library. "And don't forget to tell them how I had to muscle you out the door to go make some tea for us because you were so wrapped up in these maps."

Darian entered the library and found Camilla poring over some A3 documents, which had to be said maps. She was holding onto a large, illuminated magnifying glass and wore her reading glasses.

Now Camilla waved them over. "Put down the tray for a sec, Brandon, and tell me what you see."

He hurried over and accepted the magnifying glass. Camilla tapped the map and then ran her perfectly pale-pink nail a few inches toward her. "That, my friend, looks like a tunnel."

"Could it be part of a sewage system?"

"In the 1810s? No. I seem to remember they were early to introduce sewage here, especially because they were so far from civilization, but probably not until the latter half of the 1800s, if that. This tunnel is on a map dated 1812."

"Could it be a mine?" Darian pulled up a stool and sat down perpendicular to her grandmother. Samantha did the same and ended up on Darian's other side.

"Let me see," Samantha said and frowned. "Let me just...wait. That's the lake. So..." She let her finger follow next to Camilla's. "No. There are no mines there. They'd be flooded. See how they're aligned?"

Darian rested her chin in her hand. "Yeah. That's weird. Why would anyone blast a tunnel in this area that's bound to be flooded?"

"We can't just assume they're actually flooded," Brandon said. "Maybe they aren't connected."

"We know they were good at masonry," Darian said. "I mean, just look at Town Hall, which they started building in the late 1790s. And the rock in your basement—and Walker's. That's as amazing as the way the Egyptians chiseled rocks and built the pyramids, if you ask me."

"Agreed," Samantha said. "Which makes me want to show you something else that's kept in the part of the town hall archive where our oldest artifacts are stored. And it's not the only one. I found tons of them." Samantha went over to the bag she'd brought and returned with what looked like a box with a built-in cylinder on the side. "Now, be careful. This is not a replica. It's the real deal, no matter what it is."

"The markings!" Darian pointed at some raised patterns on the box. "I recognize that one from the journal." She ran her finger across it. "See?"

"Now I do." Samantha paled. "Now I don't know what to think."

"Does it open?" Camilla gently touched the cylinder part. "This looks like it might unscrew or something."

"I doubt it's that easy," Samantha said. "Or it might be. I really have no clue."

Darian turned the item around to look at the cylinder. "There's a strange edge here. Like a jagged set of—what?" She flinched when Samantha yanked the box back.

"Sorry. It's just…it's the western mountain chain seen from the town. See? There's the tip of Mount Corma. And that's Mount Tepor." Tapping the jagged raised pattern, Samantha covered her mouth with her free hand. "And that's where the lake is."

"You're right," Camilla said quietly. "It's obvious when you know." She looked back and forth between Darian and Samantha. "What did you find in our basement? I was so eager about the maps, I didn't think to ask."

Darian explained about the rock, the heat, and the pulsating light.

"Like in the lake?" Camilla said, doubt in her tone.

Darian and Samantha exchanged glances. "Oh, God," Darian said. "Of course. Could that be connected? I mean, strange tunnels on maps close to the lake, pulsating lights in the lake on an annual basis, and flickering, or pulsating, lights coming from a damn rock."

Samantha lowered her hand from her mouth and then slammed it into the table, making the others jump, and the artifact as well. "I've had so many questions about this town for so long, but nobody has ever been all that interested. Everybody's so happy to just go through their days as if every single discrepancy—"

The box moved, and then two pegs on either side of the cylindrical part extended with a loud snap. The cylinder rolled away from the box, and only Brandon's quick reaction kept it from falling off the table's edge.

"Jesus," Camilla said weakly. "I'm going to need something stronger than tea."

CHAPTER SIX

Samantha placed a trembling hand on the cylinder. Was it just her nerves from all the excitement, or was this item warmer? Perhaps she'd been unduly influenced by the hot rock wall in the basement and now projected her reaction onto the artifact.

"Wow." Darian shook her head in obvious disbelief. "I don't think alcohol will do the trick."

"Does it contain anything?" Camilla held one of her hands over her mouth.

"I don't dare shake it, and I have no clue if it opens." Samantha turned the item over in her hands. "Unless we find more magic buttons."

"Lots of signs, kind of like code." Darian scooted closer to Samantha. "What's that there?" She pointed at a long, raised ridge that ran along the cylinder. "There's a fine indentation in the center of it."

"I swear this thing is warming up too. Am I losing it?" Samantha murmured.

"Hey, why not? Everything else here is either glowing or warming. Some both." Snorting, Darian gently nudged Samantha's shoulder with hers. "Just try something. That or we could compare the signs with what we found in the journal."

Suddenly afraid, and without knowing why, Samantha put the cylinder down on the table and took a deep breath. Then she did as Darian suggested, felt with her index finger along the ridge. At first, nothing. She raised her hand and was just about to do it again, this time with more force, when lights began shining through pinprick-sized holes.

"God." Camilla steadied herself with both palms against the table. "What kind of sorcery is this?"

"Do it again," Darian whispered. "Remember it has sat in the archive for God knows how long."

"All right." Pushing her fingertip, harder this time, Samantha felt the texture against her skin. This time she took care to start just before the ridge and go past it at the end, making sure to cover it all.

The cylinder gave a clicking sound, and the ridge dislodged. No, not quite, but it moved, pulling something thin, of the same width, with it.

"What's that?" Brandon leaned forward.

"A paper, or cloth?" Darian asked.

"Should I pull it?" Samantha gazed around the table, but the other three seemed transfixed. "I take that as a yes." She tugged gently at the ridge, which was now more like a smaller cylinder attached to something that looked like a plastic sheet. As she pulled at it, Samantha saw it was textured and covered with more of the symbols. "Damn." She could barely breathe.

"It looks pristine." Camilla carefully touched one of the symbols on the plastic-looking sheet, and it gave a faint hum and glowed. Camilla yanked her hand back. "What did I do?"

"It's sensitive to touch." Darian rubbed her forehead. "This can't be from some two hundred years ago! It's impossible."

"Yet it is. All of these…these…cylinder boxes, for lack of a better description, are covered in dust and have been in the archive for a very long time. Hardly anybody goes into the oldest part, since the Elder Council insists on protecting the artifacts of our first ancestors here. I always dreamed of cataloguing that area one day, but dealing with the other part of the basement has had to take precedence." Samantha pulled at the thin cylinder until she had uncovered more than two feet of, well, she supposed she could think of it as a document. Line after line of different signs and figures filled it. There seemed to be more, but she was afraid of damaging it.

"How many more cylinder boxes are there, do you think?" Darian asked.

"I counted them. With this one, seventy-six." Samantha was slowly calming down. "And if all of them hold a scroll, or whatever we should call this cylinder part, it makes me wonder…are they all the same, or all different?"

"And what's in the flat box?" Brandon pointed at the box that sat on its own in front of them. "And how does that open?"

"Is there another slider thing?" Darian carefully nudged the box and made it pivot. "Not that I can see," she said, answering her own question.

"But several raised points in the corners." Samantha gestured toward Camilla. "Your turn. You made the cylinder glow, which means you have the touch."

"Ha. Oh, well, in for a penny…" Camilla gripped the box with trembling hands and lined it up in front of her. She pressed at the upper left nodules and then went around clockwise, but nothing happened. "Guess it would have been too easy," she murmured. Repeating the touch, she did it counterclockwise. Nothing. "All right. What about this?" She pressed the nodules at the top corners first and then the bottom. Still nothing. "I must have jinxed it."

"Keep trying. You'll figure it out, Gran." Darian put her hands on top of Camilla's for a moment. "Just don't hurt yourself."

"Diagonally then." Camilla winked at Darian and pressed on the upper left and lower right, and then vice versa. The glow through small holes and cracks made everyone gasp collectively.

"Camilla—you are amazing." Samantha gaped. "Want to try opening it?"

"No. My job is done. My nerves can't take anymore. Darian, you go ahead." Camilla pressed her trembling hands to her chest.

"Oh, why not?" Darian felt around the top, and after she tried to lift, and push, from different angles, suddenly the box gave a high-pitched chime and slid open. The lid went up as if an invisible hand had moved it, stopping at a forty-five-degree angle, leaning away from Darian.

The inside of the box was, like the cylinder, pristine. Not a speck of dust hid the objects from them. Darian leaned in, her shoulder once again brushing against Samantha's, and stared at the strange items. "No fucking way these things are two hundred and fifty years old. No way."

"Agreed," Samantha said, her voice weak.

"Are those some sort of tendrils?" Brandon reached into a pocket and pulled out a small LED flashlight. Switching it on, he directed the beam at the contents of the box.

On what looked like a gel type of bed, a flat, metal oval glimmered understatedly. It was about one inch across and one and a half inches long. Bilaterally, thin silicon-looking filaments—Samantha counted eight on each side—ended in small, flat, metal circles, maybe an eighth of an inch in diameter each.

"What about that?" Darian murmured and pointed at the inside of the lid. "It's illuminated."

Samantha shifted her focus. Darian was right. The inside of the lid looked like a circuit board, although more advanced than any she'd ever seen. "Damn," she whispered. "Camilla, do you have any idea what this may be, or where it comes from? Anything at all?"

"No." Camilla pressed her lips together. "But the more time goes by, the more I remember from my youth. I left here when I was just twenty years old. After I worked my way down to Los Angeles and began to gain some success as a writer, I, well, didn't forget about Dennamore, exactly, but it got pushed into the back of my mind. Strange. I thought of home occasionally, but in the abstract. I married. Had my son. You came into the world, Darian, and about seven years ago…this yearning to return to a home I hadn't really given a second thought to for so long appeared. My memories are returning, not from obscurity, but as through a kind of mist. Like Alzheimer's in reverse, you could say." Camilla pulled her cardigan closer around her. "It's rather unsettling, but part of me is also curious. I'll let you know if and when I remember anything relevant to this." She motioned to the box on the table. Darian reached out and stroked her grandmother's arm.

"Dare we touch it?" Darian looked around the table. "If it's as old as we first thought, I mean?"

Samantha felt it was up to her to decide. "I've already risked a lot for this box, and we have to figure this out. Especially if all the boxes I saw contain similar items."

"You're the boss," Darian said, a smile forming on her lips. "I volunteer."

Samantha held Darian's glance. "All right. Just be careful."

"I won't break it."

"I meant with yourself. We don't know what this is." Samantha colored faintly at the unintentional emphasis in her tone.

Darian's smile grew bigger. "I will be." Cautiously, she extended her right index finger to the oval piece in the center and ran it along the surface. "Smooth. And you're going to kill me, but it is warm. I mean, more than room temperature."

"Of course." Samantha laced her fingers to keep herself from touching it as well. One at a time was a good idea.

Darian felt around the edge of the oval. "There's an indentation where I think you're supposed to pull it out." She motioned to the short ends of the oval. "I'm going in." Gripping the oval, she tugged, and it let go of its case with surprising ease, taking the limp filaments with it. "It's very flat. Thin, but not sharp." Holding it up for the others to see, Darian wiggled the filaments gently. "Wonder what they're supposed to attach to."

"It's not more than a sixteenth of an inch thick. The little circles, even less." Brandon had pulled out a magnifying glass. Did that man have everything in his pockets?

Camilla gently touched one of the small ends of the filaments.

"Whoa! I felt that." Darian's eyes grew wide as she looked at the oval. "Do it again."

"I'll do it." Samantha touched another of the filaments.

"Yup. It's like it pinged. Damn. Whoever put this in the archives must have added a hell of a battery to the box, like a charger. You sure it was covered with dust?" Darian lifted the oval higher so they could look underneath. "I don't dare flip it and get those tendrils, or whatever they are, tangled."

"They were all covered in tons of dust. Considering anyone rarely goes there, not much dust is stirred in that part of the archive, which means they've been there a long time."

"Could we have them carbon-dated?" Camilla asked.

"I'm afraid that procedure applies only to something that was once organic," Brandon said. "This looks to be all metal and, what is that? Gel?" He indicated the casing.

"Appears like it." Samantha gently poked it. "And you guessed it. Warm."

"We need to anticipate one strange thing after another if we continue this search for the truth," Darian said solemnly. "We've stumbled upon technology that looks futuristic to me, and I would imagine, to all of you, yet the technology appears to be ancient as well."

"Yes. Exactly that." Samantha held out her hand to Darian. "May I?"

Darian placed the oval in Samantha's palm. It sat there for a moment, and then the filaments wrapped around Samantha's hand.

"Shit!" Darian reached for it, but Samantha pulled her hand out of the way.

"No. Don't touch it," she said. "It's not painful."

"But it's attaching itself!" Camilla gripped Brandon's hand as if needing him to steady her. "For heaven's sake, have neither of you seen *Alien*?"

Snorting nervously, Darian didn't take her eyes off Samantha's hand. "I don't think we need to worry about this thing implanting an alien monster embryo in Samantha."

"Nothing is penetrating the skin, I can assure—" Samantha flinched. Staring at her hand, she then shifted her gaze to the scroll that lay next to the box.

"What's wrong? Pull it off." Darian raised her voice and took hold of Samantha's wrist. "Samantha?"

"Stop. Let go." Samantha squinted at the scroll. Not the endless rows of strange signs, but the scroll itself. It also held some signs, as they'd noticed before, but they seemed to be moving before her eyes. Wiggling, almost.

"Oh, dear God, child." Camilla groaned. "What's going on?"

The signs seemed to right themselves somehow. At first, they didn't make sense at all, the differences between them too small to notice. But soon Samantha could see them clearer, as if she had put on glasses despite having perfect vision to begin with. Moving her gaze to the inside lid of the box, she perused the circuit-board-looking layout. The same thing happened. The small signs seemed to mean something. And the glowing lines produced something that resembled the profile of…a skull?

"Talk to us, Samantha," Darian said, taking her free hand. "No offense, but you're acting a little scary."

Blinking, Samantha regarded the piece of technology attached to her hand. "That was quite something."

"Tell us." Camilla cupped Samantha's cheek.

"Well, I don't know how I know this," Samantha said slowly and raised her gaze to look at the others. "I think these are meant to attach at the base of one's skull."

As an LA cop, Darian had seen more than her fair share of strange things, heinous crimes, and the worst—and best—humanity could accomplish. Yet, nothing, absolutely nothing, could have prepared her for the item that looked as if it had attached itself to Samantha's hand. Darian wanted to rip it from the stoic woman next to her, but something in Samantha's eyes, a calm that had replaced the nervous energy from only moments ago, kept her from doing it. "What are you talking about?"

Samantha caressed the raised symbols on the inside of the lid. "These symbols. I'm not saying I can read them, that'd be a lie, but I can see how they indicate the outline of a head. A skull."

"Those things?" Camilla whispered. "All I see is a pattern. Like decorations."

"No." Samantha moved her hand, making the oval glimmer.

"Does it hurt?" Camilla asked, a catch in her voice. "I'm starting to wonder if we're smart to do this by ourselves."

Samantha shook her head. "Not at all. I can't even feel it's there."

"Well, you're not putting that thing anywhere near your brain," Darian said firmly. "We might be a bit nuts, all of us, but let's not be stupid."

"I wouldn't dream of it. Around my hand is one thing, and if that can somehow make me understand the symbols more—"

"You should take it off for now." Darian hoped that darn thing would actually dislodge without them having to cut off Samantha's hand.

"Let me just try to look at the cylinder. I won't even attempt to understand anything about the document, just the cover."

"All right." Genuinely concerned, Darian restrained her protectiveness and pushed the cylinder over to Samantha.

Samantha gripped it gently and looked at it for a good minute. Like before, she ran her fingertips along the symbols, as if they were Braille letters. "Comprehension." Squinting, she sucked in her lower lip between her teeth. "Propensity?"

"That's cryptic." Darian looked over at Camilla. "What do you think?"

"I have no earthly idea." Camilla snorted, but it wasn't a happy sound. "Brandon?"

Brandon placed a gentle hand over Camilla's. "Before we discuss more, Ms. Tennen, may I fetch your medication?"

A quick frown came and went, but then Camilla nodded. "Just indulge me first. What do you think?"

"Those words made me think of education." Brandon didn't take his focus off Camilla. Darian knew he had a sixth sense when it came to Camilla's health and needs. She too could see that Gran was starting to fade a bit.

"Education!" Samantha uttered the word almost simultaneously with Brandon. "Whoa."

Darian gaped. "This is a learning tool? What the hell?"

"I'll be right back," Brandon said calmly and got up.

Camilla leaned back in her chair and adjusted her hair in an automatic, familiar gesture. "And there are seventy-six of these. You understand what you girls need to do next, right?"

"Yeah," Darian said. "We have to open more of them. Compare the signs."

"Not only that," Samantha said casually, but Darian could tell she was tense. "At one point, one of us will have to put one on the correct way." She gently gripped the oval and pulled. Nothing happened.

"Oh, shit." Darian half stood, set on fetching a knife, when Samantha instead wiggled the oval a few times back and forth. Suddenly the filaments loosened and let go. Hanging limply, they remained that way as Samantha carefully put the item back in its case.

"Let me see your hand." Darian didn't wait but took Samantha's hand and turned it over, studying the parts of it where the oval and the filaments had touched her skin. "Looks all right. How does it feel?"

"Normal. Absolutely." Sounding breathless, Samantha pressed the oval into its compartment, and the tendrils seemed to sort themselves and slip into their respective slots.

"Now that takes the cake," Camilla said, sounding out of breath. Brandon picked that moment to return, and she took the pills he brought her, not even looking at them, and downed all the water.

"Glad to see you liberated," Brandon said. "When are we fetching more boxes?"

"You heard that, did you?" Camilla asked, giving a tired smile.

"No, but I know you and Darian well enough, and Samantha seems to possess her own sort of madness." Brandon sighed.

Darian could tell he was only half joking. Yes, perhaps they were rushing into this mystery half-cocked and with a certain recklessness, but what other options did they have? If they told the wrong person about this, they might never find out what was going on.

"That's going to take some finagling." Samantha answered Brandon. "I risked a lot taking this one. I'm afraid I can't carry anything from the archive without the elders finding out. Mr. Miller is probably suspicious as it is. If I'm seen hauling stuff around, we'll lose all access because I'll be fired on the spot."

"Who else can we trust to help us?" Darian asked. "I mean, Walker is already sort of in on things, but who else?"

"Phileas Beresford. Do you remember him, Camilla?" Samantha asked.

"Phileas? Oh, Philber." Camilla smiled and looked marginally less tense.

"Excuse me? Philber? Are we talking about the same person?" Samantha closed the lid on the box.

"We are. Phileas Beresford was a handsome young devil back then, and everyone combined his first and last name like that. Phil-ber," Camilla said and chuckled.

"Well, Mr. Beresford, or Philber, is a renowned researcher and has written several papers about Dennamore folklore and traditions. He has such unhindered access to the older archive because he intimidates Mr. Miller. The same can be said for Walker, of course." Samantha pushed her hand through her hair and disheveled it in a way that made her look much younger.

"Anyone else?" Darian asked while reminding herself that she couldn't keep staring at Samantha like this, especially when they were discussing such important matters.

"Actually, I think Carl Hoskins might be a good choice. You met him that first day you came to the library," Samantha said. "He's strong, has a keen mind, and knows his way around Dennamore."

"Hoskins…" Camilla pursed her lips. "I knew a Bertie Hoskins."

"His grandfather. Carl's the youngest of four siblings. And the smartest, by far." Samantha nodded. "I can recommend these two, and we can ask Walker next time we see him—Camilla?"

Camilla had colored some and now straightened the cuffs of her cardigan meticulously in a way that made Darian raise her eyebrows.

"I'm having dinner with Geoff the day after tomorrow. I could ask him if you like. If you girls don't have anything else planned, why don't you meet us here when he drives me home?"

"Go, Gran." Darian grinned broadly. "I'll be here." She glanced at Samantha, who nodded.

"Nothing could keep me away." Samantha took Camilla's hand. "I'm glad you're starting to reconnect. It suits you."

Camilla huffed, but Darian could tell her grandmother was pleased. And so was Darian. Her grandfather had died more than twelve years ago, and Camilla had often seemed lonely, despite her large circle of friends in LA.

"Please look some more at the maps if you have time," Camilla said to Darian and Samantha and then stood, with Brandon's help. "I'm afraid I can't even pretend to feel all right, so I need to go lie down."

"Want my help, Gran?" Darian stood.

"No, no. I'll be fine once I get downstairs." Camilla kissed Samantha's cheek and then gave her a stern glance. "And listen carefully. You do not experiment with that little thing when you're on your own, my dear. You don't know what it can do to you. All right?"

"Yes, ma'am," Samantha said, nodding seriously. "I'm very curious and eager, but not a fool. I promise."

"Good." After kissing Darian on the forehead, Camilla made her way out to the mezzanine, with Brandon supporting her. Darian sat down again.

"Are we tiring her too much?" Samantha asked.

"I would say yes if I thought we had any say whatsoever regarding what Gran does or doesn't do. She's told me in no uncertain terms that if she wants to run herself into the ground for whatever reason, that's her business. I mean, she was more subtle, but that was the gist of it. She allows me to hover a little bit—with the emphasis on *little*."

"All right. I just wouldn't forgive myself if she got hurt." Samantha sighed.

Her belly warming at the care in Samantha's voice, Darian patted her arm. "Me either, so that won't happen. And she was right, just so you know. You can't experiment without me."

Samantha opened her mouth as if to speak but closed it again. Then she cleared her voice. "Without you?"

"Well, yeah. I mean, seems you and I are at the forefront, at least for now, in researching this. Or have I misunderstood?" Feeling stupid now, Darian waited for Samantha to shoot her down.

"We are. And no, you haven't. I'm not a fatalist at all, but for some reason I believe it was fate you joined your grandmother, even if you weren't born here, and literally ran into me like you did. Now we just have to be careful and smart about how we do this. Desmond Miller likes to think he's royalty around here. Being the chairman of the Elder Council is quite prestigious, and all the portraits of former chairmen, or chairwomen, hang in the town hall upper corridor, where his office is, for a reason. We learn their names in school when our local history is taught."

"Wow. That's rather posh for a small town. Guess people here are proud of their heritage." Darian took the cylinder and tried to figure out how to get the rolled-out part back inside it again. "Here again?" She tapped the protruding parts on the ends. "Think it'll work?"

"Try it." Samantha rested her chin on her laced fingers.

Darian pushed at the cylinder and nearly jumped back when a soft whirring sounded, and the document slipped back into it. It took less than two seconds, she figured. "Damn."

"My thoughts exactly." Samantha laughed. "I'm sorry, but the look on your face…"

"Hm. I bet. Stop smirking, and let's put this thing back together. How do we reattach it?" Taking the cylinder, Darian held it next to the box, but nothing happened. "Do we need to press anything?"

"Let me try." Samantha held out her hand. "It's hard to judge what are cracks or deliberately made slots on these things. But if we line them up like this…" Samantha turned the cylinder around and placed it parallel to the box. Pushing them together with a grip that seemed firm and decisive, she blinked and let go when the cylinder snapped into place. "Ah. There we go."

"That easy, huh?" Darian gently bumped Samantha's shoulder with hers.

"We need the map Gran was studying when we got here." She rose and pulled the map onto the table. The copying process had been successful, and Darian thought the original must be in good shape. She soon found Camilla's house and, after some searching, Walker's and Samantha's.

"Here's the lake. And the potential tunnel." Samantha bent over the table and followed the markings with her index finger. "Is there a scale on this thing?"

Darian scanned the bottom edge. "I'm not sure. Wait. What the fu—" Staring at the lines that could perhaps be an attempt at a scale, she also saw five of the strange symbols. "Look." She pointed.

Samantha gave a muted gasp. "I should have kept the darn thing on. What can those mean? And what are they doing on the map?"

"I couldn't begin to guess." Darian looked over at where Camilla's house sat. "Wait. If we imagine that the structures are all in the same scale as the landscape around them, and I happen to know that Gran's house is seventy feet wide…damn, is there a ruler around here?" Jumping up, she went over to a smaller desk that stood by the window, pulled out drawers, and eventually found an old wooden ruler that showed both inches and centimeters. "Excellent." After she returned, she measured the house on the map. "And on the map, Gran's house is a quarter of an inch…" She measured the width of the tunnel. "Holy crap. The tunnel has to be at least ninety feet wide!"

"Impossible. I mean, this is an old, *very* old, map. How long is it?"

Darian's hands trembled as she moved the ruler to measure the length of the very straight tunnel. Pulling up her cell phone, she taped the calculator app. After recalculating twice, she slumped back in her chair. "Approximately three miles."

Samantha and Darian made it down the stairs, where they met Brandon, who was coming from the kitchen.

"How's Gran?" Darian asked.

"She's fine. Tired, but otherwise she's all right now that her medication's kicked in properly." Despite his encouraging words,

Brandon looked apprehensive. "It's going to be impossible to keep her from overexerting herself, considering everything that's going on."

"I know." Darian sighed. "But the only thing that will be even worse is if we keep something from her to protect her. She'll see through that in a second, and then all hell will break loose."

"Ain't that the truth." Brandon's shoulders lowered as he seemed to relax some. "I'll keep an eye on her."

"You're the only one that can get away with that," Darian said, snorting. "Samantha and I made an interesting discovery, to say the least, after you and Gran left."

"Oh?" Brandon pointed at the parlor. "Care for something to eat? You can fill me in if you want."

"Just a sandwich or something. What about soup?" Darian looked over at Samantha. "Please stay."

"Thank you." Samantha still felt shell-shocked about their discoveries and had been happy to let Darian and Brandon talk alone. "I need some sustenance before I drive home. I have a lot to think about and doubt my brain will slow down any time soon."

"Mine either." Darian put her arm around Samantha's waist and gave her a quick squeeze. The touch was unexpected, but Samantha found it more reassuring than she'd ever thought possible. Darian pointed to the settee in the parlor. "Let's sit and just chill while Brandon fixes something to eat. I'd offer to help, but he'd kick me out in a fraction of a second."

"All right. Sounds good." Her legs shaking now, Samantha realized her blood sugar must be low. She sometimes suffered from hypoglycemia and normally carried dextrose, but she couldn't even remember if she had any with her.

"You look pale." Darian took Samantha's hand. "Please tell me, how are you really, I mean after what we learned and you went through upstairs?"

"I'm okay. Just a bit low on my blood sugar. I'm not diabetic. Just prone to dips. Perhaps the experiences tonight took more of my energy reserves than I realized. Something to think about in the future."

“No kidding. Here. Lean back.” Darian pushed a small round pillow behind Samantha’s neck with her free hand. “Once you eat, you’ll feel better.”

“I know.” Gratefully, Samantha leaned back. “Tell me about LA. It’ll take my mind off the fact that the room’s rocking right now.”

“What?” Darian blinked. “Oh. LA. Sure. Well, I was born there. Lived there all my life, so you can imagine it was something of a culture shock to come to Dennamore with Gran. Went to public school, despite Gran’s objections. Came out in high school. Partied a lot in college. Decided against law school, which had been my parents’ dream for me, and went into law enforcement. Got a tiny studio apartment in West Hollywood to stay close to Gran after I moved out. I worked in a precinct that saw a lot of gang violence, and I was used to being in the fray, adrenaline rushing and so on. Before coming here, I fully expected it to be a sleepy little town where absolutely nothing happened.” Chuckling, Darian shifted until she sat sideways on the settee, facing Samantha.

Samantha realized they were still holding hands but didn’t mind. Darian’s touch anchored her when the world wouldn’t stop moving. “And when you weren’t at work, what did you do?”

“I’m an avid reader. I also like working out. You?”

“Also a reader. Of course.”

“Well, duh. Librarian.” Darian hit her own forehead. “I skip true crime or crime novels though. I tend to read historical romance novels. Or memoirs and biographies.”

“Really?” Samantha ignored her dizziness and turned more toward Darian. She squeezed Darian’s hand and smiled. “Memoirs and biographies are my thing too. And historical nonfiction. We have a lot in common after all.”

“What do you mean, after all? Were you thinking we wouldn’t have?”

“That first day when we ran into each other, I admit I let my biases rule my thinking, but the more I get to know you…I don’t.”

“And what biases were those?” Darian looked uncertain now, and Samantha chastised herself for not explaining properly.

"That you would consider me too stiff and meek." Feeling ridiculous now, Samantha groaned. "I know it sounds silly, but some people find me standoffish and rigid. It is rather remarkable that I can be so at ease around you and Camilla. It doesn't come easy to me, normally."

"That can be interpreted as shyness on your part and an awful lack of understanding from people who just don't get it. The fact that your beauty is only surpassed by your intelligence can intimidate people." Darian shrugged. "People react weirdly sometimes. Being a female cop is a lot about proving yourself in a way that male cops rarely have to. Even to this day."

"I can understand that." Grateful that Darian seemed to understand without any further explanation made Samantha squeeze her hand again. "Thank you."

"What for?" Darian looked down at their joined hands as if she only now realized they were touching.

"For the lovely compliments." Samantha had to smile when Darian raised her gaze and blushed.

"Here we go, ladies." Brandon stepped into the parlor, carrying a tray of soup, sandwiches, water, iced tea, and a fruit platter. He placed it on the small rectangular table by the window.

"Thanks. You're a godsend, Brandon," Samantha said and allowed Darian to pull her up. "Oh, good. Sugar. I'll sweeten some iced tea, I think." Sitting on one of the antique chairs, she reached for the pitcher.

"Allow me," Brandon said before Samantha had a chance to pour. "You look a bit pale, if you don't mind me saying so." After a glance at Darian, who sat down next to Samantha, he smiled. "And you look flustered."

"Bite me." Darian crinkled her nose at Brandon, who merely shook his head and poured iced tea and sugar into a glass for Samantha before sitting down across from them.

They ate in silence, and then Darian filled Brandon in about their measurements regarding the map. He listened patiently and scratched his head.

"Damn it if I understand any of this. I have never lived in a town with such an old history and so many ancient, well-preserved buildings, but I'm sure not all of them have these things lurking in basements or stashed in secret archives." He bit into a cheese-and-ham sandwich and chewed forcefully.

The added sugar was already benefitting her system. Now she had to laugh at Brandon's expressive manners, something she hadn't seen so much of until now. "You're right, of course. These items are unique, but before we explore them further, we can't even begin to speculate."

"We need to divide into teams, provided that Philber and Carl actually want in." Darian lowered her spoon. "Excellent tomato soup, by the way."

Brandon nodded.

"How do you mean?" Samantha asked.

"We need to examine more of the scroll-looking things. And there's the tunnel leading to the lake. And our basements." Darian counted on her fingers.

"All right." Samantha thought fast. "What if you and I take the scrolls, Walker and Philber the basements, and Brandon and Carl try to locate the entrance to the tunnels?"

"We'll meet up and sort it out, but that sounds like a good idea." Darian finished her soup. Samantha noticed how efficiently Darian moved, even when eating. Her movements were precise, and in the basement, working the tools, Samantha had seen firsthand how strong she was.

"I need to get back home. I have several meetings, one with Mr. Miller," Samantha said and made a face. "I better keep him calm, and falling asleep in the middle of our conversation won't accomplish that."

"He sounds rather horrible," Darian scowled. "How did he ever get elected?"

"He's not a bad man," Samantha hurried to say. "He just has his own ideas and, I guess, agenda, when it comes to the future of Dennamore. Part of me can't exactly blame him because his predecessor was at the other end of the pendulum, slacking off and not staying on top of budget matters and so on. I think that's why a more hard-nosed, enterprising person like Miller was elected.

People were fed up with the previous one." Samantha hesitated. "And, if you ask me, something also changed in Miller's demeanor after he took office. He was never very forthcoming when it came to how he reached his conclusions, but after he was sworn in, he has loomed or hovered over anyone who works in Town Hall. At first, I thought he was doubting the way I did my job, but I realize that he, and his closest council members, do in fact loom."

"Perhaps they know something is out of the ordinary in the archives." Brandon put their used dishes back on the tray.

"If he does, he hasn't let on. As far as I know he's been down there only in my company, and we certainly didn't go all the way to the back and into the oldest part. Besides, no dust had been disturbed where the scroll boxes were located in many years."

"We'll have to keep tabs on him, either way," Darian said solemnly. "When are your meetings done tomorrow?"

"Around two p.m." Samantha stood, happy to feel entirely well again.

"I'll come to get a library card and borrow some books, and if Miller's not in sight, we can pop down into the basement and snoop around some."

"Come at four thirty. Miller usually leaves around four." Samantha turned to Brandon. "Thank you for helping. And for the food."

"My pleasure. Drive home safely." Brandon nodded, lifted the tray, and walked toward the kitchen.

After slipping into her jacket in the hallway, Samantha sent a glance up the stairs. "I ought to take the box back to work, but I don't dare carry it around. If Miller is suspicious, and I may be reading far too much about it into the way he acted today…I'm probably blowing this way out of proportion."

"I doubt it. You're going with your gut, and that's a good thing if we want to have a chance to discover what this is all about. I'll go up and cover it with a blanket or something and put it away. Nothing will happen to it."

"All right. Thank you. And the copied maps."

"Absolutely."

They stood in silence for a while, and then Darian wrapped her arms around Samantha and hugged her. “Glad you’re feeling better.”

“I’m fine. Thank you.” Samantha hesitated for a few moments but then returned the embrace. “Be safe working in the basement tomorrow.”

“I will.” Pulling back slowly, Darian pushed her hands into her back pockets. “And I second Brandon. Drive safely.”

“It’s a matter of a few blocks.” Samantha had to smile. Darian looked half embarrassed, and half flustered where she stood, shifting her weight back and forth on her soles.

“Even so.”

“All right. Even so. Good night.” As Samantha stepped out into the cool evening air, she knew it would feel strange to return to her house alone. So many thoughts of what had taken place tonight fought for room in her brain, and amid all the mystery was the image of how Darian had looked after the hug. *I came out in high school.* Darian’s voice echoed inside Samantha. She had never come out, not like that. A few brief relationships, most of them before she returned to Dennamore, had not built her confidence when it came to letting anyone in. She had gone out with both men and women, but she preferred her own gender. The last six years, she had fallen into a rut, dedicating herself to her research and telling herself it fulfilled her more than the confusing world of dating could ever do.

And yet, as she drove back to her house, she couldn’t stop thinking of Darian.

CHAPTER SEVEN

Samantha stepped out of the meeting with the Elder Council and the members of the small but innovative Chamber of Commerce that her hometown boasted, trying not to let her sigh of relief be too obvious. Desmond Miller had been in rare form and gone through every item on their protocol with a fine-tooth comb. Some of the others among the council had begun looking pained, and Samantha had suffered with them. She hadn't gotten much sleep last night as images of what she'd experienced with the oval-shaped object with the tendrils had mixed with ones of Darian.

Checking the time on her cell phone, Samantha lengthened her stride. Darian would arrive any minute, and she was eager, and nervous, to see her. One of the thoughts that had kept her awake had been about the constant touching between them last night. Yes, it had been mostly about reassuring that the other one was all right, but that didn't exclude the fact that the sensation had lingered. Something about Darian's dynamic personality, combined with her strength and how she moved, and, not to forget, how tender she could be with Camilla, was piercing the layers upon layers of self-preservation Samantha had constructed over the years. That, together with the strange situation they found themselves in, was like a powder keg waiting for Samantha to strike a match.

She rounded a corner and saw Carl's familiar figure as he entered Town Hall. She hadn't tried to call him yet, as he had school during the day. Now was as good a time as any.

"Heading for the library?" she asked Carl as she met him halfway.

"Oh, hi, Ms. Pike," he said brightly. "Yeah. Our math teacher got sick, and they couldn't find a temp that fast. We got the mother of all homework instead. I thought I'd do it here. It'll go faster."

"Can I have a word first?" Samantha had to smile at his sudden expression of concern. "No, you haven't done anything wrong. At all. I have an extracurricular assignment for you, perhaps."

"Really? In the library?" Carl brightened. "Anything to keep me away from my pesky siblings. They're at *that* age, to quote my mom."

"Well, come along. I'm expecting Darian—Ms. Tennen, if you remember? She'll be able to help fill you in."

"That LA cop that lives at Brynden 4? Sure. She's cool." Carl looked a little starstruck.

They entered the library, and after saying hello briefly to her colleague who manned the reception desk, Samantha found Darian sitting in an armchair by the window, reading a magazine. She looked up, and the smile she gave Samantha made her nearly stumble on her three-inch heels.

"Careful there, Ms. Pike," Carl said and gallantly held her by the elbow. "Those shoes are lethal weapons if you ask me."

"Hear, hear," Darian said and stood. She seemed to size Carl up, which made the young man blush.

"Don't scare him, Darian," Samantha said and motioned for them to join her in her office. "Anyone else desperate for coffee? The Elder Council members are all about tepid, diluted tea of unknown origin."

"Bleh." Darian made a face. "I can do a coffee-shop run really quick if you want."

"No. I have a machine here. Hang on." Samantha pulled out an espresso maker from a cabinet.

"Wow. Impressive, Ms. Pike," Carl said, grinning broadly. "But why hide it? It's not like you're making moonshine."

Darian chuckled. "Good question."

"You two clearly don't know Mr. Miller and some of his more conservative sidekicks. An espresso machine on display in the library, heaven forbid."

Darian took the pitcher sitting on a shelf. "I'll return with water. Nearest source?"

"Restroom in the hallway." Carl pointed. "But I can do it."

"Nah, that's okay. I think Ms. Pike has something to discuss with you." Darian left, and Carl turned slowly back to Samantha.

"Now I'm super curious. What's up?" He slipped out of his backpack and put it on the floor next to one of the visitors' chairs.

"Please, do sit," Samantha said and did the same after having prepared the machine for the beans and the water. "How are you about confidentiality matters? Would you say you're trustworthy?"

"Yes," Carl said calmly. "When you live in my house, you learn that pretty fast. If I told you anything about all the embarrassing things I hear through paper-thin walls, nobody in my family would ever be able to show their face. Trust me." He gave a lopsided smile, but Samantha guessed he was only half joking.

"That's reassuring. When Darian returns, we'll close the door, and that way we can discuss this situation, if not in minute detail, at least enough for you to decide if you want to help us. And please know that whatever you decide is fine. That goes without saying. Most important is that you realize you cannot share this with anyone."

"Shit…sorry, Ms. Pike. But shit." Carl's eyes showed mostly pupils now, and she could tell he was intrigued.

Darian came back and closed the door behind her without asking. "Here you go." She handed Samantha the pitcher. After starting the fully automated machine to make two lattes and a double espresso, the latter for herself, Samantha sat down behind her desk. Darian had taken a seat next to Carl.

"You don't live in one of the original Dennamore log houses, do you?" Samantha asked Carl, just to make sure.

"No. We live in a pretty sad house from the sixties. I'm sure it's full of radon and other nifty things slowly killing us." Carl drummed his fingers against his jeans-clad knees.

"Darian does. She, Chief Walker, and I found something interesting in their respective basements that just doesn't make sense. It is old, from the late 1700s, but it looks as if made with advanced technology. We've also found a map showing a tunnel, we think, that I've never heard about. There's also an artifact that looks just as futuristic as what we've found in the basement, in its own way." Tilting her head now, Samantha studied Carl's face. The young man looked mesmerized. "Does this sound like something you'd like to help us research?"

"Hell, yeah. Damn it. Sorry again. Yes. Absolutely." Carl nodded eagerly, making his mop of thick, black hair bounce. "When can I have a look at these things?"

"Any time you want, when it comes to my house," Darian said. She rose and fetched their beverages. "I'll tell Gran and Brandon who you are and so on. When it comes to the artifact, you can't fiddle with that on your own. We'll show one of them to you."

"Excuse me? One of them?" Carl gaped.

"There are seventy-six." Samantha sipped the espresso, her energy beginning to surge again.

"But…but where?" Carl scratched the back of his head.

"Basement." Darian pointed to the floor. "Old archive."

"Didn't even know there was an old archive. Just an archive." Drinking from his mug, Carl sat in silence for a few moments. "What can I help with, exactly?"

"My grandmother's employee, Brandon, is someone I think you'll like. We thought you and he could try to find if it really is a tunnel, and if that's the case, where the entrance and exit are. From how it seems, it starts somewhere near the lake and stretches toward this building."

Carl looked hesitant, and who could blame him? "Wait a minute. Are you sure? I've never heard of a tunnel in Dennamore. I mean, the entire town is built directly on bedrock."

"We've asked ourselves the same thing. But think about it. Have you been down at the archive in the basement?" Darian asked.

"No. That's off-limits for most people, according to Ms. Pike." Carl shook his head and sipped his coffee again.

"Well, I've been there once. That day I saw you at the computer. This enormous archive, I mean it's huge, with super-tall walls, is also somehow blasted out of the bedrock, and this building is ancient," Darian said, motioning around her.

Carl sat quiet for a few beats. "Yeah. You're right. Wow. So, me and this Brandon, then?"

"If you're interested." Samantha hid a smile.

"You're joking, right? You couldn't keep me away with a pitchfork." Carl slumped back in his chair. "When do we start?"

"Darian and I'll slip into the archive in a little bit, but for now, I just want you to do your math homework and look as if all is business as usual." Samantha emptied her small mug. "I think Mr. Miller and the Elder Council have gone home, but in case they haven't…" She shrugged.

"Not even Mr. Miller knows?" Gaping, Carl looked over his shoulder as if he expected Desmond Miller to grab him by the neck.

"No. It's the three of us—plus Camilla, who is Darian's grandmother, Brandon, Walker, and, I hope, Phileas Beresford."

"That scientist who you always keep taking stuff to? Yeah. He'd be good to have, I suppose. A bit old, maybe." With a youth's slight disdain for someone middle-aged and above, Carl nodded approvingly.

"Ageism's alive and well, I hear," Darian said lightly. "Don't talk like that around my Gran, just as a tip. She'll read you the riot act."

Carl blushed such a deep red, Samantha took pity on him. "It's all right. Carl's a gentleman."

After they finished their respective coffees, which had the added bonus of allowing extra time for the Elder Council members to leave the building for the day, Carl sat down at one of the tables in the library and pulled out his math books.

"Poor kid. I wonder if he'll get anything done," Darian murmured when Samantha returned after informing her colleague, who was busy putting books back farther into the library, that she was leaving for the day. "His mind must be spinning."

"Ah, he's young and a good deal more adaptable than me, that's for sure." Samantha looked over her shoulder. "Cindy is in charge of locking up tonight. I told her I'd go home after I've returned things to the archive." She held up the maps she'd copied the day before. "These are our alibi."

"Cool. Still, let's hope we don't run into anyone." Darian opened the door and looked out into the corridor. "Nobody." She walked ahead of Samantha and had just started down the stairs toward the basement when an all-too familiar voice made Samantha jump.

"Ah. Excellent. You're bringing more of the originals back down again." Desmond Miller appeared like a fast-growing mushroom in the woods. Samantha turned around and made sure she stood between him and Darian, who was already halfway down. She gestured behind her with her free hand for Darian to continue.

"Mr. Miller. Heading home for the day?" Samantha spoke calmly, but her heart raced so fast, she was certain he'd be able to see it if he came closer.

"Yes, actually. We're having company from out of town, which is a nice change." Miller thankfully looked rushed. "We'll talk more tomorrow about the budget cuts I suggested. I better hurry."

"Have a nice evening, sir." Samantha waited to turn around and walk downstairs until he was halfway to the front door. When she reached the basement level, she found Darian waiting, looking worried.

"All's well. Mrs. Miller's infamous razor tongue has him hurrying to get home on time."

"Damn, that was close. I mean, we could have lied through our teeth, but still." Darian tightened her ponytail.

"Agreed." Samantha turned the large key in the lock and punched in the code. "Here we go." After switching on the lights, she closed the door behind them. In the lead, she guided Darian into the back recesses of the archive, until they arrived at the small oak door with a code lock. She pulled out her card and entered the digits.

"Now this is kind of creepy." Darian looked around, her eyes huge. "And dusty."

"No cleaning crew is allowed in this part. When they clean the outer archive, they're supervised. I've tried a few times to get rid of the worst of it, but I don't have time. I don't think my great-aunt ever did either, not as long as I worked with her anyway."

They walked among the shelves, and Samantha placed the maps where they belonged. Farther in, they finally reached the back wall.

"Which direction did we walk to get to this wall?" Darian slowly approached one of the shelves.

"Um…northwest." Samantha joined her. "Any box in particular you want to explore?"

"Let's take one each. Any table in here?"

"No, but there's a couple of empty shelves right to our left. And some stools, I think." Samantha dusted off the shelves, and Darian helped her pull up two ornate stools, the seats covered in cracked leather. After fetching two of the scroll boxes, they sat down and opened them. They were pristine on the inside, like the one kept at Camilla's house. Samantha pushed the two protrusions on the cylinder and, like before, a plastic-looking document rolled out. This time she kept her fingers on the nodules until it stopped. About half a yard showed, and it was densely packed with symbols.

"So far so good," Darian said, her voice trembling a little. A quick look at her face reassured Samantha she was more excited than afraid. She wished she could say the same.

Darian gently set the scroll aside and pulled the case closer. Examining the oval, as far as she could see, it looked identical to the one still at Camilla's house. "I want to try one on." She shot Samantha a look. "And before you freak out, I'm not talking about putting it on my head. When that happens—"

"When? You're so certain we'll ever do that?" Samantha seemed apprehensive.

"What's all this for if we're not ready to explore the entire truth about these things? Or are you having regrets?" Darian ran her finger over the oval.

"I'm...conflicted, a little bit." Opening her case, Samantha clenched her hands as if to keep them from touching the object. "Last night was pretty overwhelming, and if I can feel like that after having it on my hand, can you imagine what it might do to a person who attaches it to their head?"

"You have a point," Darian said. "But are you ready to hand this over to, let's say, the US government to explore? And perhaps have it become classified and, because of that, never find out a damn thing?"

"No, of course not," Samantha said promptly. "Absolutely not. If I'm not ready to share this—yet—with the Elder Council, of course I don't want these things to disappear in some government archive and have someone throw away the key."

"I'm going to try it on my hand. That way, if we're interrupted, I can just tuck it into my pocket and be all casual like."

Snorting, Samantha covered her eyes for a moment. "Casual like. Hm."

"Here goes." Darian gently bumped Samantha's shoulder with hers. "Be prepared to take notes if I start speaking in tongues."

"Don't worry. I'll pull out my cell and film the scene," Samantha replied, sounding entirely composed.

Darian was about to stick her tongue out for emphasis but thought better of it. Slowly, she picked up the oval and examined it on both sides. Samantha had actually pulled out her cell but used its flashlight mode instead of filming.

"Wait." Samantha held up her hand. "Wiggle it a little."

Darian was holding the oval with the concave side up and did as Samantha asked. The tendrils swayed with the movement but stayed limp.

"I'll be damned," Samantha said.

"What?" Darian pulled the oval closer to her to see what Samantha had discovered.

"Keep holding it like that." Samantha flipped her cell phone over and filmed a short clip of the back of the oval with the flash on.

"Let's see." Tapping the screen, she played the clip, pulling Darian to her. "Look. See?"

Darian watched the light from the flash catch on what looked like finely chiseled lines. "Something written?" She squinted. "And…are those the same type of symbols?"

"It's too hard to see. We'd need better magnification." Samantha switched off the flashlight.

Darian scrutinized the oval. "I'm going to try a slightly different placement. Still on the hand, but right here." She placed the oval on the inside of her wrist, and for a few seconds, nothing happened. She felt a sting of disappointment, but then the filaments snapped around and attached themselves to the back of her hand.

"Whoa." Darian lifted her gaze to Samantha, who appeared transfixed. "It was like someone snapped a rubber band against me, but it didn't hurt."

"Right."

Vertigo hit out of nowhere, and Darian reached for Samantha, swallowing hard against an unexpected bout of nausea. "Ew."

"Hey. You all right? I can pull it off—"

"No. I'm good. I'm good. Just chill for a bit." Darian closed her eyes but snapped them open, as that made it worse. Samantha's arms went around her in a firm hug, which seemed to help. "Thanks." She moved her head carefully. "Better. Got nauseous, but it's going away."

"Good." Samantha kept holding Darian and stroked her back. "Just take a few more moments."

Darian did and then straightened on the stool. "There. All better." She shifted her gaze to the scroll they had rolled out. "Holy crap."

"Yes? See something you can interpret?"

"Those signs," Darian managed to say as her gaze flew across the symbols. "They're almost glowing. So clear." After moving the box out of the way, she tugged the scroll closer. "I don't know what you saw or how much you could, well, read, but this is kind of scary."

"Tell me. And yes, I'm filming."

Darian didn't take her eyes off the scroll. "Instructions."

"What? It says that? Instructions?" Samantha's voice sounded distant, and, unsettled by that sensation, Darian reached out and placed her hand on Samantha's knee.

"Yes. Or perhaps not instructions exactly. I think…manual. Yes. Or guide."

"I get it. The words are related. Keep going." Samantha's voice was now closer, as if her lips were against Darian's ear.

"There's a large paragraph where I can make sense of only a few signs, but then there's the next header. Aptitude. Predisposition. Establish."

"So damn cryptic," Samantha muttered. "Will this document establish the user's predisposition—in that case, for what?"

"We most likely won't know until we place it where it's supposed to go. It probably has to attach to our head to read our minds or something. As morbid as that sounds." Darian let her finger guide her down the rows of strange signs. And then she froze. "That can't be right." She felt along where the symbols made up three words. To her, their meaning was obvious.

"Dar?" Samantha's lips actually touched the shell of Darian's ear this time, bringing her out of her reverie.

"See here?" She pointed at the symbols. "It says star chart, exploration, and velocity."

"Star chart?" Samantha whispered.

Darian looked up from the scroll. "Am I losing my marbles or…does this suggest that what we're messing with is—"

"Extraterrestrial." Samantha's eyes had darkened, or perhaps it was an optical illusion in the old basement. "That's the only thing that makes sense. These things have been stored down here for God knows how long. And even if they were just put here, think about it. This technology doesn't exist, to my knowledge. The language, or whatever the symbols represent, is certainly nothing I've come across."

Darian chuckled weakly. "You're saying that the Mayans or some Sanskrit-typing people haven't been up here in the mountains and invented this?"

Getting to her feet, Samantha began pacing. "That's what I'm saying. This just got a whole lot more complicated. If I thought of any chance we could share this, at this point, with more people than we first agreed on, I know we'd all be considered mentally impaired and, at best, a laughingstock. I mean, really. Aliens? Back in the 1700s?"

"Come back here. I can try for a few more words." Concerned at Samantha becoming agitated, which didn't feel like her at all, Darian patted the stool next to her.

"I'll do one better. I'll put the other one on my wrist, like you."

"Glad you don't insist on your head. We would have had words." Darian watched Samantha open the other scroll box and attach the oval. Once it was in place, Samantha turned on the filming feature on her phone again and leaned against Darian, who wrapped her free arm around Samantha's waist.

Samantha pressed the ends of the scroll, and the document shot out. "Let's see," she muttered. "Oh. Yes. You're absolutely right."

"Can you make out the smaller symbols?" Darian directed Samantha's attention to the densely packed paragraphs.

"No. Not really. Their meaning feels just barely out of reach, though."

"Exactly."

They kept looking for the bigger symbols together. Darian thought her senses might overload, part of her mind focusing on the signs and the rest of it acutely aware of Samantha's presence.

"Here. Synaptic charge," Darian said after staring at a particular row of symbols for a good half minute.

"What could that mean?" Samantha huffed. "I suppose we won't know more until we can put them on the right way. Which I refuse to have anyone, including myself, do before we can have a physician present."

"Agreed. Have anyone in mind?" Darian said absentmindedly. She had spotted two other emphasized words.

"We have a small clinic in Dennamore, which has been run by the same doctor since I was little. He has two colleagues working with him, and the youngest is freshly returned from New York, where he worked at one of the free clinics. He's a voracious reader of everything science fiction." Samantha glanced down at Darian's finger. "What does it say?"

Darian moved her finger out of the way.

Samantha bent closer. "Extinction Prevention." She jerked. "Is that what you got as well?"

"Yes. That sounds ominous." Darian rubbed an aching spot between her eyes. "I need to take this thing off. Not sure how you feel, but my forehead's beginning to ache."

"I've had a headache for a few minutes, yes." Samantha straightened and pulled at her device, which let go with a soft pop. Darian pulled at hers and began to get nervous when it took two attempts before it dislodged.

"Damn. Let go, already," she muttered. Returning it to its case, where it folded its filaments neatly into the slots, she sighed and carefully tipped her head to the side a few times. "Ah, better. I wonder if it'll do that to us when we snap those suckers in at the back of our heads."

"Either that, or they'll work better when we use them correctly." Samantha gently rolled her shoulders. "Ow."

Darian wanted nothing but to jump up and massage Samantha's shoulders, but she was afraid such a move would seem too intrusive. She was still not over how close they'd been sitting, and the touching…even if it hadn't been in a romantic, or a passionate sense…was still engraved in her mind. Samantha smelled so good, Darian could barely detect the dust and old, musty books and items around them.

"How big is your backpack?" Samantha, who clearly hadn't been lost in thought about any touching, asked.

"Pretty standard." Darian forced herself to focus and lifted the backpack from the floor. "Here."

Samantha took it and opened it. "Empty. Good. We should be able to fit in five or six of the scroll boxes."

Darian could hardly believe her ears. "We're stealing more?" Samantha had been adamant about them being careful. This didn't spell cautious approach to her.

"Stealing? I prefer to see it as borrowing," Samantha said firmly. "And I'm the head librarian. I know Council Chairman Miller thinks he owns this town in general, and Town Hall in particular, but he's wrong. Not very many people have read this town's rules and regulations, but I have. When I became a librarian, before my great-aunt retired, I made it my business to know what my duties and rights were when I one day would take over. I hadn't even seen the door to this part of the archive then. So perhaps that was a hunch. And I do have the right to bring items out of the archives to be catalogued and for Phileas Beresford to examine, but not to take them home with me." Her green eyes became opaque. "This is something extraordinary, and it's part of the Dennamore history. The scroll boxes, the fact that someone managed to build this basement into bedrock two hundred and fifty years ago and, not to mention, build whatever the strange glowing rocks in your basement are, and the potential tunnel…and let's add the seasonal lake lights as well."

"You think they're all connected." Darian didn't offer her own opinion just yet.

"I do. I can't even begin to fathom how, but it's one of the few things that seems logical." Samantha raised her chin. "And you?"

"Hell, yeah. With me, you're preaching to the choir. You know so much more about this town than I, or even Camilla, do. If you'd asked me just the other day, my pragmatic ass would have deemed you beautiful, but eccentric."

"And today?" Samantha murmured.

"Today you're beautiful and brave." Darian caressed Samantha's reddened cheekbone without realizing that's what she'd meant to do. "So very beautiful, inside and out."

"Darian."

Feeling that Samantha made her name sound like the prelude to a rejection, Darian wished she had used more caution. "We better tuck the scroll boxes into your backpack and get out of here," she said huskily.

"All right. These two and three more?" Darian walked over to the shelves. "Any of them?"

"No. Wait. Let's take the ones from the far end. I know we've disturbed the dust already, but it might be less obvious all the same."

Darian carried the boxes over to Samantha and saw she had made the document retract again and was already packing up. After adding the last three scroll boxes, Darian tugged at the drawstring, but then she changed her mind and pulled her sweatshirt off, tucking it on top and around the boxes.

"Probably won't do us much good, but it'll at least not be too obvious." She shrugged.

"Agreed." Samantha replaced the stools and then scooped up some dust from a corner shelf and blew it across the empty shelf they'd just used as a desk. "As you were saying."

After making their way through the entire archive and locking everything behind them, they stood in the basement for a few moments, listening. The library was closed, and everything was quiet.

"The alarm is on, but I have my code, so we'll be able to get out. But it'll show that I was here this late. They can't know that I simply didn't just work late in my office though. The only lock that logs our presence is the one at the front door, thank God."

"Sounds good. Do you often stay late?" Darian walked next to Samantha but slipped in behind her when they reached the lobby.

"Five or six times a month, perhaps. Mainly I take work home." Samantha halted at the top of the stairs. "Empty. We only have a security firm that checks Town Hall on a schedule at nights. Let's just go."

Crossing the lobby, Darian glanced around her, not seeing anything or anyone. "When you think about it...why are Miller and the Elder Council so adamant about Dennamore's old artifacts staying tucked away? I mean, why not open a museum and display stuff like every other normal small town? Just like the lake light is a tourist attraction, I mean. It's strange. Not logical, I mean."

"I don't know what information the Elder Council sits on. Perhaps they know more about these things than we can imagine? And if they do, perhaps they're afraid of Dennamore becoming some weird place that believes in extraterrestrials. Like Roswell or something." Samantha pressed a touchpad next to the front door and slipped outside. After looking around, she waved for Darian to follow. She reset the alarm, and then they strode down the stairs and over to the parking lot where Darian's car was parked next to Samantha's.

"Are you going straight home?" Samantha pulled out her own car keys.

"Yes. I want to get this backpack placed somewhere reasonably safe before someone catches me with the contents." Darian hesitated but then leaned in and kissed Samantha on the cheek. "Are you going home too?"

"No. I plan to swing by Phileas Beresford's first. I'll call you when I'm home. Please text me when you're at the house?"

Darian smiled and nodded. "Of course."

Before Darian could react, Samantha cupped her cheek and lightly kissed her on the lips. "Please be safe."

Darian momentarily forgot how to breathe. "I will," she croaked. "You too."

Samantha stood by her car until Darian had tucked the backpack into the passenger seat and started the engine. As Darian drove off, she saw the headlights on Samantha's car switch on. Driving toward Brynden 4, Darian wasn't thinking about any extraterrestrial creatures. Instead, her lips burned from Samantha's chaste kiss.

CHAPTER EIGHT

Samantha stood outside Phileas Beresford's log house, another of the remaining original houses from the first settlers. As she raised her hand to pull the chain hanging by the door, it opened, and she found herself staring at the apron-clad man covered in flour.

"Mr. Beresford. I'm—"

"I know. You're Ms. Pike." Beresford tsked. "Well, don't just stand there. Come in. I've got to mind the oven. It's got one temperature, and that's full speed ahead. My cinnamon rolls need supervision."

"Thank you, but I meant to say that I'm sorry to disturb you this late." Samantha stepped inside and closed the front door behind her as Beresford hurried into what had to be the kitchen. It was at the opposite side compared to Camilla's house, so perhaps this was a mirrored version. Hesitantly, Samantha joined him.

"It smells wonderful, Mr. Beresford."

"Oh, for the love of everything under the sun, call me Philber. People do it to my face and behind my back anyway," Philber grumbled. He bent and peered into the oven. "If I miss the time by as much as fifteen seconds, they'll be positively nuked."

"Oh, my. That's some oven." As far as Samantha could see, it was the same kind as the old one in Camilla's or, rather, Brandon's kitchen.

"Tell me about it. My mother burned so many pot roasts over the years, it wasn't even funny. Here goes!" Flinging his hands into large oven mittens that looked like welders' gloves, Philber pulled out the sheet with the buns. "Ah! Perfect."

Samantha counted twenty-five buns, baked to perfection, judging from their golden-brown color.

Philber put the sheet on a grid on the counter and then turned off the oven. Removing the mittens and the apron, he pivoted and squinted at Samantha. He was a large bear of a man, with thinning gray hair. Dressed in green corduroy pants and a green-and-blue plaid flannel shirt, he looked like he was more used to plowing than using his brilliant mind for scholarly work. "Well?"

Samantha blinked but pulled herself together. "Would you be interested in helping me sort out a complete mystery that might affect our town for the foreseeable future?"

Philber's blond, bushy eyebrows rose. "You, Ms. Pike?"

"Samantha, please."

"You have discovered some mystery, and you think I have time for that?" Huffing, Philber made a big production of slapping flour from his hands.

"I'm not the only one involved in this, and considering that we've stumbled onto hard-core artifacts and evidence that there's a lot we don't know about Dennamore, I think you, as a scientist with a special interest in our town, would be interested. At least to a degree where you'll hear us out."

"Us. I thought you said it was just you?" Philber began tidying up his kitchen table, but Samantha had the feeling he wasn't as disinterested as he made it sound.

"Would you be interested? I'm not sure I should tell you who else is part of our research group before you at least let me know that." Realizing she was baiting him now, using the word research and also hinting at that he might not get a chance to learn the details unless he showed genuine interest, Samantha hoped she sounded as sincere as she felt.

"By all means. I'm the local expert. And since nobody outside of Dennamore gives a rat's ass about this godforsaken place, then I'm the only expert."

Not to mention humble. Samantha forced herself not to smirk. "Do you remember Camilla Wells—her last name is Tennen now? She used to live at Brynden 4." Samantha studied the quick surprise that flickered over Philber's stark features.

"I do. Has she returned?" Sounding noncommittal, almost too much so, Philber washed his hands and wiped them on a terry-cloth towel that hung over the backrest of a kitchen chair. As if the chair in front of him reminded him of his lack of manners, he pulled it out for Samantha. "Take a load off."

Not very cordial wording on his part, but Samantha sat down. "Thank you. And yes, she has," she said, answering his question. "She is back with her assistant and her granddaughter, Darian, and all three are part of this group. The others are Carl Hoskins, a local student, and Chief Walker."

Sitting down across from her, Philber appeared to have lost most of his disdain and cynicism. "Camilla. She was a bit older than Geoff Walker and me, but everyone adored her. I thought she might be among the few who never got the yearning."

"Oh, she did. And so did her granddaughter, even though she's never set foot here."

"What about her children?" Philber folded his large hands on the table.

"Her son and daughter-in-law were killed in a car accident when Darian was very young." Samantha wondered what amazing power Camilla still had over these men who used to know her. Then again, as she was getting to know the charismatic woman, Samantha acknowledged that she had already joined the ranks of admirers.

"Who is Carl Hoskins? Does he belong to the Hoskins in the townhouses?" Philber made a face when he asked the question, but Samantha guessed it had more to do with the less-than-fantastic architecture of said townhouses than the Hoskins family.

"Yes, that's him. He's a senior in high school. Brilliant boy."

"And Camilla's granddaughter. What does she do?"

"She's on a leave of absence. Detective at the LAPD."

Philber looked surprised. "An investigative mind. Can be useful."

"And Brandon, who is Camilla's assistant, is certainly no fool either." Samantha leaned forward, placing her arms on the table. "Philber, we found an old journal in Camilla's private library. It dates back to the late 1700s and contains symbols we have only begun trying to decipher."

It was educational, to say the least, to watch the transformation of Philber's expression as it changed from cynicism to mild interest, and now, as if being lit from within, utter surprise.

"A private journal found at Brynden 4?" He clenched his hands.

"Yes. I know you've worked your way through a lot of documents and objects kept in the archives, but this is something that has sat on that shelf for God knows how long. I found it by chance when I was skimming the spines of the books, as Camilla wanted me to catalogue them." Samantha spoke of how they had read through a few pages that first evening. "At the same time, we found an, well, an anomaly, in the basement. A smooth piece of rock that looks as if made by modern-day machines. And it emanates heat. Geoff has the same in his basement…what?"

"Does it glow?" Philber asked quietly.

Samantha stared. "Yes," she whispered. "A warm, yellow-tinted glow. We haven't freed all of it at Camilla's because we keep finding new things, and it's hard to know which to focus on first. Are you saying you've seen it before?"

"Yes. In my own basement. We can go down later, and I'll show you, if you like." Philber wiped his forehead. "You said there's more?"

"Maps showing a tunnel stretching from the lake toward Town Hall. At least we think it's a tunnel. And…in the oldest, locked part of the archive, very high-tech-looking artifacts that you have to see in action to believe."

Philber coughed. "Excuse me? In action?"

"Yes." Samantha smiled, starting to feel how tired she was. "Do you want to be part of—"

"Yes, yes. Don't be ridiculous. Of course I do. With the exception of you, I doubt any of the others know how to catalogue information in a way that scientific deductions can be made in a safe and methodical way."

"Thank you. I'll call you when we're getting together. We had an idea about how to divide the assignments among us, but we're open to suggestions." Samantha stood. "Can we take a look at your basement, and then I'll be on my way. It's been a long day."

"Yes, you do look tired," Philber said, sounding matter-of-fact. "This way." He showed her to the stairs leading down to the basement, and when Samantha stepped up to the old furnace, which looked identical to Camilla's and Walker's, she saw the smooth, nearly glass-like surface. "May I?" She motioned to the wall.

"By all means."

Samantha pressed both hands against it. Smooth and warm. Check. Humming faintly. Check.

"Notice the faint vibrations?" Philber asked from behind her.

"I do." She looked back at him. "What's on the other side?"

"I thought you'd never ask." Philber, eager now, waved for her to join him.

As they rounded the rock wall, she saw he had no wooden shelves or covering on the other side. If something had been there at one point, Philber had removed it. Samantha walked past him and stepped closer to the wall. "Oh, my God." She couldn't believe her eyes. There was indeed a warm, yellow glow, but it was so much more than that. The glow wasn't as faint as in Camilla's basement, since it was in plain view here. The yellow-toned glow originated from distinctive lines in intricate patterns, looking like a huge circuit board.

"I doubt any deities are at work here, but when I found this, five years and four months ago, I too wondered." Philber stepped closer to Samantha. "Especially when I noticed these." He ran his finger along the glowing lines. Samantha followed it, entirely mesmerized when she saw how the movement created different nuances of the yellow on different parts of the wall.

"What can make it do that?" she whispered. "Are you sure it's safe to play with it like that?"

"I've done it a lot, and I'm still alive," Philber said lightly. "Do any of your artifacts match this?"

"Yes. Absolutely." Samantha nodded, feeling dazed.

Philber patted her gently on the back. "Relax and take a deep breath. You can relax now. I'm definitely in."

Darian was climbing into bed after spending time with Camilla and Brandon in the kitchen, updating them on what she and Samantha had been up to. Having placed the bag with the five scroll boxes in one of the cabinets in Camilla's library that boasted a sturdy lock, she now placed the key under her pillow. It felt like something out of a ridiculous adventure novel and entirely astute at the same time.

After half an hour of tossing and turning, Darian realized sleep was not going to happen yet. Too many images of what she'd experienced in the old archive with Samantha played out on the inside of her eyelids. The symbols, some vividly clear, others still eluding her, had made her head hurt. Would that get even worse if and when they tried the damn things on their heads? Either way, Darian was relieved that she was the custodian of the ovals since she could picture Samantha putting them on while alone, for research reasons.

Her cell phone buzzed on the nightstand, and Darian sat up in the old four-poster bed and tapped the screen.

A text from Samantha made Darian's heart pick up speed.

Are you awake? Know it's late.

Darian pushed the pillows up and tugged the duvet closer.

Awake. Can't sleep. Too much to think about.

I know. Same here. Can I call?

Darian wasn't sure why her cheeks suddenly warmed, but she simply dialed Samantha's cell instead of typing back.

"Well, that answers that," Samantha said huskily. "Glad I caught you before you did fall asleep. I promise I won't keep you very long."

Ah. What a shame. "I'm glad too. That you texted. And called. Or I called." Oh, shut up, Darian told herself. Just stop rambling.

"Are you all right? You sound exhausted." Samantha must have been speaking closer to the phone, as she sounded louder.

Darian closed her eyes. "I am. I have a bit of a headache. Think it can be the ovals?"

"I do too, so yes, perhaps. In my case, it could be from inhaling a fair amount of flour."

Darian snapped her eyes open. "Excuse me? Flour?"

"Philber was baking cinnamon rolls as if he were disarming a nuclear device. Lots of flour."

Chuckling, Darian pictured the elegant Samantha trying to avoid getting flour all over her suit. "Is this guy on board with what we're doing?"

"I have to say, at first, he was his usual arrogant self, clearly not thinking much of any of us. He's sometimes quite full of himself, but he can also be most generous and kind. Don't tell him I said so though. I have no doubt he's taking those cinnamon rolls to the nursing home where his wife spent the last years of her life." Samantha's voice grew throatier, and she cleared it gently. "Anyway, he got very interested when I mentioned some of what we've found so far. He's agreed to join us tomorrow after I get off work. He, like Walker, remembers Camilla fondly."

"Of course, he does." Snorting, Darian knew there were few people who weren't ready to walk on water for her grandmother, not that Camilla would ever ask that of anyone. "I'm going to work on exposing more of the rock in the basement."

"I was getting to that. Philber lives in a similar house to yours. He knew about the rock, and his is exposed," Samantha said, sounding more energetic. "The glow is from these lines, or whatever you want to call them, and they change when you touch them. It was the oddest thing. Actually, the lines looked like the inside of the lid of the boxes. Like a strange sort of circuit board, remember?"

"Really?" Darian sat up straight. "If it wouldn't wake up Gran, I'd go down now and use a damn ax on those boards covering ours. I want to see that."

"You need your rest, Darian. I'm very psyched about all this, but I know I have to rest, or I'll run myself into the ground. I tend to do that if I don't watch myself."

Darian grimaced. "Yeah, me too. My lieutenant has had to send me home when I've been staying too long, too many days in a row."

"In other words, we're both A-type personalities." Samantha sighed. "Can we make a pact to look out for each other, so we don't make ourselves ill? I don't have a boss per se to tell me to go home at the library."

"All right. I'm game," Darian said readily.

"Speaking of tired. How's Camilla doing?"

"Gran's been exploring the maps more today, which means that Brandon and Carl are good to go. She also worked some on the journal, going through it and finding names, she said. She's planning to brief us tomorrow."

"That sounds exciting. I'm hoping it'll shed some light on some discrepancies I found when helping people look for their family tree."

"I know these things we've stumbled upon seem random, but I have a strong feeling they're connected. Even the lake lights." Darian moved her pillows until she could curl up on her side and pull the duvet closer around her.

"Agreed. Not sure where the lake lights fit in, but perhaps we'll find some information about that when we decipher the part of the journal that's not in English." Samantha yawned. "I'm sorry. Long day."

"Yes." Hesitating, Darian wanted to say something to Samantha that didn't have to do with their curious finds. "I like working on this with you, though." Did that sound as lame as it felt?

"I enjoy your company too."

"Good. I know you must have considered me a pesky brute for running right into you that first day." Darian sighed.

"I did nothing of the sort. Just an accident—and as it turned out, one that led to all this. I haven't felt this engaged and alive in ages," Samantha said quietly. "Getting to know you. And Camilla and Brandon too, of course." She cleared her throat again. "I don't mean to sound presumptuous, but I honestly feel like you and I are at the apex of all this. So, that run-in was a lucky one."

Darian was tongue-tied long enough for Samantha to ask if she was still there.

"I'm here." Pressing her hand against her stomach, Darian wasn't sure what to say. "That means a lot. To hear you say that. I feel the exact same way."

It was Samantha's turn to go quiet. Darian waited as patiently as it was possible for her eager nature.

"Good. Excellent." A new warmth permeated Samantha's voice. "With that, I think I can relax and try for some sleep. I'll see you after work then. I'll call Carl and have him take his bike over to your house at that time, if that's all right."

"It is. What about the doctor?"

"He's next on my list."

Darian wished it wasn't up to just Samantha to bring people together, but she was the one who knew everybody. She thought fast. "Walker will be here too, remember, as he and Gran are going out to dinner. They'll be here a bit later though, but we'll fill them in."

"Perfect."

"Good night, then." Darian stifled a yawn.

"Good night."

Putting the cell back, this time remembering to charge it, Darian pulled a pillow into her arms and let the soft mattress engulf her. It had been special to listen to Samantha's voice as the last thing she did before nodding off. Perhaps a little too exciting to be soothing, but oddly calming just the same.

Closing her eyes, Darian could easily picture Samantha's green eyes, shadowed by long, mascara-enhanced lashes. Her eyebrows formed perfect arches above those beautiful eyes, and when Samantha raised them while questioning something, Darian wanted to pull out her cell phone and snap a picture. Framing Samantha's oval face, that rich, strawberry-blond hair offset her eyes even more. And her lips…curvy and full…were to die for.

Reeling herself, and her heated thoughts, in, Darian told herself that becoming friends was the best she could hope for. Sure, at moments they got stuck in each other's gaze, for a second or two, but when it came to Samantha, Darian's gaydar seemed to malfunction. Meh. Who was she kidding? Back in LA, once she grew tired of one-night stands, partying, and short, combustible relationships, she hadn't used her gaydar at all. Now, when she needed it, she was afraid to plug it back in.

It was kind of weak to think this way, but as long as she didn't know for sure what Samantha's sexual orientation was, she could harbor a tiny hope. Darian flinched. Hope for what, exactly? Recoiling, she shoved the pillow away and rolled onto her stomach. Sleep, that's what she needed. Not the slippery slope down the road of wishful thinking.

CHAPTER NINE

Doctor Raoul Viera looked mystified but gave Darian an easygoing smile where he stood in Camilla's hallway as part of their newly formed team. A tall, gangly man in his late twenties, he boasted short, dark-brown hair. Clean shaved, his olive-tinted skin looked flawless, and Darian decided that his long, black eyelashes would make a lot of women jealous.

"Hi, I'm Darian," she said and extended her hand. "So glad you're willing to give us all the benefit of the doubt. Samantha's due any moment, and my grandmother, Camilla, will be home in about an hour, with Geoff Walker. This is Philber and Carl. We don't bother with titles or last names."

"Raoul." He shook her hand and then repeated it when he greeted the two other men who had arrived just before him. "I know of you, of course, Philber. Nice to meet you, Carl. Samantha hasn't told me very much other than how you need medical supervision during an experiment." He looked concerned as he rocked back and forth on his soles. "As intriguing as it sounds, it seems rather dangerous."

"Sorry about the secrecy. I have my reasons for it, and we'll explain everything as best we can once she gets here," Darian said. "Why don't I show you all to the library? It's right up the stairs to the mezzanine."

They climbed the stairs, and Darian found it reassuring that Philber moved as lithely as the two younger men. He was handsome, and if she hadn't been used to dealing with huge guys armed to the teeth in LA, she might have found his demeanor intimidating. Carl absolutely seemed in awe of the old scholar.

Darian had carried up another table and made room for eight chairs. If their group grew any larger, they would have to meet in the parlor. She hoped not, as eight seemed like a nice even number, for now.

"Here, take a seat, please. Brandon's in the kitchen, as he insisted on fixing us something to eat. He'll join us in a bit. Why don't you look over the maps here. We've marked what we can't figure out, or at least what isn't readily visible at present. I'll be right back."

Philber pulled a map closer and put on reading glasses. Carl and Raoul leaned in, both looking puzzled. Darian heard the door chime and hurried down the stairs. She opened the door, and the sight of Samantha, dressed in a powder-blue skirt suit and with her hair in a low bun, stole her breath. Perhaps a very good thing they had a doctor present if this kept happening.

"Welcome. We're missing just Gran and Walker." Darian's cheeks stung. She must be displaying a face-splitting grin.

Samantha's smile was a good deal softer, but the warmth in her eyes made Darian's cheeks burn. How could green be such a warm color? Or hot, on the verge of fluorescent? "Thank you. Glad they're prompt. I had to do a bit of a song and dance around Miller again. If I didn't know better, I'd swear that man is a mind reader. He pops up at the most inopportune times."

"Weasel," Darian muttered. "Want to lose the jacket, or…?"

"Yes, please. I want to lose the jacket and the shoes. Why I torture my feet for vanity, I'll never know." She glanced at the floor. "You look much more comfortable."

"Crocs would do that for you. Gran swears by her fluffy slippers, but I draw the line at pink feathers and stuff on my feet."

Samantha threw her head back and laughed. "I'll say." She toed off her pumps and let Darian hang her jacket in a small closet by the stairs. She turned to Darian but seemed to hesitate. "It really was nice to talk last night. Sort of rounding the evening's events off. Perhaps it helped that it was a shared experience."

"Yeah." Darian gently touched Samantha's arm. She was wearing a short-sleeved blouse, and the sensation of her skin against Darian's fingertips sent a shiver up her fingers.

"Are they in the library?" Samantha didn't take her eyes off Darian.

"Yes."

After keeping her gaze locked on Darian for a few more beats, Samantha sighed. "We should go up. We have a lot to brief them about. And Philber is bound to have tons of questions."

"Yay. Like school." Darian grumbled half-jokingly. "At least we don't have to repeat anything when Gran and Walker get here. They're already informed about pretty much everything to date. Gran wasn't entirely pleased that we experimented in the archive at Town Hall, but she calmed down."

Samantha started up the stairs. "Thank God."

The men all stood when they entered the library, but Samantha waved her hand as if warding them off. "No, no. You don't have to keep doing that. Sit back down so we can begin."

Darian absolutely loved this side of Samantha. Authoritative, but calm and with a friendly tone, she took a seat next to Carl after acknowledging them all. "I see you've been looking at the maps. What are your thoughts?"

"Without knowing what to look for, I can see a clear difference between this and the oldest maps I've studied until now." Philber rubbed his chin. "The places you marked are of interest. I found a few more."

"What? Where?" Darian took one of the markers and handed it to Philber.

"Here. And here. And here." He marked eight small dots next to what looked like buildings. Darian drew a quick breath when she realized that one of the dots was right next to Camilla's house. "Couldn't that be some sort of old basement or something? For storing food, I mean?"

"I know for a fact that there are no traces of such a structure on my lot." Philber shook his head. "If you look at the precise location," he said and handed Darian a magnifying glass that he plucked from his breast pocket, "you'll see they're perfectly aligned with the glowing walls."

Darian and Samantha leaned in together as Darian held the magnifying glass over Camilla's house. It only took a second for Darian to concur. "You're right. But you say there's nothing there in your yard?"

"Not where I've had the crew, who put down drainage, dig. But they dug about four feet deep. This might go a great deal deeper than that." Philber reached into a briefcase. "I have some photos of my wall in the basement, as Samantha thought you needed to see it firsthand."

"Excuse me. What are we talking about?" Raoul was leaning on his elbows against the tabletop, staring at the map and then the faces around the table. "This looks like copies of old maps of Dennamore, but I've never seen anything like them before. And what are these glowing walls you're talking about? I feel very out of the loop here."

"Raoul. I'm sorry." Samantha straightened and placed a hand on his shoulder. "I should have informed you more when we spoke, but I was in a hurry. We have found maps, artifacts, and a journal that suggest something extraordinary once happened here. We're being careful because we have indications that the Elder Council would object and perhaps vote to restrict access to our oldest archives. They have that power and we…" She glanced at Darian, and there it was again, that long, curious look, "…we are very keen on discovering the truth. I hope you don't think we're some conspiracy-theorist fools. I assure you we're not."

"But glowing walls?" Carl's eyes gleamed with interest. "In Philber's basement?"

"Never crossed my mind that either of you are conspiracy nuts." Raoul smiled. "Still want to hear about the wall, and clearly so does Carl." He then looked down at the map. "I live in one of the older houses, where I grew up. It's not as old as this one or Philber's, but from the mid-1800s. I haven't noticed anything strange."

"That's three generations after the first settlers, which would suggest that what we've found stems from them. Or what happened to them." Philber handed out the photos. "Here you can see what's glowing."

Darian slumped back in her chair when she saw the distinct, bright lines. She had only managed to uncover about a third of their own wall in the basement, but with each board, the glow became more intense. Was this what she would find? “You’re right,” she said to Samantha. “It does resemble the inside of the lid of the boxes. Not exactly the same, but similar.”

“Yes.” Samantha pointed to the center of Philber’s uncovered wall. “See those? I’m not certain, but that looks like a few of the symbols.”

“Which part?” Philber got up and rounded the table. “Show me.”

“Wait. I should get one of the scroll boxes before we continue, or this will sound too academic to you guys.” Darian stood and retrieved the first box they’d examined. She placed it in the center of the table and pressed the protrusions that made the cylinder detach. “This contains a scroll of sorts.” She ran her finger along the ridge and the document, for she had no other word for the plastic-looking sheet, rolled out. In the meantime, Samantha opened the box and displayed the oval with its filaments.

“Oh my god,” Carl said. “And that was in the archives all along? That’s some sci-fi stuff, if you ask me.”

“My thought too,” Darian said, snorting. “Philber. See these symbols. In the center of the glowing lines on your wall, doesn’t that look like something similar?”

Philber didn’t speak for several moments. He walked back to his chair and sat down in a way that made Darian think his knees had just buckled. “Damn it, girls. What the hell have you stumbled on?”

“That’s a good question, Phileas Beresford,” Camilla said in her sonorous voice from the doorway. She stood next to Walker, who held a hand against the small of her back. Darian thought she could see a new light in her grandmother’s eyes. Was this caused by reconnecting with Walker? If that was the case, Darian was both happy for Camilla and worried.

“Camilla Wells…no, sorry, Tennen. Welcome back.” Philber stood but didn’t walk over to the couple at the door. “Walker. Good to see you.”

"Philber. What do you think about all this? Camilla said you have the same strange wall as she and I have in the basement." Walker and Camilla stepped into the room, and Darian motioned for them to sit down.

Now they were all gathered, and the knot in her stomach was tightening. She knew Samantha was insisting on being the first to place the oval where she claimed it was meant to go, at the base of the skull.

After Philber updated Camilla and Walker of what he'd noticed on the map, a brief silence fell on them. Raoul still had an expression of disbelief, and Darian couldn't blame the guy. He hadn't been informed beyond the fact that his expertise as a doctor might be needed, and here he sat faced with something that indeed looked like something out of a science-fiction movie.

"I have written down a roster of sorts, and if all of you are on board with it, it'll give you a specific task." Samantha pulled out a stack of papers. "And I know, I'm a born list-maker, and I hope you can abide by it. That said, I don't want any documents leaving this room, if possible. It's not that I don't trust you—I don't trust the council, or at least not our current chairman."

"My parents both sat on the council back in the day," Camilla said. "Neither of them was ever elected chairman, and I remember my mother saying she wouldn't be caught dead running for that particular office. My father was the local prosecutor at the time, when we still had a courtroom in Dennamore."

"We were the last to have one, actually," Carl said. "It was unusual."

"Exactly. I think it ended when my father died in 1944."

Darian knew that her great-grandfather had died in World War II, before Camilla was born. Walker briefly touched Camilla's folded hands, and Camilla in turn gave him a reassuring smile.

Samantha handed out her list. Darian already knew what it said but still read through it. Samantha and she would be the first to attach the ovals and try to decipher the scrolls and the journal. Carl and Brandon were going to try to find remnants of the potential tunnel. Walker and Philber would work more on the walls. Camilla would assist with everything they documented along the way. Raoul would monitor Samantha and Darian, at least initially.

Raoul, slightly wide-eyed at this point, turned to Samantha. "Surely I can be of more use than this. You can't just dismiss me after letting me in on all this, once we know any procedure is safe, I mean."

Samantha looked around the table and then nodded. "Of course not. If you want to participate and contribute more of your time, we're grateful. We might need more hands-on work done as well. I'm glad you're curious enough to want to hang around."

"Are you kidding? This is the most fascinating, hell, the only fascinating thing that's happened since I returned. Don't get me wrong. I enjoy being a family physician, but after living in a big city, Dennamore is…quiet."

"We like it that way," Philber said.

"So do I, but you have to agree that this is exciting." Unfazed, Raoul nodded at the map.

Philber huffed but nodded reluctantly.

"To not waste time, I'm going to put on the oval now," Samantha said, her voice stark. "We need to know more. We have to find out where to look for more evidence of what occurred here two hundred and fifty years ago." She pulled the box to her and then turned to Darian. "Will you assist me?"

"Yes, but…I wish you'd let me go first." Darian was nervous now. What if something happened to Samantha or they couldn't get the item off? She tried to think of how easily it had dislodged from her hand yesterday, but it didn't help much.

"No. I instigated everything. I need to do this." Samantha reached back and undid her bun so that her hair spilled down in soft waves around her shoulder. Using one of the pins to part it in the back, she then put it back up in two smaller buns on either side of the part line. She placed two fingers at the base of her skull. "Here. From what I saw the first time, this is where it needs to go."

"Got it." Darian looked at Raoul. "Do you have your equipment ready?"

"Right here." Having pulled out a stethoscope, he now attached a blood-pressure cuff around Samantha's right arm. On a small stainless-steel tray, he had brought several other gadgets, including four marked syringes. He nodded, his eyes sharp now.

Darian removed the oval from its case, and the ones who hadn't seen it like that before gasped quietly.

"That's a strange-looking thing," Walker said huskily. "Samantha…"

"It's going to happen," Samantha said. "I'll be fine."

Darian prayed she was right as she shifted her grip of the oval and slowly moved it toward the back of Samantha's head. "Which way do you think? Horizontally? Vertically?"

"Vertically. Absolutely," Samantha said.

Swallowing against her suddenly dry throat, Darian gently held the oval against Samantha's skin. Small baby hairs curled underneath it, and Darian hoped that wouldn't matter. It would be a crime to cut them.

She thought she imagined a tremor coming from the oval, but then it moved fast between Darian's fingers and snapped onto Samantha, who flinched.

"Damn it. You okay?" Darian kept her fingers hovering right next to the device.

The filaments hung limp for another few moments, and then they went rigid and slid the small round metal feet into Samantha's hair, where they disappeared.

Raoul had kept two fingers against Samantha's carotid and still did. "Pulse 92, but that's all right. She's stressed."

Samantha clenched her hands, tipped her head back, and then slumped to the side, just as Darian sat down in time to catch her.

CHAPTER TEN

Samantha had never known such vertigo. Everything was spinning and swaying, but at least nothing hurt. She felt Darian's arms around her, but she couldn't speak to reassure her. Darian frantically called out her name over and over, as did Camilla.

"Fuck it. Get that thing off her," Brandon said, sounding oddly far away.

"Nn-no!" Samantha managed to say, fumbling for Darian's hands, squeezing them. "Don't."

"Her blood pressure is 140/90." Raoul's voice was a welcome calm in the storm. "Pulse still in the nineties, but strong and steady." Steady fingers pried her eyelids open one by one, and a sharp light shone against her eyes. "Pupils reactive and normal."

"Please, Samantha, slow your breathing," Darian murmured close to Samantha's ear. "You're hyperventilating."

She was? Samantha kept her eyes closed against the spinning room and deliberately drew a deep, slow breath through her nose and out through her mouth. "Room is spinning. Nauseous."

"Keep breathing like that. That's it," Darian said, sounding calmer. "There you go."

Slowly, the vertigo stilled, but Samantha didn't let go of Darian's hands. She opened her eyes and realized she was lying in Darian's arms. Held by strong arms, she knew she had never been at risk of falling. She began sitting up, smiling faintly. The cuff around her arm inflated again. "Better. Much better. Room's not spinning anymore."

"BP going down. Pulse also. Color returning to normal. You were a bit flushed there for a moment, Samantha." Raoul let the cuff remain around her arm. "Let's just keep it there for now."

As she sat up, Samantha met the startled eyes of the men and women around the table. "Now that was a trip." She tried to joke but was met with concerned looks. "What? Did I grow a beard while the device was attached?"

At least Carl chuckled, but he was still pale. "Nah. A small mustache. That's it."

"Ah. How becoming." Samantha rolled her shoulders and stretched her arms. "I'm a little sore, but otherwise I feel fine now. I'm not lying." She was grateful she hadn't thrown up.

"All right," Camilla said. "I know you wouldn't, as Darian will put one on at some point."

"Exactly." Samantha pulled the cylinder with the document hanging from it toward her and let her eyes follow the signs. She could understand more words, but nothing made sense. She flattened the plastic-looking material against the table. "It's so clear to me, but I can't make out what it means." She tried over and over. "It's like the words are out of order. Like a puzzle." Disappointment washed over her, and she began to tremble. Solving this mystery meant so much to her. But why did it? None of them had really questioned why this was so important. Yes, the joy of discovering something new and exciting, sure, but this drive that she'd felt ever since Darian and she went down to find Camilla's blueprints that day showed more than that. Were they making each other obsessed, or what was going on? If anything, the urgency had gone up a notch since she put on the oval…no, the word oval wasn't sufficient. The neural interface.

"Samantha?" Darian wrapped an arm around her waist. "What's going on?"

"We're obsessed." Samantha shook her head. "I actually think Philber was the first to react. So adamant about his research into Dennamore. Then, when I started showing some of the inhabitants here how to look for relatives and ancestors, I was bitten. Then you came, Darian, and once I took you to the basement in Town Hall, the feeling grew that we needed to figure this out."

"And now when you're wearing the oval?" Darian asked gently.

"It's called a neural interface." Samantha blinked and then closed her eyes. "It connects to me, but it doesn't do as much as I hoped, or dreamed of."

"You could have a look at the manual," Carl said, pushing the box toward Samantha. "There are tons of symbols, lines, and indentations on the inside of the lid of this thing."

Samantha took the box and examined the signs. At first, she could see only what she'd already noticed when she attached the neural interface around her hand. Then it was as if the signs trembled, and when she moved her eyes from the bottom right corner and up, everything finally began to make sense.

"I should place my fingertips into the indentations for my aptitude test. At least I think that's what it says." Samantha squinted at the signs. "There are three indentations." She pointed to them.

"They're pretty shallow. Are you sure?" Darian murmured, shifting restlessly next to her.

"No, but since Raoul says my vitals are all right, I'm going to do it." As the faint indentations were arranged with the middle one a quarter of an inch higher than the other two, Samantha placed her middle finger in that one, and her ring and index finger in the ones on either side.

It was like flipping a switch. No vertigo. No elevated heart rate or hyperventilation. Instead, when Samantha looked at the box, the symbols made perfect sense, as if they were written in modern English. She pulled her fingers free, somehow knowing the shallow indentations had served their purpose.

"This device is an expertise connector." Energized, Samantha straightened and looked at the people around the table. That was an odd sensation in itself. They were her family, friends, and, in a way, cohorts in crime, but she now regarded them with fresh eyes.

"A what?" Camilla raised her eyebrows.

"An expertise connector. That's what it says." Samantha pointed at what she now thought of as letters rather than symbols. "Below it, it says it will provide the, um, carrier, with the expertise required for the mission at hand, and that it's personal once it recognizes you."

"Holy crap," Darian said. "And how are you feeling?"

"Never better. Honestly." Samantha smiled and hoped her confidence would set the concerned people in the room at ease. "I now know why it says aptitude, or propensity, at the top. It'll sound crazy, I'm sure, but I have knowledge that I didn't have a few moments ago."

"Knowledge about what?" Philber leaned forward. "To read this material?"

"Yes, that, but more. I know exactly how to navigate." Samantha only had to close her eyes, and it was so easy. She opened her eyes again and looked at the map still on the table next to the scroll box. "Like here. I see it so clearly, as if it were 3D-generated. It's hard to explain."

"Can you read the document?" Darian pushed the scroll to Samantha.

"I'll try again." Samantha pulled it to her. At first, it was as jumbled as before, until she realized that when she'd read on the inside of the lid, she had started in the lower right corner and read vertically from the bottom and up. She shifted her gaze, and now she grew rigid with excitement. "Once provided with a NIEC, that must mean neural interface expertise connector, the individual in question may not attempt the procedure with any other device. It is personal. If the individual expires during the journey, a new, unmatched person must take over the device to provide continuity in the knowledge base. Once the journey has commenced, it is vital that the person utilizing the NIEC not remove it until the ship has reached its destination." Samantha stopped reading for a moment.

"Ship?" Brandon said, rubbing his bald head. "I can't imagine that anyone coming over on the *Mayflower* brought these things."

"Continue, Samantha," Philber said, and Samantha noticed how he was writing in his notebook in a frenzy.

"The station the NIEC suggests for the carrier is determined after a multi-faceted neural scan, where the individual's aptitude is determined. If the NIEC goes dormant and spontaneously detaches, no match was found, and the person in question is dismissed."

"Picky little things," Carl murmured.

"I need to use one as well." Darian didn't wait for anyone else to respond. She rose and fetched one of the other five boxes. When she retook her seat, she first looked at Camilla and then Samantha. "I'm doing this. Want to put the blood pressure cuff on me, Doc?"

"Yes." Raoul repeated what he had done with Samantha. "Pulse eighty-five, respiration twelve, blood pressure 120/75. You're good to go from a medical standpoint," he said after performing the tests.

Darian worked quickly. After parting her hair in the back, she opened the scroll and the case. Plucking the NIEC from its compartment, she handed it to Samantha, who received it with great care. "Just slap it on there."

"Funny." Samantha placed her free hand on Darian's shoulder. "Don't rush it. Remember how I nearly crumbled. It'll take a little while to figure things out."

"Sorry. Okay." Darian bent her neck. "Go ahead when you're ready," she said, sounding calmer.

Samantha exchanged glances with Raoul, who slid closer and nodded. He was ready. Placing the NIEC against the indentation just below Darian's cranium, she watched in fascination how the filaments first hung limply, but then straightened as if electricity ran through them and slipped into Darian's hair. Samantha carefully felt among the silky tresses where the little metal circles ended up. Startled, she realized she couldn't feel them. Her hands flew up to her own scalp, and it was the same thing there. The filaments and small round metal dots were not distinguishable against her skin.

"What is it?" Camilla asked, and Samantha could see that she was trembling. Walker had his arm around her.

"Nothing. I'm fine and…Darian?"

"Hold on. Push the box closer," Darian said, speaking through her teeth. She fumbled for the indentations and shoved her fingers into them. The vertigo must be bad. Within seconds, she was straightening and tilting her head back and forth as if working out the kinks. "Whoa. That was a trip. All better now." Darian pulled the documents from her scroll closer. "What the fu—sorry, Gran. I mean, why don't these make much sense to me?"

Samantha guided Darian in how to read, and it soon became obvious that Darian's scroll said exactly the same thing. Samantha thought of something. "The scroll says that we're not supposed to use anyone else's NIEC. We should mark the cases just to be safe."

"But how?" Philber looked at the artifacts, and now he was quite pale. "You can't damage them by carving your initials or anything."

"I know." Camilla turned to Brandon. "Please fetch my blue makeup bag."

"Of course." Brandon disappeared for a minute and returned with a sizable makeup kit.

"What are you thinking, Gran?" Darian asked as she held on to her scroll box.

"Nail polish. I have every nuance known to mankind." Calmly, Camilla snapped the lock open and displayed an impressive array of high-end products. "This won't hurt the surface, but it'll show clearly which box belongs to whom."

Philber nodded. "Acceptable."

Picking a green polish, Darian placed one drop at the top left corner outside the lid. Samantha chose a pink and repeated the maneuvers with hers.

"Using these NIECs is obviously voluntary," Samantha said, but she stopped talking when Carl nearly bounced off his chair.

"I want to try one."

Samantha held up her hand. "I know you're legally an adult, Carl. Just consider this…you still have another seven years to go before your brain is fully developed. I couldn't live with myself if something happened to you. If it damaged you beyond repair."

"But, Ms. Pike…"

"No buts. And, please, call me Samantha."

"Samantha, I really think you should reconsider…" Carl looked so disappointed, Darian ached for him. If anyone had told her that she couldn't experience this enigmatic technology, she would have been crushed. She thought of something and turned to Camilla. "Same with you, Gran. You know what I mean."

"Not that I was about to volunteer, but you're right. I know that." Camilla patted Walker's hand. "I have had a few minor blood clots in my brain and am on blood thinners. I'm fine, but attaching some strange device onto my head is not a good idea. Yet you know what that means, don't you, Darian? You're going to have to read aloud for me, from the journal my ancestors kept."

"No problem, Gran." Darian looked relieved. Perhaps she had expected the feisty, if frail, Camilla to insist on a NIEC of her own.

"Anyone with any illness or condition like that should be excluded." Samantha injected all the authority she could manage in her voice.

"I suffer only from spite and sarcasm," Philber said calmly.

Camilla chuckled. "Nothing changes much in Dennamore."

Darian slapped her palm against the table, making everyone jump. "Security. Martial-art moves I've never learned. Weapons' knowledge." Her eyes huge, she turned and looked at Samantha. "What the hell?"

"Your aptitude. Well, it makes more sense than my sudden knowledge of navigation, maps, and charts."

Raoul had sat next to Darian and quietly monitored her. Now he shoved his fingers through his thick hair. "I know you only invited me for my medical expertise, but I need to do this."

"But who will monitor you?" Walker asked.

"Both you and Darian, being cops, have first-aid knowledge. I have everything set up and labeled. Epinephrine for allergic reactions, adrenaline if someone's heart stops, etcetera."

"Heart *stops*?" Darian gaped. "Was that what you anticipated?"

"No, but I wanted to be prepared. I'm healthy. And I need to do this." Raoul looked calm but showed a determined intensity that Samantha recognized within herself.

"Who else in this room wants to try this, if not tonight, then later?" Samantha asked.

"I do," Philber said.

Walker shook his head. "If I didn't sit next to the woman I dreamt of for many years, I might have been so inclined, but I'll help in any other way I can."

"I want to try," Brandon said. "All this fascinates me, and I might be a stand-in of sorts for Ms. Tennen."

This remark made the others smile.

"All right then. Raoul and Philber, to begin with." Samantha looked at the devastated Carl. "And if we find evidence that this is safe for younger people, we might reconsider. I hope you respect this decision and still want to be part of the group."

Carl relaxed visibly. "Yeah. Hell, yeah. I thought for a moment you might kick me out altogether."

"Absolutely not."

Darian fetched boxes for the three men. "Why don't we just go for it? Philber first, so Raoul can be there for him. No offense, sir, but you are of a mature age, after all."

Despite that fact, Philber went through the process with fewer side effects than any of them, it seemed. He stuck his fingers into the indentations, and within seconds, he seemed to look younger. His posture and entire demeanor altered. "I'll be damned," he said, running a hand over his face. As he read the lid, and then some of his scroll, Philber's eyes shone with enthusiasm. "I think anthropology comes closest to what is now permeating my brain. I see patterns in the things I've already studied that I couldn't detect before. And I know of other cultures that I've never even heard of!"

After Philber calmed down to mark his box with an orange nail polish, it was Raoul's turn. To Samantha's relief, he easily overcame his vertigo. They had found the method of not waiting to stick your fingers into the lid to be preferable.

Sitting perfectly still, his eyes brightening, Raoul then began to smile. "Still a doctor, but I remember medical procedures, instruments, and illnesses that I know I've never seen, or even heard of…and now I just know." He marked his box with a light-yellow dot.

Samantha glanced over at Darian and noticed the pensive look on her face.

Brandon was the only one not having to part his hair, being bald. Samantha held his NIEC against the base of his skull, but to her surprise, nothing happened. The filaments didn't move.

"It could be malfunctioning." Darian fetched another scroll box, but the result was the same.

"I'm sorry, Brandon," Samantha said, "but I can't get it to work."

"I wonder why this is." Camilla took Brandon's hands between hers. "There has to be a reason."

Philber looked up from his notes. "I think it's pretty obvious. Brandon's not from Dennamore. I mean, he has no ancestors here. It's the most obvious conclusion."

Samantha frowned. "We haven't tried this on more than a handful of people. It's too early to draw any conclusions at all."

"Perhaps," Philber said, "but it's the best I can come up with at this point. Unless you want to round up people and conduct some double-blind study."

"I can tell the NIEC didn't alter your acerbic personality," Camilla said. "Good to know."

"Oh, I don't mean to sound dismissive, but that's the logical conclusion for now." Philber had the good taste to at least try to look regretful.

"Now to another matter." Darian reached around her neck. "Let's see how these things detach. "Something tells me that we should have tried that before we started handing them out like freaking candy."

"You're just going to pull?" Camilla looked aghast. "How about reading the damn manual first, child?"

"That's what we did when we tried them on our hands. But you have a point." Darian pulled the scroll to her again. Samantha did the same. "Hm. Wait. Let's see," Darian muttered. "Ah. Here. For removal…allow vacuum seal to break." She locked her gaze on Samantha. "Is that what you have too?"

"Yes," Samantha said, having found the paragraph as well.

"Same," Raoul said, and Philber nodded.

"Not sure what it means exactly, but I should be able to gently pry it loose." Samantha moved in behind Darion. She slid her blunt nails around the edge of the NIEC. "Just relax and envision it detaching. All right?"

"Yeah. Envisioning." Darian leaned back against Samantha, her shoulder blades touching Samantha's belly.

Pulling gently, she thought at first that it did seem stuck, but she didn't let on since Darian didn't express any discomfort. Then the NIEC came loose, and the filaments dangled after creeping out from Darian's hair.

"Oh!" Darian gripped the edge of the table. "Damn."

"Vertigo?" Samantha sat down next to Darian, still holding on to her NIEC.

"No, not really. Just a whoosh…and then, well, I feel, not empty, exactly, but depleted? The knowledge went away. Or the brunt of it, at least." She ran her finger along her NIEC. "Put it back again. Please."

"You sure?"

"Yes."

Samantha repeated the, by now, familiar procedure and was still just as fascinated by how the filaments wormed their way along the scalp and into Darian's hair.

"Ah. Good. It's all back." Darian grinned. "Obviously after the initial attachment, we don't have to go through the whole thing with placing our fingers exactly right and so on."

"What is the purpose of these items?" Brandon regarded the boxes with a certain exasperation. "I mean, of this elevated knowledge?"

"I think Darian and Samantha have started to figure it out. To me it's obvious." Philber crossed his arms over his chest. "This is required knowledge when you're putting together a crew."

CHAPTER ELEVEN

A crew. Darian stood by the window in the parlor, trying to wrap her mind around Philber's laconic words. They had merit, but still, how could it be? When the people who once founded Dennamore arrived in this part of the world, no matter how forward thinking they might have been, they couldn't have used, let alone, constructed, this advanced technology. Still, these aptitude neural interfaces had enhanced her proficiency for police and security work, which would be useful on any ship. Samantha as some kind of navigator? The woman was methodical and more organized than anyone Darian had ever met, that was true. Raoul would be a given as a ship's doctor, which was only logical. Philber, in turn, the scholar among them, had been pegged as the person most able to make sense of a new world. How the hell had their ancestors used these devices when coming over from Europe? Just thinking about it gave her a headache, and it didn't help that she still was wearing the NIEC. She planned to take it off once they'd looked at how far she had come in uncovering the glowing rock below.

"Darian. Raoul and Carl are ready to go down into the basement. Let's get that over with so we can remove the NIECs. We probably need to get used to them little by little." Samantha came up to her, placing a gentle hand on Darian's shoulder.

Normally, Darian's heart would have skipped several beats from the unexpected touch, but now she just kept looking out the window at the starry sky. "Little by little? Are you kidding me?

We're running headlong into this, and before you say anything, I know I'm as head over heels about this as the rest of you." She waved both hands in the air to indicate what she meant—which was everything. "What if we get addicted to the NIECs? The way I reacted when we took it off me bothers me."

"Hey. Come here." Samantha put her arm around Darian's waist. "I think it was the novelty of it—and that you and the rest of us feared you might not get the knowledge back when we reattached it. Now that we know that you did, we'll be more relaxed."

Darian gave something between a snort and a huff. "Really. Relaxed. I haven't been able to think about anything else. The knowledge. It's been many things, but relaxing isn't one of them."

Samantha stood quietly for a moment. "True. I've felt the same, but perhaps it's different for me since I was actually born and bred here. You're as much a part of this town as I am, and the others here, but you don't have the same connection to it. No wonder you're hesitant. I promise you, I'd never dream of putting any pressure on you to continue with this—"

"Stop right there." Darian pivoted within Samantha's arm and glared at her. "That's not what I mean. I'm in, all the way, just like before. I'm just worried that things are happening too fast and that we're rushing in. You were the one who set the limit when it came to a young person such as Carl. I didn't even think about that. When you brought it up, it made total sense. Well, perhaps not to Carl at first, but to the rest of us, me included. We need to be less pushy and more reflective."

"Hear, hear," Camilla said from behind Samantha. "I couldn't agree more. Why don't you two take our guests into the basement to look at that thing? Then I want you all out of those little machines."

"Yes, ma'am," Darian said, briefly pressing her forehead against Samantha's shoulder before she stepped away. "Let's go."

The men were already walking down the stairs when Darian and Samantha joined them. Brandon had installed excellent lighting in the basement, and Philber didn't need any guidance as he rounded the wall to the old pantry.

"Ah. Just as in my basement. You've been hard at work, Darian." Philber regarded the large pile of discarded boards on the floor. "Those things are massive."

"Tell me about it." Tension gripped Darian's upper arms just thinking about the logs. "I've uncovered about a third of the smooth wall, or stone, behind it. If you look here—oh, shit!" She stared at the wall.

"What is it?" Samantha was right behind her and now gripped Darian's arms firmly.

"I couldn't make that out before. I couldn't see the words. Is it the NIEC at work? It has to be."

Philber and Raoul joined them, and the four who were outfitted with NIECs stood side by side, trying to figure out the meaning of the words.

"Think of it this way," Philber said. "We're reading from the right bottom and up, and that means we're starting somewhere in the middle here and just getting the last thirty percent of what it says."

"What about the lines?" Samantha placed her finger along one in the middle. Immediately, the coloring of the light shifted faintly, and some lines moved marginally. "Wh-what was that?" Samantha yanked her hand back. "I suppose this is what you meant by acting before thinking," she said as she took Darian's hand.

"Yeah, yet I want to try that too." Darian sighed. "Unless someone else feels the urge."

"Allow me," Raoul said and put his entire palm against the stone surface, in a different spot. Some lines shifted to a blue-green light, and a couple of the words glowed stronger.

"Alert zone one. Pathway gates ready." Samantha read aloud. "Better let go, Raoul."

Raoul backed up. "I'll say."

"Let's not experiment with this one," Philber said calmly. "In my basement, this part is entirely exposed, and we tested it in a more structured way."

"What did you think your smooth wall was about before we reached out?" Darian asked.

Philber grimaced. "You sound as if we know what it is right now. I realized I was on the verge of discovering something remarkable but had no way of knowing where to begin, or how to continue from where I was. I've touched my wall all over. It's never switched colors or showed any words or warnings." He glanced at Walker. "Why don't you place your palm in the same place as Raoul did?"

"All right." Walker did as asked without hesitating. The glow remained steady and nothing reacted. "One probably needs a NIEC to use this, whatever it's meant to do."

Darian squeezed Samantha's hand. "We need to rethink who works with whom."

"Agreed." Samantha let her gaze move around the basement, a slight frown on her forehead. "We need one NIEC wearer in every team. How about Carl and Raoul deal with the tunnel survey, and Philber and Walker explore Philber's basement wall? When it comes to the journal, Darian and I can work with Camilla and Brandon, as it is her book, after all, including the map and other documents we might come across."

"You're the born organizer," Darian said, still not about to let go of Samantha's hand. She needed something to steady her, help her through her doubts and, yes, downright fears. "Sounds good to me." She hoped she and Samantha would automatically work together as they'd be in the same place, when Samantha wasn't busy with her day job.

"Agreed," Philber said. Raoul nodded and so did Walker.

Carl didn't look as if he'd been paying much attention. He was still mesmerized by the wall.

"Carl? That okay with you?" Darian asked.

"Hm? Sure." Carl was now tapping on his phone.

"What are you doing?" Philber sounded annoyed. "If you're on social media then—"

"What?" Looking surprised, Carl snapped his head up. "Social media? Not my thing. No. I'm just writing down what Samantha read just now. I had a thought. I know I'm not trusted with a NIEC, but I can still think, Mr. Beresford."

"Philber. I told you." Philber huffed and scratched the back of his head. Darian interpreted this response as possibly as close as the stubborn man would come to an apology. "What were you thinking?"

"Samantha read: *Alert zone one. Pathway gates ready*. Right. Pathways can be tunnels. If you go with that thought—couldn't gateways be these things? Or the odd things Mr. Be—Philber—spotted on the old map by your old houses?"

Philber slapped Carl hard enough on the back to knock him off balance. "You're not the measly asparagus you pretend to be, kid."

"Philber." Walker covered his eyes and then shook his head.

"Thank you. I guess," Carl said dryly, but he smiled.

"I think this is as far as we'll get tonight." Samantha glanced at Darian. "I don't know about you, but I'm tired, and we probably need to rest our heads from these devices."

"Agreed," Raoul said. "I admit, I've got a bit of a headache."

Darian walked ahead of the others up the stairs, where she found Brandon waiting. He had placed the scroll boxes on a dresser for their convenience, and she kissed his cheek. "Thank you."

"Of course." Briefly touching her arm, he stepped out of the way. "I'll put them in one of the large cabinets in the library when you're all done."

Samantha had already pulled her NIEC off and now let it settle into the casing. One by one the other three followed suit. Afterward, they all seemed subdued. Darian looked at Samantha and saw dark circles under her brilliant green eyes, which looked bloodshot. Feeling like she must look even worse, Darian tried not to slump until the men had told them good night and left.

"Would you mind staying for a little while, or are you very tired?" Darian prayed Samantha would say yes.

"I was going to ask just that." Samantha peered into the parlor. "However, Camilla and Brandon are settling down in there, and I don't want to disturb your grandmother. She must be tired."

"She is, but clearly not tired enough to forgo a game of chess with Brandon. One day I'll tell you about their long ongoing torment of each other." Darian hesitated. "If you're okay with it, we can use my room. The room Camilla intends to use as a family room is undergoing major work."

Samantha blinked. "Naturally. If that's all right with you."

Darian wanted to groan. "Sure thing. Hang tight." Darian poked her head in and told the two who were focusing on the marble chessboard that she was heading back upstairs with Samantha.

"That's fine, dear," Camilla said absentmindedly and waved dismissively.

Turning back to Samantha, Darian crinkled her nose. "I think she heard me."

As they ascended the stairs again, this time taking a right turn when reaching the mezzanine, the thought of being alone with Samantha in her room made her pulse race faster than it had when she attached the NIEC.

Samantha stood motionless just inside the door of Darian's bedroom. It was a good-size room, albeit with the lower ceilings typical of the era when it was built. In here, the logs were visible, and it boasted exposed beams. A four-poster bed dominated the room. No curtains attached to it, but it still added to the old-fashioned ambiance of the room.

"We invested in new mattresses, naturally. I mean, the old ones were thrown out a long time ago, which was a relief, since I'd never sleep on a mattress from the sixties or something." Darian stood by the bed, her hands deep into her back pockets. She was speaking faster than normal, which suggested she might actually be suffering from a sudden onset of nerves, just like Samantha was.

"I totally agree. Good move." Samantha took a couple of steps into the room. A beautiful blue-and-white rag rug adorned the wooden floor by the foot of the bed. "That's a lovely rug."

"Yeah. It came with the house. We found several in a closet and had them professionally cleaned. I refused to kill the old washing machine by pushing those heavy things into it. Little did I know that appliances in this town seem to live forever."

Chuckling, Samantha relaxed and walked closer. “I know. It never used to occur to me, but the way things are going, we might have to add that to our list of oddities.”

“Have a seat.” Darian motioned toward the bed, while pulling up the chair belonging to the small desk by the window. “Gran says she used this desk and chair when she did her homework as a teenager.”

“Thanks.” Samantha sat down on the foot of the bed. “And I can picture it.” She wasn’t exaggerating. She’d looked up Camilla’s schoolbook picture the other day, and though the black-and-white photo probably didn’t do the stunning girl justice, it was obvious why any young man, or woman, for that matter, idolized and desired her. Her eyes had glowed in the photo, and knowing how blue they were, Samantha easily envisioned them piercing the person who enjoyed her attention. At the same time, it wasn’t hard to figure out that the same glance could eviscerate someone who displeased her. Darian’s brown eyes could do the same.

“How are you feeling?” Darian pulled up one foot onto the seat and leaned her chin against her knee. The move made her seem impossibly young, but the exhaustion on her face did not.

“Tired. Headache, though it’s better. At least I’m not having a sugar low this time. And what about you? Can you elaborate on what you were thinking earlier in the library when you seemed hesitant about us doing this? Worried for us?”

“I’m not sure. I’ve been so at it, you know, hungry for more knowledge about symbols, letters, signs, artifacts, and so on, that I haven’t stopped to think about if we even *should* look into this. I mean, looking into it is one thing, but when we were in the library, this voice in my head, well, not an actual voice, obviously,” Darian laughed and pulled her elastic out of her hair. “But anyway, as I said, my thoughts made me question if we’re going too fast. If we’re hurting ourselves, or each other, by pressing on.” Darian ran her fingers through her hair. “Yet I know this needs to be done. I mean, how can I know that for certain? Is this another part of that damn yearning you Dennamore inhabitants keep talking about?”

"We don't just talk about it. It is a valid point. Something even you have experienced, which can't be explained away by 'buying into the hype' or something. The returnees, like Camilla, sometimes are resentful, even, when they come back. They feel they didn't have a choice. Do you think we need to add that to the ever-growing list of peculiarities we keep coming across?"

"Perhaps. I know it's real. I'm just frustrated that, so far, we have so many questions, but no answers. Or very few."

Samantha had to smile. "You do realize we've been at this only a few weeks, right?"

Darian pressed her forehead against her pulled-up knee for a few moments, before glancing back up at Samantha. "I do. Although, why, then, does it feel like I've known you for much longer?"

"Well, when you're in the crazy-trenches together, perhaps that slows time down?" Samantha tried to joke the question away, but in her heart, she knew Darian was right. She too felt as if she'd met and cared about Darian for a lot longer than a few weeks. Mustering courage, she nodded. "I feel that way too. You're not just a new acquaintance that shares a hobby of mine."

Darian's cheekbones colored a soft pink. "Good to know. I'm not sure why, but with you, I'm afraid of overstepping."

Puzzled, Samantha folded one leg over the other. "What do you mean?"

Darian lowered her gaze to Samantha's exposed knee but then returned her focus to her eyes. "I suppose I'm simply afraid of goofing up and risking our friendship." The sentence ended just above a whisper.

Samantha reacted without thinking. Sliding to the side, she patted next to her on the bed. "Come here."

Darian merely stared for a few beats, but then she moved and did as Samantha asked. "Yes?"

"Listen." Samantha forced herself to focus. She hadn't been prepared for how it would feel when Darian sat two inches away from her. Granted, they had sat just as close together in the library, but this was Darian's *bed*. "I don't want you to have to second-guess yourself around me. We truly are in some form of trenches together, as we're experiencing things that we can't explain or share with very many people. But that's not all. I would value your friendship no matter what. Even if we just met at the coffee shop by the square." Samantha took Darian's hand and felt it tremble in hers. "You matter to me."

Darian's gaze seemed to have gotten stuck on their joined hands. Samantha let her thumb run along the back of Darian's hand, in what she hoped was a reassuring way. "Dar?"

Darian looked up through her long lashes. "You've called me that once before. Dar."

"I have? Do you mind?" Samantha hoped not. She hadn't paid attention the first time she said it, or this time.

"Not at all. On the contrary. I like it." Smiling now, and relaxing again, Darian squeezed Samantha's hand. "And I like this." She motioned with her chin at their hands.

"Me too." That was a huge thing for Samantha to say. Not always a very tactile person, she could often cringe when someone spent too long a time within her personal space. And yet, here she was, being the one who had invited Darian to sit this close and hold hands. "Another thing that's special about you."

"How so?" Darian tilted her head, her brown eyes so warm, it was as if they calmed every frayed nerve-ending after the last two days' explorations.

"I know I come across as formal, at best, and rigid and aloof, even, sometimes." Samantha found enough security within herself to laugh. "Perhaps it was your hands-on approach to knock the wind out of me that first day that allowed me to at least not chill you to the bone."

Darian returned the smile, but she waited so long with her reply that Samantha was just about to get nervous again, when she slowly shook her head. "Who told you these things? Aloof and rigid, and able to chill anyone to the bone?" Her voice was slightly huskier than usual, but so very soft.

Samantha didn't know how to explain that those had been only a few of the epithets used about her being a cold fish, throughout her life. "Not everyone. Of course not. But enough for the words to stick and have an impact. Most likely because there is some truth to them. I'm not easy to approach all the time. I enjoy my personal space."

At that, Darian's eyes grew wide before she seemed to inwardly measure the tiny distance between them. "Then I take this as a vote of confidence."

"Good." It was, but it was more. Samantha wasn't ready to even explore what this "more" consisted of, but it was still true. "No matter where our studies and explorations lead us, I want to say that getting to know you is the big win for me."

Tears rose so fast in Darian's eyes, and made them unimaginably more beautiful, that Samantha gasped.

"Darian! What did I say?"

The fat teardrops ran down Darian's cheeks, and she swallowed hard but still didn't say anything. Samantha let go of Darian's hand and now wiped at the tears with her thumbs.

"Please. I'm so sorry." Samantha felt her own eyes sting but refused to let it go beyond that.

"No. Don't be sorry." Darian cleared her throat. "I just wasn't prepared for you to say that."

"What?" At first, Samantha couldn't remember her words, but then she did. "Oh." She carefully stroked away the last drops. "So, good tears then?"

"Yes." Without warning, Darian wrapped her arms around Samantha. "And please don't think I'm usually this unhinged. It's just…this evening…and then you…" She drew a deep breath and slowly let it go.

Surprised by the unexpected hug, Samantha hadn't managed to gather her thoughts quickly enough to return it, but now she slid her hands up Darian's arms to show she didn't mind the brief embrace—to the contrary. "I see." She leaned in and placed a very quick kiss on Darian's cheek. "I really do."

Darian suddenly smiled broadly, her gaze darting back and forth to either side of Samantha. "I really do like this Princess Leia do you've got going on."

"Excuse me?" Taken aback, Samantha felt her hair and realized she was still wearing her hair in two side-buns. "Oh, God." She moved her fingers, trying to find the pins.

"No, don't. It really is cute." As full of tears as Darian's eyes had been only moments ago, now they glittered with joy.

Cute. At first, Samantha thought there was no way she was keeping this silly hairdo, but the way Darian looked at her made the commonplace self-consciousness on her part evaporate. She lowered her hands but couldn't help but roll her eyes. "Honestly." But even so, after they said good night and she started to drive home through Dennamore's streetlamp-lit streets, the way she had made Darian beam was more on her mind than their amazing finds.

CHAPTER TWELVE

The spine of the journal creaked ominously when Darian opened it. Across the table from her, Camilla sat ready to take notes on her laptop. She could barely hold a pen, but after being a writer for most of her life, the muscle memory in her hands still worked flawlessly. Darian suspected that they still hurt, but if she pointed that out, Camilla would not appreciate it.

"All right." Darian had put on her NIEC and opened the page she'd browsed with Samantha that first evening, several weeks ago. "I've got to admit, I'm nervous. Yikes."

Camilla reached around the screen and patted Darian's hand. "You'll do fine."

"From your lips to—" Not wanting to involve any sort of deity in this venture, and not sure why, Darian lowered her gaze to the page. You wouldn't expect this type of penmanship during the era the journal was written. In 1775, people wrote in cursive, and quite ornately, as far as she remembered from history lessons back in high school. This handwriting was precise, and also cursive, but entirely vertical, which made it look unusual. "Here goes. This first page mostly contains strange letters, or code…whatever."

"I'm ready." Camilla pulled her chair closer to the table.

Darian still could hardly believe how easy it was to interpret the writings.

"*My name is Bech'taia. I start this journal to document this stop in our journey, which was unexpected. The Elders have decided we must remain, but I know most of us want to return home at one point. Coming to this new world is surely an adventure, but aren't adventures meant to be shared with the ones we left behind? I believe that to be the case, and so does my beloved Gai'usto. He talks often of his sisters and worries how they fare while living in the capital with their aunt. Being out of reach, unable to communicate since the Elders have forbidden this until further notice, weighs heavy on him. As far as I know, my family is intact, but given the way politics were creating chasms between the wealthy and the less fortunate, who can be sure?"*

Camilla typed steadily while Darian read, but now she looked up. "Is she talking about the British? She must be, right, since the rest of the text is in flawless English. I've browsed it some, and the further you get into the journal, the less she uses the symbols."

"I suppose." Darian turned the page and found more symbols. The part that was in English was more factual, about the efforts of cutting down trees and building dwellings. The ones written in code spoke more of feelings, positive or negative, and sometimes of criticism, even resentment.

"*It has been two months, according to the lunar cycle. We have roofs over our heads, all of us, and the ones not joined with a mate are residing in barracks. They are the younger ones among the crew and—*"

Darian stopped. "Crew. The ship's crew was stranded here, by their Elders? That sounds odd."

"Agreed." Camilla rested her hands in her lap. "I wonder how big their ship was. What it was called. Perhaps we can find that in the journal."

Darian cleared her throat.

"*—and I expect they'll eventually begin pairing off once they realize the decision for us to remain here is permanent. For now, the members of the council the Elders have formed are the only* *ones that are informed. Gai'usto agrees with me that this is an error in judgment. Once the truth is revealed, there are bound to be repercussions. I worry about it. Gai'usto and I were chosen to be on the council mainly because we are the heads of the agricultural department. If we had held lower positions, no doubt we'd be just as oblivious."*

"They kept their people in the dark about these matters?" Camilla looked appalled. "That doesn't make sense. Surely those who came to the New World in the Americas did so expecting to stay and create a better life for themselves. Unless they arrived as convicts or slaves, naturally. I don't get the impression that these 'younger ones among the crew' are slaves, though. Or convicts. They are sailors."

Darian nodded. "I agree. This is nothing like any of the history I remember learning. And you, having grown up here, is this part of the local history? Did you read about any of this about the first settlers?"

"Not at all. I've always loved history, you know that, and this is new to me."

Darian kept reading about how the small settlement grew as the younger people formed what Bech'taia referred to as "new family units." She turned the page and sat up straighter. "Here. Wow.

"1777, the 2nd of March. Today the entire crew met in the meadow that will one day be our square. This is a traditional way of trading in our new home—in a square in the center of a town with vending stalls where they sell their merchandise. This is, however, not our mission today. The Elders have now shared their decision that all of us will remain here for the foreseeable future. They also insist on naming our settlement after our home. Gai'usto loathed the idea, and he and I fought long and hard to reach a compromise. The Elders resisted us, but as we are instrumental in our immediate survival here, they surrendered to the idea, to us, for obvious reasons. If we are to blend in, to call this home, we need to have it sound more like the language they speak in these parts. Young

Ensign Tre'Main, who sometimes goes to barter for supplies to the closest settlement—which is a three-day walk—told how they asked where he comes from. Not knowing better, he told them. They mispronounced it as Dennamore."

Not sure why, Darian's eyes stung. "Oh, Gran. Bech'taia and Gai'usto wanted to return to their country. The Elders stranded them here."

"Hm. Yes. It sounds like it. Is there more on that page?" Camilla rubbed her knuckles.

"Just a brief paragraph. You okay?"

"Yes.

Knowing when to stop fussing, Darian continued after quickly wiping at her damp eyelashes.

"*It saddens me, even if this is the best way under the circumstances. We will soon have procured the same type of garments as the people who inhabit this world. We will eat the same food, live very similar, hard lives, and thus blend in. Once the Elders decide that it is time to bury the ships, we will also stop using the tools we brought with us. Time will pass, generations will shift, and, eventually, nobody will remember Dwynna Major.*"

Camilla stopped typing. "What?" she whispered.

"It's what it says. There's no other way to read this. Dwynna Major."

"Dwynna Major. Dennamore." Camilla spoke the words slowly and then slumped back in her chair, covering her cheeks with her hands. "Is that where the Dennamore settlers really came from? I've never heard of it."

"Trust me. Neither have I. Doesn't it sound a bit Irish?" Still unable to think clearly, as the text had squeezed her heart as if to stop it, she said, "I'll have to Google it. Do you think anyone ever returned there? And why would they bury their ships? What was their port of entry? New York? Boston? Perhaps Plymouth?" Darian rubbed her temple. "Did they sink, no, bury, their ships? Was that really what Bech'taia meant? She wrote *buried*."

"I…I suppose we might find out later, if it's in the journal." Camilla's hands were trembling now. "I think I need a break, if that's all right."

"Me too. I—" Darian's cell phone rang, and Raoul's name showed up on the screen. "Wait a moment, Gran. I'll help you down the stairs, but I just need to take this. It's Raoul." She tapped the screen. "Hi, what's up—?"

"You need to come to Philber's house. Samantha too." Raoul sounded out of breath.

"What? But she hasn't gotten off work yet." Confused, Darian raised her eyebrows at Camilla, who was standing up, mouthing "wait for me" to her.

"You've got to call her. I'd do it, but I'm busy here. It can't wait. Philber says so, and I agree. Carl as well."

"You have to tell me something." Darian stood. "What's wrong?"

"Nothing's wrong exactly, but we think we found a way into the tunnel." Raoul drew a deep breath. "And by the way, wear your NIEC and bring Samantha's."

Samantha rushed through the doors and down toward the parking lot outside Town Hall. She had hastily told her colleague that she intended to work from home, which was a half-truth, if you weren't too particular. Darian had given very little additional information other than what Raoul had mentioned over the phone.

Getting into the car, she had to will herself to calmly put her briefcase on the passenger seat and strap herself in. She gripped the wheel with one hand and turned the ignition with the other, relieved that her car didn't have one of its moodier days and started willingly.

The drive to Philber's house took less than ten minutes, despite roadwork in the area. As she drove up by his house, she saw Darian's car behind what had to be Raoul's. A bicycle leaned against Philber's hedge. As Samantha stepped out, another car pulled up behind hers, and Walker exited. Samantha hoped all these cars wouldn't attract too much attention among the neighbors.

"You were summoned as well?" Walker held up his bag. "I was here earlier but felt I needed more of my gear. It's important we document what's going on."

Samantha could hardly believe she hadn't even given that aspect a single thought. Darian had worked on the journal today with Camilla and mentioned how they had translated and written down several pages worth of coded text. Of course, they needed to document visually as well, when appropriate. "Thank God you thought of that," Samantha said and walked up Philber's garden path with Walker. She was about to ring the doorbell when someone flung the door open.

"Damn. I'm sorry. Didn't mean to startle you. I saw you from the window." Darian stepped back and let them in. "I just got here and haven't gone down to the basement yet. I had to let myself in."

Samantha was about to ask why when she heard the raised voices below. She couldn't make out what they were saying, but someone, most likely Philber, was causing a commotion.

Carl appeared in the doorway to the basement stairs. "Oh, good. You better come down before Philber has a heart attack. He doesn't want to wait much longer. Better slap your NIECs on first."

"I've got mine." Darian pulled a box out for Samantha. "Here's yours."

"Good." Samantha opened it and lifted her hair in the back. The NIEC attached instantly, and she waited a few seconds to see if the vertigo hit, but it didn't. She felt an odd possessiveness. This NIEC was *hers*.

Walking downstairs, Samantha was able to make out words from behind the smooth rock wall.

"This is my damn property, and if I want to press the damn sensors, or what the *hell* these things are, I should be able to do that without some damn doctor—"

"Philber, we have no idea what'll happen." Raoul sounded calmer, but he clearly had to raise his voice as well, to be heard. "And we owe it to Samantha and Darian to insist they be here. This is their discovery. Their baby, if you will."

"And we're here," Darian said and hurried around the wall. "Calm down and fill us in."

"Took you a long time," Philber muttered. His eyes were narrow slits, but he seemed to try to harness himself.

"Fill us in." Samantha waved Walker forward.

"Come over here and tell us what you see," Raoul said, and pointed at the wall. "This showed up when Philber and I pressed one of the outer glowing spots each, at the same time."

Samantha felt her eyes widen when she saw the grid that had appeared on the rock. It seemed perfect to her. "Have you measured the grid squares?"

"Yes. They're 3.3 centimeters. Well, actually 3.33333, to be more precise," Philber said, rubbing his chin. "It's unfathomable how a rock that sits in a house built in the seventeen hundreds..." He shook his head and didn't continue. It was rare to see Philber speechless.

"And the map ought to be just as accurate," Darian whispered, indicating the detailed map of an old version of Dennamore. "Here we are." She pointed at where Philber's house was shown with a sharply edged rectangle. She did the same with Camilla's house and Walker's. "Here's Town Hall. The lake. And...the tunnel?"

Samantha felt for support and found Darian's shoulder. Bracing herself, she let her gaze follow the clear marking of a completely straight tunnel, or whatever it was, that led from the lake to the town hall. In four spots, lines seemed to lead from the tunnel to the homes of Philber, Camilla, and Walker, and one more. "This house, and yours, Walker, and Camilla's, are located south of the tunnel. So is the fourth house. Who lives there?"

"That's the one they tore down, remember?" Philber nodded at the fourth rectangle. "The Normans' house."

"Ah. The other two remaining log houses are north of the tunnel, with no lines to them. Perhaps they don't have these rocks either." Samantha turned to Philber. "Are you saying you think these lines indicate access points to the tunnels?"

"Yes. Yes!" Philber flung his hands up. "Now to the next part we discovered." He stepped up to the wall. Placing his palm against another bright dot at the edge, he pushed up, thus moving, not scrolling, the entire grid.

"Holy crap!" Darian gaped.

"And this." Raoul used two spots and pulled them apart. The map grew bigger. "Now the grid is 6.66 centimeters. You can get it up to twice that size." He zoomed in farther, keeping Philber's house in the middle. "See?"

Samantha did. She was trying to think above her sudden dizziness, which she suspected came from learning too much too fast. "It behaves like the map on my cell phone does," she said quietly.

"Look at that." Darian pointed to what Philber thought was an access point from his house. In the center of his house were two smaller but distinct glowing dots.

"I'll be damned," Walker said behind them. "Perhaps I need to utilize one of those interfaces after all. There are markings at my house as well." He motioned to his house, just visible to the far left. "And at Camilla's."

"Is this what the argument was about?" Samantha asked. "You wanted to push these markings and see what happens?"

"It's my house," Philber said grumpily.

"It is. And still, don't you agree that we need to be prepared when we take such a huge step?" Speaking in her best librarian voice, soft and calm, Samantha locked eyes with Philber.

"Like you were so prepared when you put on the NIEC the first time," Philber said, not without triumph.

"Touché," Samantha said. "I did take a risk. A personal risk. If you touch the markings and cause your house to fall on us—isn't that something we need to at least consider?"

"Make the house collapse? Ridiculous." Philber huffed.

"It might be, but it is worth a few extra minutes while we discuss the possibilities. We're a team here. I don't suggest that I'm the leader of our group—" Samantha blinked as Raoul and Darian both guffawed. "What?"

"You are so our leader," Darian said brightly. "This is your show, Samantha. The rest of us are equally important to our, well, um, quest, but we need a leader, and that is you. I know Gran feels the same way. Anyone else here have a different opinion?"

Everyone shook their heads. Even Philber.

Carl patted him on the back. "Now that we're gathered, you can better make your case. See how that works."

"Don't push your luck, kid," Philber said, but Samantha could tell he was mostly joking. Mostly. "All right. I don't think anything will level the house. If this is an access point, someone must have accessed it back in the day, and obviously the house is still intact."

"Yes. But it's also older," Walker said.

"My house is in perfect condition." Philber hit the logs that made up for the outer wall for emphasis.

"True. It is." Walker had pulled out his tripod and was now attaching his camera. "If you've decided to do something, I need to set up properly, to document."

Philber brightened. "Now we're talking."

Samantha raised her hands. "If we're going to do this, we're going to do it by the book."

"What book is that exactly?" Carl asked while looking at the grid. "Would that be the 'steps to not getting killed while investigating crazy sci-fi shit'?"

Everyone chuckled. "That'd be the one," Darian said.

"I want the ones not touching the markings at a reasonable distance. Over by that other wall." Samantha pointed behind her. "Raoul, I assume you have your medical equipment with you?"

"Yes." Raoul pointed at a shelf by the back wall.

"Good. Philber, since you'll be doing the deed, so to speak, you'll have to back up instantly. No antics." Samantha turned her head around, not even blinking, and made sure the stubborn man knew she meant business.

"Got it," Philber said, probably worried she might pick someone else for the task.

"Carl. Your mother will kill me if I let you get hurt. You stay over by the stairs, and if I tell you to, or if something looks off, you hightail it out of the house. Understood?" Samantha repeated the look when homing in on Carl.

"Absolutely." Carl nodded and moved to a safer spot.

"Have your cell phone ready," Samantha added. "Just in case."

Philber was already positioned by the grid on the wall. Samantha stood between Darian and Raoul, barely able to breathe.

"Hold on to your lucky drawers," Philber said, and suddenly his voice trembled slightly. Whether it was from an onset of nerves, or from excitement, was anyone's guess, Samantha thought. Perhaps both. Philber chose to use both index fingers and pressed them against the markings for a moment and then pulled them away. Nothing happened. "I'll try again and keep them there." Philber raised his hand but then stopped in midmotion and cast a glance at Samantha. "Boss?"

"All right," Samantha said, hoping she sounded calmer than she felt.

Philber repeated the maneuver and kept his fingers in place. Samantha found herself counting the seconds, and when she hit five, a gentle rumble grew in intensity. Philber let go and jumped back toward the rest of them. Over by the stairs, Carl stood wide-eyed and clutched his cell.

Then the wall shifted. The grid wasn't visible anymore, merely the lines that Samantha recognized from before, the ones that looked like a circuit board. Now the wall folded in on itself, slowly, rumbling like distant thunder during an electric storm. When it stopped, it had created an opening from floor to ceiling, wide enough to easily fit a person through. Behind it, a soft light came from below.

"Unbelievable," Darian whispered. She took a few steps forward, and Samantha's first reaction was to grab her arm and yank her back, but instead she joined her. "A hole in the floor." Darian pointed. "Or, rather, an opening. See?"

"I see it." Samantha bent forward and peered down the hole. "Steps. And light. How can there be light?"

"You're asking that, after all we've seen lately?" Darian snorted. "I have no clue. None."

"We have to go down." Philber, of course, was obviously ready.

"We will, but not yet." Samantha could see Philber gear up toward another frustrated exchange of words. "And before you blow another fuse, I'm just saying, we need to have the right gear with us. We need people on the surface, as in Camilla and Brandon, to know where we are in case something happens."

Philber deflated. "Yeah. All right. Damn it."

Darian nudged Samantha's arm. "And one of the people with a NIEC has to stay up here in case that thing suddenly closes itself. Who knows if it opens from inside?"

Samantha shuddered. She had never been keen on closed-off areas, and the idea of being trapped underground was not appealing. "Good point."

"And," Darian said, raising her voice some, "I think it's vital that I read you what Camilla and I translated today. It might help us once we're down there. You never know."

"Who'll stay behind?" Philber said, his fiery eyes making certain everyone knew it wasn't going to be him.

"I'll do it," Walker said. "I'll go back with Darian and have one of the NIECs fitted. I'll bring Camilla back with me, and we'll keep watch while the rest of you go down. Those who want to, that is."

"I'm going," Carl said and pointed to the opening with an open hand. "This was part of my assignment from the start."

Nobody else offered to stay behind. Samantha thought it was as if the mystery they were unfolding had them in a tight grip. Even she, who took some pride in being levelheaded and who led a quiet life, normally, couldn't imagine not going. Glancing at Darian, she knew the fact that she was in on this played a big part in her decision.

"Let's sit down a bit," Philber said and pointed to the far end of the basement. "I have some stools in there. I want to hear what Darian and Camilla found."

As they sat in a semicircle in Philber's laundry room, Darian read the translation from the journal.

"Dwynna Major," Samantha said. "Dwynna Major became Dennamore in early 1777."

The rest of them sat in silence. Clearly, the translation was about all their brains had room for. Eventually, Walker stood. "I suppose it's time to start if we're going to do this today. I'll drive over to see Camilla and fill her in."

"I'm right behind you." Darian stood but waited for Samantha.

Samantha rose slowly. "Philber. Please don't be tempted to go down alone."

"I won't." Philber seemed somewhat subdued. Was the enormity of their discoveries dawning on him?

"I'll stay here," Raoul said. "I've got hiking gear in my car. Enough for you too, Carl."

After agreeing to meet back at Philber's house in an hour, they all walked upstairs. Samantha kept close to Darian. "Drive safely," she said. "I'm not going into that hole without you."

Darian lit up. "Same goes for me." She smiled. "I can't believe we're going to enter some underground tunnel with no, and I mean *no* idea what we'll find." She took Samantha's hand. "So, you be safe too."

"Before we go, did you notice something else oddly familiar about the text you translated?" Samantha squeezed Darian's hand.

"No? What are you thinking of?"

"Probably nothing to do with our explorations, but isn't it kind of odd that Bech'taia and Gai'usto are critical of their Elders? I don't mean I'm critical of our Elder Council as a whole, but I'm definitely not on the same frequency as Desmond Miller."

"Oh, right. Of course. Their Elders sound rather like they make the decisions as if none of the other settlers have a say in the matter. That's probably what your Miller would love to have happen in Dennamore too."

"He's not my Miller." Samantha made a face.

"Ah, you know what I mean." Stepping close, Darian ran the back of her curled index finger along Samantha's arm. "See you back here in an hour then."

Samantha nodded, distracted by the goose bumps on her arm. As she made her way back to her car, she thought of the tunnel they hoped to find, but also, how Darian only had to be even remotely close to her personal space for her to forget about scrolls, maps, and NIECs.

CHAPTER THIRTEEN

Darian took in the eclectic mix of people that had once again gathered in Philber's basement. Raoul, the doctor who was unaware of the incomprehensible finds only a couple of days ago, had now changed into climbing gear and looked the part of an adventurer for sure. Carl, the young man who was a frequent flyer at the library and quite the individualist as he walked his own path in life, could probably not even spell "peer pressure." Brandon, also geared up, had been with Camilla and Darian since Darian moved in with her grandmother at age six, more than twenty years ago. Now he was ready to brave the unknown, not even being from this town, and Darian knew in her heart that it was because Camilla needed Darian to be safe. Brandon wasn't young, but he was strong and a jack-of-all-trades.

Walker stood next to Camilla, clearly set on being the protector when it came to her grandmother, as well as the gatekeeper of the opening before them. Philber stood next to it, unusually subdued, and he too had changed clothes and strapped on a backpack.

Samantha was reading something on her phone where she stood beside Darian. Dressed in jeans, T-shirt, and, holy crap, a gray hoodie, she too wore a backpack. Each of them carried their own scroll box, something Samantha had insisted on. They had no idea what to expect when going down the stairs. Camilla had insisted Darian put the journal in her backpack, and they had taken great care to protect it in double-plastic, zipped-up bags.

"It's time to go," Samantha said and tucked her cell phone into her back pocket. "Everyone ready?" Solemn nods and hums answered that question. "Good. Darian goes first. I know this is Philber's basement, but she's the only one who's armed."

"What?" Philber blinked.

"Just as a precaution. I don't expect us to run into that type of trouble, but better to be prepared and not have to use my weapon." Darian patted her shoulder holster encasing her Glock. "So. I go first."

Samantha pointed to the others, one by one. "Raoul is next. After that it is me, Philber, Carl, and Brandon. Chief Walker, you have your walkie-talkie set on channel four? Remember, anyone can listen, but we have no other means to communicate."

"Got it." Walker wiggled the radio. "Camilla and I will be here."

"Excellent." Samantha nodded at Darian. "Let's go then."

Darian kissed Camilla's cheek. "Stay warm, Gran. Glad Philber brought down an armchair for you."

"I'll be fine. Be safe, sweetheart." Camilla cupped Darian's cheeks.

Darian patted Walker on the shoulder and then walked over to the opening in the wall. She looked at the sides where the smooth rock seemed to have folded in on itself but couldn't see where it had tucked the pieces of the wall that it moved. Right now, it appeared to be two wide, rectangular columns on either side of the hole she was about to climb into. The glow from underneath made it possible to see the black steps. She put down one foot and then the next on the first step. It didn't tremble or shift, which gave her courage to start walking downward.

On either side of the narrow staircase, the walls were as smooth as the rock above. She had brought her favorite LED flashlight but didn't need to take it out yet as the light from below was more than enough. She hoped they would find the energy source for all the items they'd come across.

Turning her head, Darian could make out Raoul's silhouette at the top of the stairs. "It's fine. Let's go." She kept walking and felt, rather than heard, the others enter the staircase, following her down.

"I'm counting the steps," Carl said. "Just in case it matters at one point."

"Good thinking." The tension in Samantha's voice didn't seem to come from nerves. Darian knew how eager Samantha was to learn more about Dennamore, but she was also aware of the risk Samantha was taking professionally. Not that anyone expected a member of the Elder Council to pay Samantha a visit to check up on what she might be working on at home, but the mere idea that it might happen had to be nerve-racking for someone as dutiful as Samantha.

As they kept descending, and it grew increasingly colder, Darian was grateful for her fleece hoodie, but also for the lightweight sweater she'd packed in case she needed layering. Above her, the ceiling of the staircase glowed with enough light for them to still see the steps and where to place their feet. "How many steps now, Carl?" she asked.

"Seventy-seven" came the laconic answer. "That's almost four floors in a modern house. Ish."

"Thank you." Four floors below ground. Darian tried to not consider the idea of tons and tons of gravel, dirt, and rocks above them. "Tell me when you reach a hundred."

"Sure thing." Carl, perhaps because of the thirst for adventure that comes with youth, chirped the words out. It took him only a couple of minutes. "A hundred."

"Call them out every twenty steps," Philber said from behind. "Going back up is going to be a bi—bummer."

Suddenly grinning at Philber's rather moving attempt at being cordial, Darian let her hand slide along the smooth wall and kept her eye on every step. If she fell, she had no idea how long that tumble would be.

"A hundred and twenty," Carl called out. "Forty. Sixty."

The staircase ended around step two hundred. A rectangular opening a few yards ahead was lit up by small LED-looking lights around the perimeter. "I've reached a floor level, guys," Darian called out. She walked up to the opening but stopped, wanting to wait for Samantha before they explored what lay ahead.

It took only a few moments for the rest of the team to reach Darian. Samantha and Raoul flanked her as they carefully stepped through to the next part. Darian unzipped her jacket, a motion that was part of her after being a cop for years. Unfastening the snap on the holster, she felt better for having it ready.

One by one they entered something they'd never been able to imagine.

"Is this…is this the tunnel?" Samantha whispered, yet the acoustics carried her voice easily. She turned around, making a full circle. "It's huge."

Darian looked at the vast space. Even if they had estimated the width as being thirty yards, it was something entirely different to stand in the center of it. It was impossible to fathom how it could even exist. The rock walls looked as smooth as the walls in the basements. She tipped her head back. "Damn. How tall is that ceiling?"

"Let me check." Philber pulled out a laser measuring tool. Pressing it to the ground, and then the wall where they had exited, he soon had the readings. "Twenty-eight yards wide and fifteen yards tall."

"What the hell did they use to build this thing?" Raoul kept turning around as if the motion would help him fathom the size of the tunnel.

"Can we even call it a tunnel?" Brandon asked. "It feels more like a hall."

"I have no idea what to call it," Darian said. "Now that we're down here, which way do we turn?"

Carl stepped closer. "That way," he said and pointed to their right as they faced away from the opening, "is Town Hall. That way is the lake." He shifted and pointed to the left.

"What do you think?" Darian turned to Samantha. They had talked about what they might find, but now she wasn't sure.

"Not Town Hall. Not this time. It's still early enough for people to mill around in the building. What if we trigger something and a whole wall opens up in Miller's office?" She snorted, but it wasn't a happy sound. "No. I vote we go left."

"So, do I," Philber said. "Now that we're on a flat surface, my knees are much happier." He did sound happy, clearly having gotten his second wind.

"Left it is," Brandon said. "I'll keep taking up the rear."

Darian was grateful for that reassurance. Brandon could handle himself. "Good. I'll be up front with Samantha. Let's keep a little distance between us. If something happens to one or two of us, we'll have a fair chance that it doesn't happen to everyone." She pulled out her walkie-talkie and prayed it would still work. "Darian to Walker. Over."

A soft crackle lasted far too long, but then Walker's voice came through. "Walker here. Over."

"Checking in," Darian said.

"Are you…having fun?" It was Camilla, and Darian could picture her grandmother snatching the radio out of Walker's hand and trying to keep the conversation casual.

"We are. We'll get back to you later."

"Got it." Walker was back on the radio.

"Darian out." After attaching the radio to her backpack, she was ready.

"Let's go," Samantha said. She began walking, and Darian fell into step with her. Around them, the walls glowed enough to keep the space lit. Their footfalls were barely audible, as they all wore shoes or boots with thick soles, but a definite echo occurred when they raised their voices.

"I can't help but think it should be colder down here," Darian said to Samantha. "I mean, we're eight floors down, approximately. Then again, I have no knowledge about the physics when it comes to ancient bedrock."

"Another thing, too," Samantha said. "What about ventilation? Shouldn't the air down here be stale, at least? And what about the risk of flooding? It ought to be damp."

"Yeah, but nothing about this has made any sense from the beginning. Why aren't our interfaces telling us what we need to know about this, as they do with the texts and how to use the console in the basement?" Darian sighed. "I suppose there might be tons of places down here where we could stick our fingers or press our palms, and we just can't see them."

"If there are any such places," Philber said from behind, "I have confidence they'll light up when we get close, somehow sensing the NIECs."

"I hope so," Darian muttered.

"I started a step counter to keep tabs on how far we've walked at any given point," Carl said, "and right now, we've covered about two hundred yards."

"And how long to reach the area around the lake?" Samantha asked.

"Given the proportions of the map," Philber said, looking up from one of the copies in his hands, "I'd say it's about two and a half miles."

"It should take us about an hour at the most," Carl said. "Unless there's a steep incline or something we haven't counted on."

Darian laughed. "This has been one long string of 'something-we-never-counted-on', but I hear you, Carl."

The others chuckled as well, which made Darian relax a little. They were heading into the complete unknown, and if something happened to them, the risk was great that help, if it came at all, would be too late.

An hour later, they stood by a massive wall. The tunnel had come to an end and had apparently led to nothing. Samantha dropped her backpack on the floor, rubbing the small of her back. She considered herself to be in good shape but was growing increasingly tense.

"Fuck." Darian let go of her backpack as well. "This can't be it."

"It looks as if whoever built this ran out of steam right here. Or they hadn't counted on the lake."

"Either way, it's time to check in with Walker and Camilla," Brandon said and pulled the radio from Darian's backpack. He had to try twice before he heard a faint voice through static. "All is well.

I repeat, all is well," Brandon managed to say before the static took over completely.

"I'm sure they heard you," Darian said and patted him on the arm.

"Hey, guys, is this something, maybe?" Raoul asked. He was standing at the left corner, feeling along the edge. "It's like a ridge."

Philber hurried over, and Samantha and Darian took their backpacks and followed, along with Carl and Brandon. Raoul and Philber stepped back to let Samantha move closer. She pulled out her flashlight and directed the beam against what he had found. "You're right. And it's as smooth and well-constructed as everything else we've discovered."

Darian stepped nearer and rested her hand against the wall to reach in as well. They all jumped when a bright light around her hand erupted in lines and different shapes. Darian yanked her hand back, but the rectangle, approximately three feet wide and two feet tall, kept blinking and lighting up. Unlike the golden glow on the ones in their basements, this section was even more defined and multicolored.

"So, not the end of the tunnel?" Carl asked, his voice faint.

"Apparently not." Samantha focused on the text along the lines. "Do you read the same as I? Are we going to be able to ascend somewhere around here?"

Philber put on a pair of reading glasses. "I'll be damned. Yes."

Samantha willed herself to relax. She was far too tense to focus. Somehow it felt important to allow the NIEC to do its job and not fight it. She followed the lines, read the labels of the smaller circles, all stating something that at first seemed quite cryptic. "Struts. Perimeter. Safety distance. Winch…wait. Winch? Can that be something?"

"Try it." Philber nodded, then he seemed to remember they were a team. "Or?"

The others merely nodded.

"Everyone, take a step back." Samantha motioned with her hand, and everyone but Darian did as she asked. "You too."

"Just press the damn thing." Darian clearly wasn't moving.

Holding her breath, Samantha placed her palm against the circular symbol that said winch. The floor immediately jerked under their feet.

"Shit." Carl gripped Philber's arm and helped the older man remain on his feet.

Samantha and Darian stepped away from the wall and joined the others.

"We're moving." Brandon felt the wall. "Slowly, but we're moving."

"I can see it," Samantha said, gazing at the console she'd just used as it seemed to lower against the floor and then disappear. "We're picking up speed." She looked behind them. "Doesn't it seem like the entire tunnel's moving? That can't be right." Trying to see how far back the floor of the "elevator" went, she simply couldn't determine the distance. Her chest ached because of her rapid pulse. This situation was potentially dangerous, and she felt responsible for everyone. Inching closer to Darian, she gazed toward the ceiling. It hadn't gotten lower. What a relief. At least they might not be crushed.

"I agree about the floor," Brandon said. "A very large part of the tunnel seems to move upward."

"What if we end up in the lake?" Carl murmured.

"I doubt it. No water. Not even dampness in the tunnel, remember?" Darian said. "No, we're going somewhere else." Her tone was stark, and Samantha hoped so too. She raised her gaze and grabbed Darian's arm. "Is an opening forming?" A dark line grew at the top of the wall that was approaching faster.

"I don't know." Darian flipped her jacket back behind her holster, which was still unclasped. "Just stay away from the wall until we know."

The dark rectangle grew larger as they seemed to reach what Samantha surmised could be the floor level of another part of the tunnel. She was prepared with her flashlight, as no light glowed from this part. As their floor leveled out with the new one, Darian raised her fist, something Samantha felt rather silly that she recognized from crime shows to mean "stop and be quiet." At the same time, the elevator stopped, aligned perfectly with the other floor.

"All right," Darian said. "Flashlights on."

Samantha switched hers on and let the beam sweep back and forth and pierce the darkness before them. She was trying to find anything resembling a console like the one below. How else would they get back? Something caught her eye, and she grew rigid and stepped sideways fast enough to bump into Darian. "What's that?" Samantha's trembling hand kept the flashlight beam on a spot where the outline of a pole, or something similar, created shadows around it.

Two more beams converged with Samantha's. It was hard to judge distances in the dark, but it wasn't very far away since it was well lit by the flashlights. "I'm going in," Darian said, removing her gun from its holster and holding it on top of her other hand, which directed the flashlight.

"As are we all." Any other day, Samantha would have thought that sort of protection to be overkill, but as she walked behind Darian into what looked like a new tunnel, she had to confess Darian made her feel safer.

On either side of Samantha, Carl and Raoul kept their flashlights trained on the structure ahead, and behind them, Philber and Brandon took up the rear.

"We're closing in," Darian said. "It seems…I mean, to me it looks like some kind of metal. Ridges, something looking like rivets. I don't know."

Samantha didn't take her eyes off the metal object, which became more detailed as they neared it. When they were only three yards away, Darian repeated her fist maneuver. Everyone stopped, truly acting like a team now.

"Let's check out this tunnel before we examine that, um, whatever you want to call it. It looks like an aluminum construction beam, but very large," Darian said.

Samantha directed her light up the structure, and it took her only a fraction of a moment to find it was attached to something. The tunnel ceiling? "Look up," she managed to say, her voice husky. "We…we're standing underneath something."

Five more beams joined hers and lit up a detailed ceiling that resembled the structure it rested on. Sharp indentations and rounded convex patterns were outlined by smaller bullet-like objects, indeed looking almost like pop rivets, as Carl had said earlier.

"Hey, guys," Carl said, and Samantha was startled to see he had walked closer to the tall structure. "Look here." He had turned his light to the floor.

Darian hurried over to him. "Hey, yourself. Not cool. You have to stay behind me." She stopped abruptly. "Whoa."

Samantha had been half a step behind Darian, and now she blinked hard a few times as she looked at the object that had caught Carl's attention. The long aluminum-looking beam in turn rested not directly on the floor, but seemed inserted into a large, oval disk. As she stepped closer, a momentary bout of vertigo nearly made her trip and fall, but she righted herself and closed her eyes briefly. When she opened them, she wasn't confused about the structure anymore. "This is the left rear strut," Samantha said. "It seems in pristine condition."

Darian swiveled and looked startled. "Samantha?"

"I just know. I think my NIEC kicked into another gear, so to speak."

"This vessel has four struts," Raoul said. "It's parked with its starboard side facing us."

"What the…what are you talking about, starboard?" Philber began walking toward them, and then it was as if his knees buckled. Brandon was impressively fast and caught Philber before he slammed said knees into the rock floor. "I'm fine. I'm fine," Philber said, but his voice was weak. "Just need to sit for a moment. My backpack has a folding stool."

Brandon unfolded the stool and helped Philber take a seat. Wiping at his face with his sleeve, Brandon then looked at the strut and back up at what Samantha now knew—as clearly as she hadn't known before—was the underbelly of a vessel.

"Okay, NIEC-wearing people, fill me and Brandon in, please." Carl impatiently waved his hands. "What vessel?"

"This one." Darian stepped up onto the foot of the strut and placed her hand on the tall pillar. Samantha gasped and moved to pull Darian down, but as she gripped her hand, a flood of light blinded her. Unable to stifle a cry, she tugged at Darian, but instead of bringing her down onto the floor, Darian yanked her closer and wrapped a strong arm around her waist. "It's all right," Darian called out. "I think that was my doing."

"What the hell happened?" Philber roared and stood up so fast, his stool turned over behind him.

"Oh, fuck," Carl said, his voice sounding like a prayer.

Samantha blinked against the lights, and when her eyes got used to them, she saw. Not only four struts but, farther into the tunnel, eight. "Two," she said weakly and was glad Darian held onto her. Left to her own devices, her overwhelming emotions would have sent her to her knees. "Two vessels. Two ships."

"Not only that," Darian said, smiling broadly. "Two spaceships."

The silence between them created weird sensations in Samantha's ears, like faint, forgotten echoes, and then an incredulous, "Well, *that* just happened," from Carl broke it.

CHAPTER FOURTEEN

"Of course," Darian whispered. She was still holding onto the strut and looking up at the hull of the spaceship. She knew what every part was called, what its function was, and even the vessel's name. "*Speeder One*, Torrent-class shuttle."

"Able to transport forty crewmembers from *Velocity*, to go planetside and back again. Also able to be used as an escape vehicle for injured or ill crewmembers." Samantha turned to Darian, her eyes dark green and looking almost too big for her face. She was pale, but two distinct red spots marked the highest point of her cheekbones.

"*Velocity*?" Carl asked, as he came closer. "That the other one?" He pointed at the second ship.

"No," Darian said, but was interrupted by Raoul, who had rounded all four struts of *Speeder One*.

"That one is *Speeder Two*," Raoul said.

Darian nodded. "Same configuration. It's a ship that attaches to *Velocity* when in space or orbit. Weapons' array is the same. Canons. Nukes. Fire-pellets."

"Nukes?" Brandon flinched where he stood next to them. "You're joking, right?"

"Not at all," Darian said. "Everything is right here. Of course, the shuttles, the speeder*s*, have a limited capacity, but *Velocity* is fully equipped and ready to face any enemy."

"You guys are creeping me out," Carl said. "I know you suddenly have knowledge through the NIECs, but surely your personalities haven't changed. You have to see the problem with having nuclear weapons sitting under Dennamore!" Carl's voice nearly cracked.

Darian reeled herself in. It was as if the information that flooded her brain had been just that, like a shopping list she'd ticked off at the grocery store. Now she inhaled deeply and let the breath escape slowly between tense lips. "You're right. Sorry. Didn't mean to sound so freaky. That was quite the burst of information. As soon as I touched the ship, it was just there, from one second to the next."

"Same here," Samantha said and placed a hand on Carl's shoulder. "I promise, we're not going crazy and about to launch any weapons."

"Can you open the ships?" Carl asked, apparently reassured enough for his curiosity to win.

"Sure." Raoul glanced at Samantha. "That okay, Boss?"

"I don't see why not. Just don't touch anything that looks like it can go boom." Samantha pulled out a camera, and Darian recognized it as one of Walker's, the one he'd brought to the lake. "I need to film this." She raised the camera just as Raoul put both palms on the strut Darian had held on to. He made a twisting motion counterclockwise against two of the larger rivets, and she heard a popping sound above them. Then a hatch opened downward and extended until it reached the floor. On the side facing them, Darian counted fifteen steps.

"I'll go first. Again." Darian had tucked her sidearm away into the holster, but it was still unclasped, and she moved cautiously up the stairs. She could barely breathe. This was unfathomable. Was she in shock, since she could climb the steps toward the opening so calmly? It must be because she could understand what this was, and what everything was for. How odd for this vessel to seem so alien—and so familiar. When she had five steps left to go, she was able to peer inside. Like with the tunnel, it was lit up, and she could see five seats with what had to be computer consoles. Instead of windows, one long, curved screen showed all the information the helmsman would need to pilot *Speeder One*. The other stations included weapons, operations, engineering, and the one in the center, the commanding officer's chair. After the five last steps, Darian stood in the opening, looking toward the back, where thirty-five chairs sat in rows of five. After a few seconds, her NIEC made her see that half of them could be turned into LSC-beds, which stood for Life, Support, and Care.

Soon, all six of them stood in the center of the command part of *Speeder One*. Samantha was taking shots of every part of the stations and then the crew area.

"Do we dare sit in one of the chairs?" Philber asked, and it dawned on Darian that he had been unusually quiet since the shuttles came to life. Studying him, she could tell he was flustered, but a quick glance at Raoul showed that he was keeping an eye on their oldest member.

"As long as we don't give any commands, or attempt to use the consoles, we should be fine." Samantha pointed at the ops station and then tucked the camera away into her backpack. "Take a seat, Philber."

Philber sat down, and immediately, the part of the screen that ran by his station filled with a pattern that told Darian it was running a diagnostic.

"A diagnostic procedure," Samantha said. "I'm torn between feeling deeply worried about this sudden, obvious knowledge and completely fascinated."

Placing her hand at the small of Samantha's back, Darian pointed at the commanding officer's station. "Your seat, ma'am." She smiled as Samantha reluctantly sat down. Raoul remained standing, but Darian slowly sat at the security officer's station. Her desk began its diagnostic. Familiar swirls, jagged chevrons, and numbers flickered over the screen, none of it in English. Of course. Here, the symbols that had been a complete mystery only days ago streamed from the lower right corner of the screen, floated upward, and then moved to the left when the row was full. It was an aqua-tinted screen, and the letters, familiar despite their odd shapes, ran up along the right edge in a never-ending stream.

"All systems at operations are functional," Philber said in a laconic voice.

"Same here," Darian said after reading the diagnostic results on her screen.

"This is surreal. And not." Samantha had curled her fingers around the edge of the armrests. "I wish we could make copies of the logs, but we have no compatible equipment."

"We'll be back, now that we know they're here." Darian couldn't wait to go over everything. Even if her NIEC made it possible to understand what she was looking at, she didn't have the personal memories of the aliens who…She paused her thought. Surely the ones who had arrived in these ships, who brought the scroll boxes and NIECs and hid every sign of what once had happened, had to be extraterrestrial beings? Before regular human beings came to settle in Dennamore, these aliens…No, she couldn't keep thinking of them as aliens. Visitors. That was a better word. The visitors that came, and stayed? Or did they leave with the mothership, *Velocity?* "I know we'll have to head back soon, or Walker and Camilla will send the cavalry, but we'll be back tomorrow, right? We have to go find *Velocity.*" Darian hoped she wasn't the only one feeling this way.

"Agreed." Samantha stood. "Before we leave, we should go through the storage facilities on board this ship. If we find more documentation that we can study, or items to take back, we should do it."

"Let's divide the task between us. Look only in cabinets and storage in the crew area. We can't afford to accidentally touch something that takes us into orbit." Darian was only half joking. She turned to Samantha, who staggered as she turned to move toward the back. "Hey," Darian whispered and discreetly took her elbow in a gentle grip.

"Dextrose." Samantha felt in the front pocket of her backpack. "I tend to get sugar lows." She started to tremble as she tucked a piece of it into her mouth.

"Why don't you just sit until that takes effect?" Darian knew it would take a couple of minutes for the sugar to do the trick.

“All right.” Samantha lowered herself onto one of the seats. “Just for a moment.”

After making sure Samantha would be all right, Darian went to the very back of the shuttle, finding it eerie to have the lights come on as she made her way down the aisle between the crews’ seats. She saw what looked like floor-to-roof metal blinds, and small consoles next to them came alive as she grew closer. It took only a few moments for her brain to learn what to do. Why the NIEC couldn’t tell her their function wasn’t logical, but she knew just how to hold her finger against a blue circle and slide it along a red line upward. The metal blinds on the port side of the ship went up with a soft, whining sound.

“Whoa.” Darian looked at rows of uniforms leading far into the storage space. Above them, she saw helmets that resembled nothing she’d seen on TV when NASA sent up their astronauts. She took one down, and of course it switched on. Light blue in the back, transparent in the front, it was illuminated around the edge in between. The rim that was supposed to attach to spacesuits seemed to consist of some sticky silicone, or something similar. Darian put the helmet back and watched it go dark. Examining one of the uniforms, which looked quilted in a shiny, light-blue material, she saw it also held a thick line of “silicone” at the neckline. These flimsy things were space suits? After she pulled the suit off its hooks, it too lit up along the edges, down the sides, arms, and legs.

“Darian?” Samantha called out from farther into the back. “I suppose this is your area.”

“What?” Hanging the suit back from where she took it, Darian absentmindedly slid her finger on the console, closing the blinds again. She hurried over to Samantha, who looked bemusedly at the contents behind another set of blinds. “They came well stocked when it came to self-defense…or potential attacks.”

Darian watched in similar dismay how weapons, at least fifty rows of them, were kept in the storage unit. On smaller shelves sat canisters, which she knew were ammunition. Or what served as ammo when it came to these alien weapons. How could they look utterly futuristic and weird, yet quite familiar? She had asked herself this question so many times already, it wasn't even funny. "Yeah, enough to take out half the British army in the war for independence. I wonder if they did use them back then?"

"No record of strange people dropping from the sky and firing witchcraft weapons at the Brits as far as I know," Carl said from behind. "And those things look like they can vaporize people."

"Actually, they're mainly used to incapacitate the enemy, not kill them," Samantha said slowly. "There's a setting that will kill, but it's mostly used for hunting. Uproars and civil unrest are not considered offenses that require the ultimate sacrifice of your opponent."

Darian gaped. "That's right. Shit."

"Sounds civilized enough," Philber said. "We've found emergency rations that have long expired, and so much technology, we'll be exploring this place for the next decades."

"If we're allowed to," Brandon said. "I don't mean to rain on any parade here, but we all know what will happen the moment the government learns of this. Of what once happened in Dennamore. They'll move in, cordon it off, perhaps move the entire population by force. I'm not pessimistic by nature, but as you have all gathered the knowledge, I have contemplated what has happened in the past when something gets classified."

"Thinking about Roswell?" Carl frowned. "But that's just some conspiracy stuff."

"We can't be sure about that." Brandon shook his head. "I'm not saying Roswell really happened, but we've all heard about enough cover-ups, and they never declassify some things."

Darian knew Brandon had a past he never discussed, at least not with her. Perhaps Camilla knew more about him. The way he spoke now, assertive and serious, made Darian think he had some information none of the others in the team knew about. Perhaps Brandon had worked for one of the agencies. Or the military.

"So, mum's the word then," Darian said and squared her shoulders. "I don't want the authorities to move in and shut us out, even if the risk is minimal, since Dennamore isn't exactly a household name."

"Which is why the aliens chose this location, no doubt." Philber had sat down on one of the seats. "Access to wildlife and water. Timber. Bedrock. And remote."

"And they never left to go back to where they came from… Isn't that strange?" Samantha leaned her hip against the backrest of another seat. It was silver and white, and looked pristine. No dust had settled. "Bech'taia, who wrote in the journal at Camilla's house, seemed conflicted. Darian's translation suggested the settlers wanted to go home, and we all thought they meant Europe. We found it curious, obviously, but not unheard of. She and Gai'usto seemed part of a group that tried to get their Elders to understand this fact, but the Elders were planning to stay, for whatever reason, and blend in with the people they met. This tells us they must have looked human enough."

Something beeped, making everyone jump. Samantha held up a hand. "I apologize." She produced her cell phone. "I set a timer to remind us when we needed to return. As you've all noticed, I'm sure, it's easy to get carried away and forget about time."

Darian took in the interior of *Speeder One*. What had looked so futuristic and alien just a little while ago now looked…normal. Every console, every reading on the screens made sense. It was unsettling that all that knowledge would go away if she removed the NIEC, yet she would be glad to do so when she was back with Gran. "We need to take something back to show Camilla and Walker." Darian opened another, smaller, metal blind. In the narrow cabinet, she saw neatly stacked metal boxes. "Why not one of the crew computers?"

"Oh, yes," Samantha said. "We should take a few of them. They'll give us more answers and allow us to communicate without using easily detectable two-way radios." She shook her head and covered her mouth. "And we just know these things."

"We do." Darian smiled, trying to reassure Samantha. "The sooner we get used to knowledge being infused when we don't even realize it's happening, the better. I use too much energy being in awe and trying to figure out how the damn NIEC works."

Raoul walked past Darian and opened another cabinet. "And I'll investigate their medical kits." He pulled out a larger metal container.

Soon, everyone carried something from the shuttle. They climbed down the steps onto the floor of what wasn't a tunnel, but a shuttle bay or sorts, created by the aliens within the bedrock. It was wider than the tunnel, but the height was approximately the same.

"What's that? Over there?" Raoul pointed farther into the shuttle bay. "Looks like a small shuttle or something?"

"Darian?" Samantha turned to her. "Can you join Raoul and have a look? We need to use the elevator and start walking back."

"Sure." Darian began jogging along the wall on the starboard side of the shuttles, Raoul right beside her. As they neared the object, Darian saw it was more than one. In fact, she saw eight of them, lined up beside each other by the wall. "Those aren't shuttles," she said as they reached the first one. She took in the rectangular shape. "These are haulers."

"Hell, yeah." Raoul grinned. "And if they're in working order, we won't have to walk back."

Darian slid onto the seat of the first one, and just like with the rest of the alien technology, it came alive and she felt right at home with the controls. A sort of joystick sat at her right hand, and a maneuvering console was displayed across the transparent surface in the front.

"Ten seats in each," Raoul said as he sat down behind her.

"That makes sense," Darian murmured.

"How do you mean?"

"Seventy-six scroll boxes. Eighty seats. I hope we find the crew manifest somewhere in their database, or something." Darian gripped the joystick, for lack of a better word, and the hauler followed her every movement with ease. "I can't help but wonder about their power source. Everything works as if they'd left the things here yesterday. I hope they won't kill human physiology in the end."

"I don't think so," Raoul said. "If it was harmful, Dennamore wouldn't exist anymore, considering this stuff has been here a while."

Darian wasn't so sure. Everything had been hidden, buried, and forgotten. Now they were handling the items with their bare hands. It was something to keep in mind.

"Aliens have golf carts?" Carl said, making everyone chuckle.

"Looks like it." Darian jumped off. "This will make our return trip a lot easier. This could be why they built the tunnel in the first place, if a bit oversized."

"Hm." Philber claimed the last pair of seats. "Actually, I think they used it to move the shuttles as well. If you let them pivot ninety degrees, they'd fit."

Darian stopped in midmotion after helping load their backpacks. "And that's why the elevator is so enormous. They turned the shuttles, and somehow that elevator is strong enough to handle them. Now, why is another matter."

Samantha sat down next to Darian and studied the console. "Clever to have the controls on the windscreen…though it's not called a windscreen, of course."

"Still clever." Darian turned her head and made sure everyone was securely seated and had their gear. "All set?" After five affirmative answers, she used the joystick. No. It was called a throttle. Throttle sounded better than something that belonged to a computer-game console. She maneuvered the hauler onto the part of the tunnel that made up the elevator and stopped in the center. The screen before her and Samantha shifted.

"Ah. See that? That's the same as the elevator controls we saw below. Now that makes sense." Samantha didn't hesitate but tapped in a command. Instantly they began their descent.

"Wow." Darian knew it wasn't the most eloquent thing she could say, but the word did express a lot about how she felt.

The ride down felt shorter, but Darian guessed it had more to do with being less nervous about it than when they rode up. It took them only ten minutes to drive the hauler back to the opening that led to Philber's basement. Darian stopped just behind it and watched the hauler switch off after they all exited. Climbing the steps was hard for Philber. Brandon helped remove the older man's backpack, strapping it on top of his own. Raoul wound an arm around Philber's waist and supported him up the steps behind Darian and Samantha. Carl and Brandon took up the rear.

Darian took pride in being fit, but even she was winded when they exited the staircase. Camilla and Walker had obviously heard them arrive and stood ready to receive them. "Oh, darling." Camilla hugged Darian and then Samantha. "I'm so relieved you're back." She glanced over their shoulders. "Oh, my. Philber, come here." She pointed at the armchair. "Sit down. We've prepared food for everyone."

"Sounds. Good." Philber literally fell into the chair. "I'm going to have to start working out to make it up and down those stairs." He shook his head.

"We all will, unless we find another way into the tunnel," Brandon said, he too gasping for air, but he'd carried twice the weight of everyone else.

"I imagine you have tons to tells us," Camilla said, "but you can do it at the dining-room table. I hope it was all right that we found our way around your kitchen, Philber?"

"No. Problem."

"Just sit for a moment while I check the oven." Camilla waved her hands dismissively at Philber, who looked as if he meant to get up. Turning to Darian, she kissed her cheek again. "So relieved," she repeated.

"Me too." Darian hugged Camilla again and watched Samantha over her grandmother's shoulder. "And we have so much to tell you."

Camilla pulled back. "I can't wait to hear it all."

Everyone but Brandon and Philber made their way up the stairs to the ground floor. After washing their hands and removing the NIECs for the time being, they sat down around the table. Philber and Brandon then joined them, and Darian could tell that the two men had somehow bonded during their recon into the tunnel.

Samantha began eating but then stopped, lowering her fork slowly.

"Something wrong?" Darian asked quietly, knowing she was becoming increasingly perceptive when it came to Samantha.

"No. At least I don't think so." Samantha looked around the table. "Listen," she said, raising her voice slightly. "Is it just me, or is anyone else retaining some of the things the NIECs, well, induced into your mind?"

Darian blinked. Was she? She thought of the elevator, *Speeder One*, and the hauler. More so, she remembered some of the symbols and markings on the consoles—and what they meant. "Yes," she managed to say, not quite believing it was possible. She didn't even come close to having an eidetic memory and had always had to study like crazy in school to get decent grades. Now she had looked at alien symbols and languages, and used technology that defied all imagination, a few times, and it was beginning to stick already? She swallowed hard and put down her utensils. "Does this mean the NIECs are creating changes in our brains?"

CHAPTER FIFTEEN

As Samantha woke up the next day, she thought back to the conversation at the table. Raoul had been invaluable in mitigating fears about the NIECs, even if it was obvious that nothing could be determined without an MRI, which Raoul thought was overkill. Perhaps they were all quite eager to disregard the dangers, as the discoveries were—literally—out of this world.

She was glad that today was her day off. The library stayed open between nine and one p.m. on Saturdays, and today it was her colleague's turn to hold down the fort. Checking the time, Samantha hurried into the shower. Darian was coming over with one of the computers this morning, and they planned to link up with the others. They no longer stored all the NIECs at Camilla's, but kept them in their homes. They were afraid what might happen if the wrong person found out.

Exiting the steaming shower stall, Samantha wrapped herself in her favorite pink terry-cloth robe. She wore a towel around her hair and added just enough makeup to look alive. She was paler than normal, which came from tossing and turning last night. After finally falling asleep sometime after four a.m., she had awoken several times after dreaming she was tearing through the tunnel in a massive spaceship, unable to brake when it came to an end.

The doorbell startled Samantha enough that she nearly poked herself in the eye with the mascara wand. Staring at herself in the mirror, she then checked the time again. Could that be Darian already? But who else would turn up at this hour on a Saturday?

After hurrying through the hallway, she peered through the small window in the door. Darian. Relieved, but also concerned, she opened it.

"Good morning…oh shit, I'm really too early, aren't I?" Darian's expression went from bright to appalled. "I'm sorry. Should I come back in a bit?" She was holding her backpack, but also a box that came from the best coffeehouse in Dennamore.

"No, of course not. I'm glad it's you. I mean, that you're early." Samantha motioned for Darian to step inside. "For a moment, I saw either men-in-black or, worse, representatives from the Elder Council, in front of my inner eye."

"God. That'd be horrible at any given time, let alone on a Saturday morning when you can instead enjoy some of the best croissants in town. I hope you have a coffee machine or something, like you do at your office."

"I do." Aware that she was naked under her robe, Samantha cleared her throat. "Help yourself in the kitchen. I'll get dressed."

"Sure thing." Despite her words, Darian remained just inside the door, her eyes not leaving Samantha's.

"Dar?" Samantha tilted her head.

"Er…oh. Right. The kitchen." Darian took a few steps forward but then stopped. "Which way?"

"Sorry. Of course. You haven't been to my house." Samantha wanted to slap her forehead. "To the left. Kitchen and family room. Open plan. One of the few perks of living in a house that's not listed as a cultural treasure. You can knock down walls."

"A woman with a sledgehammer. I like it." Darian made a cute face and walked off toward the kitchen.

Hurrying back into her bedroom, Samantha tossed her robe onto the bed and pulled on some lounge wear. Gray pants and a pastel yellow top. She tugged the towel from her head and detangled her hair, deciding to let it air-dry. Taking the alien computer from under her bed, she carried it with her to the kitchen, where Darian had the coffee machine going. She had put out croissants in a basket at the kitchen island and was in the process of browsing through the refrigerator. "Butter, jam, cream cheese…" She pushed the fridge door closed with her hip and arranged the items on the counter, next to the basket.

"I made it easier for myself and used the regular brewer. That monstrosity looks like we'd need a NIEC to operate it." Using her thumb to point over her shoulder, Darian chuckled.

"It's an Italian machine. I'll teach you one day." Samantha placed the computer on the counter, glad she'd splurged on a massive island, even if she was single and a bit of a recluse.

"Oh, good. I have mine here." Darian placed hers next to Samantha's. "Want to browse around before we try to ping the others?"

"You ready to use the NIEC then?" Samantha stepped closer to Darian and held her upper arms gently. As Darian wore only a black T-shirt with her jeans, she felt the warm, smooth skin tingle her palms. "It was a lot yesterday, and you were concerned when we sat down to eat. Nobody would think badly of any of us if we sat out some parts of this exploration."

"I know that," Darian said, her eyes now a soft amber. "And yes, I was freaked out for a while, but I think it was fatigue speaking. Or emotional overload. I don't know." She sucked her lower lip in between her teeth.

"Yes. Agreed."

"Kind of like now," Darian whispered. She slid her hands up Samantha's equally bare arms, causing an eruption of goose bumps. "Or it might just be me."

"No," Samantha said, her voice barely carrying. "Not just you."

The coffee machine chose this moment to give the familiar bubbling sound that indicated it was close to done. Samantha tried to catch her breath, not sure why she kept getting caught in Darian's gaze or, like now, entirely mesmerized by the simplest touch. She stepped back, but Darian's longing expression didn't escape her. Before fully realizing her own intention, Samantha ran quick fingertips along Darian's cheek. "Coffee's ready."

"Thank God. I need something to center me." After taking the scroll box from her backpack, Darian swiftly removed the NIEC and placed it next to her plate. It looked so surreal—the fantastic piece of technology next to a gray ceramic plate from the 21st century. "If I didn't know better, I'd swear this little thing nearly jumped out to greet me." Darian shook her head.

Samantha fetched her scroll box and took out her NIEC. "I suppose we might as well." She lifted her damp hair, and the small filaments wormed their way in along her scalp. Within a fraction of a second, all the knowledge—and then some, she thought—were there. No vertigo. No pain. Nothing.

"That was easy enough," Darian said, who had held her ponytail out of the way and attached her own neural interface. "Want to hear about my weird dream?" She rounded the kitchen island and fetched the glass coffee pot.

"Absolutely." Climbing onto one of the leather stools, which boasted a short backrest, Samantha held out her mug to be filled. She saw a small milk carton next to the basket of croissants and poured some into her coffee.

"I dreamt that when I put on the NIEC, not only did I suddenly know everything about the ships and the alien technology, but I also had the personal memories of the previous owner of the device. I saw a whole lifetime of someone else flashing by. Very strange. And scary."

Samantha shuddered. "I'm glad they're not that advanced. I mean, I draw the line with having more than one conscience, or persona, in my head."

"No kidding. I've got enough on my plate just dealing with myself." After spreading butter and strawberry jam on her croissant, Darian bit into it—and moaned. "Oh, no wonder they advertise that they're the most popular coffeehouse. The croissants alone are enough for the baker to be knighted by the Queen of England."

Samantha laughed. "Agreed. Though a congressional medal of honor might suffice as well."

"True."

They ate, and Samantha could tell they both made an effort to keep up the small talk. And even if it was a bit forced, at least it helped relax her.

"Okay. All done with the croissants. Going to wash my hands and then open my computer." Samantha walked over to the sink and ran the faucet. As she stuck her hands under it, so did Darian, who had joined her, and they both jumped. Taking soap from the dispenser behind the sink, Samantha washed quickly and then began clearing the kitchen island of everything but their coffee mugs.

Sitting closer together, they opened the lids of the metallic boxes, and Samantha was relieved at how familiar the interface looked. She read the text without any problem, and the fact that its controls didn't resemble anything she'd come across before didn't faze her. A glass-like surface had replaced where her regular laptop's keyboard sat. The screen at the top was transparent and sepia-tinted when turned off.

"It's ten twenty," Darian said. "I'll try Gran and Walker. Can you believe that he stayed the night?"

"What?" Intrigued, Samantha looked at Darian.

"In the impromptu guest room, but still. Gran said it was because they needed him to wear a NIEC for the computer today, but I think she's smitten."

Samantha studied Darian's expression but saw nothing but affection for Camilla in the way she smiled teasingly. "Then try. We can use yours for communication with the others and mine as auxiliary."

"Good point." Darian let her fingertips slide and tap in intricate patterns on the smooth area under the screen. The screen lit up with lines, symbols, and a three-dimensional area, where Camilla and Walker appeared sitting close together.

"Brandon. Come here," Walker said, waving his hand in the air. "Darian and Samantha just joined us. Hello." The last part was directed at them.

"Hi. Wow. Picture and sound are fantastic." Darian grinned. "Now, let's see if any of the others are awake." Darian soon had Philber and Raoul in two other boxes. "Carl coming over to either of you?"

"He's just getting a Coke," Raoul said. "Here he is."

"Hey, everybody," Carl said and laughed. "So, apart from golf carts, the aliens invented Zoom. Fantastic."

"Geez," Philber said, running a hand over his face. "At least we're all here. What's our next plan, Boss?"

"I forgot. I'll be right back." She hurried back into her bedroom and returned with her laptop. "I made a list." She pulled up the encrypted document. "I've disconnected the wi-fi on my computer, just to be safe. From now on, I'll use the one from the shuttle."

"Good thinking," Walker said.

"Are we so sure it's such a great idea?" Philber frowned. "What if these computers send off a signal, or radiate something that NASA picks up?"

Samantha hadn't even thought along those lines. "Is that a valid concern? I mean, do the authorities scan for alien frequencies? That sounds a little farfetched…and if they did, would they scan a tiny mountain town in the Adirondacks?"

Philber shrugged. "Perhaps not. I used my old Geiger counter this morning, and there's no radiation that way, at least."

"I think it's safer to use these than cell phones and laptops," Raoul said. "Even better than hard copies of notes, etcetera."

"Okay," Darian said and moved her fingers on the alien computer. "I'm opening an encrypted set of folders on here. The NIECs should make it as intuitive for you to open them as it is for me to create them. They seem instantly accessible. You can place pictures and documents here that are visible only to *us*, even if, by some remote chance, someone else might slap on a NIEC and manage to log in. Carl, you have to settle for working with one of us until we say different. I know this is frustrating for you, but we have to find more documentation of the NIECs first."

"All right," Carl said and sighed. "I know, I know. Mom will kill you—and me—if you scramble my fabulous brain."

"Right."

"Go on with your list, Samantha," Camilla said, bringing them back on track. "What's first?"

"We have to locate the *Velocity*. If there's information on these computers, that will make it easier. If not, we have to look for clues elsewhere. The rest of the journal found in Camilla's library needs to be summarized. We should try the different consoles in *Speeder One,* to see if we can operate it or not."

"I offer to help with the tasks that don't require too much physical maneuvering. Seems the old ticker is acting up," Philber said calmly. "I'm particularly interested in the journal."

"You're welcome to join us," Camilla said. "I can't be as helpful as I'd like to."

"Brandon wasn't able to use the NIEC, but I for one know there are very few things this man can't do. Like operate the haulers, for instance," Darian said.

Samantha watched Brandon brighten where he sat just behind Camilla and Walker. Why wasn't he compatible with the NIECs? Did they have settings they hadn't discovered that might help facilitate him using one?

"Another thing that's important," Samantha said, "is the other end of the tunnel. Does it reach all the way to the library? And if it does, where does it exit? We have to figure that out too. And where would you launch the speeder*s* from?"

Camilla blinked. "Launch?"

"Of course," Samantha said firmly. "Listen, in a very short time, we have found ways to operate and understand alien technology. When we wear the NIECs, we *know*. They somehow transfer the knowledge to our brains. Am I really the only one here who is certain this is for a reason and that we know how to fly the ships?"

Samantha's conviction would have been contagious even if Darian hadn't been of the same opinion. "This is part of the yearning," she said slowly, taking Samantha's hand out of sight of the others. "Finding these items, the ships, everything. Learning about what happened here right as the United States was gaining its freedom. Somehow beings from another world landed here. We will find out why their Elders insisted on them staying—I believe there's a story there—and we'll learn why this is important to us now."

Camilla ran trembling fingers across her forehead, straightening a misbehaving lock. "You think the yearning has to do with this?"

"It's not a farfetched idea." Philber leaned close enough for his face to fill his entire part of the screen. "It would explain a theory I've been toying with."

Darian wasn't sure why his words made her stomach clench. "Go on."

"It might also explain why the NIEC didn't respond to Brandon." Philber disappeared out of view for a moment but returned with a stack of papers. "Don't worry. I'll burn these once I've added them to this computer." He put on reading glasses and browsed the papers, then switched them into a different order. "Bear with me, now. When I was a kid, my granddad told me about the yearning. It was back in the late fifties, early sixties, and it fascinated me. Granddad talked about it because three of my uncles all returned home within a few months of each other, all claiming that they *had* to. One even left his wife, who wasn't interested in leaving…um, Chicago, I think it was, to go live in Dennamore, which was of course even smaller back then. That particular uncle suffered greatly, but still never regretted returning.

"As I grew up, I heard people talk about the yearning and the returnees. The conversations made me interested in history and anthropology, and my granddad paid for me to go to college and get my PhDs. I taught for a few years, but when I suddenly got, well, homesick isn't the right word for it…I was in my forties, had a brilliant career underway, and all I wanted, no, needed, was to go back home to Dennamore. So, I did. I recognized it as the yearning, and I came home in time to spend the last few years with my granddad before he passed.

"He had, in his layman ways, done quite a bit of research when it came to Dennamore's history in conjunction with the yearning. I found his papers after he passed, and his passion became mine. I managed to obtain a grant via my university under the condition that I guest-lecture, something I did until I retired. I never retired from my research regarding Dennamore though." He looked to the side of his screen. "You have been most patient with me, Samantha."

Samantha squeezed Darian's hand. "My pleasure, Philber. Go on."

"I started looking at dates that Granddad had jotted down of when the returnees had come home. Naturally, people arrived during all months of the year, but more than fifty percent of the ones he had on his lists arrived around the time of the Lake Light Festival. You can argue that it's a Dennamore staple, our pride and joy to have something as unique as that happening here. If you're returning to your hometown, why not do it when a lot of your family and friends are off work and in a celebratory mood to begin with?"

"That'd make sense," Walker said.

"I thought so too," Philber said, nodding slowly. "Until I realized that they did so before we even started having the Lake Light Festival, before the lake lights were even considered something that was worthy of celebrating. Until after the first world war, the lights were a local curiosity, at the most."

"We returned just before the festival," Darian said slowly, looking at Camilla, who nodded. "Was that happenstance, Gran? What do you think?"

"I don't know. I thought it had to do with the sale of the condo, but…I'm not sure. I did tell my realtor that I wasn't interested in an endless bidding war between the people who were interested in it. I just wanted to go…home."

Darian let go of Samantha's hand, mostly because sweat broke out in her palms and down her back. "I never understood why I was so willing to give up my career that I fought so hard for, to go with you, Gran. I mean, I didn't even think twice about it. My captain said my job would be waiting for me, but I knew that was mostly bullshit. When someone eager, hungrier, shows up ready to fill your spot…" She shrugged. "Even talking about it should have made me go nuts, but I just want to be here." Glancing at Samantha, she felt her cheeks warm. "It's the truth."

"That's a really good example, Darian," Philber said. "And you're not the only one who longed for 'home' without having ever actually lived here. I've found at least a dozen others, which, I'm sure, is far from everyone."

"What was your theory before the last turn of events?" Brandon asked.

"It has given me a lot of sleepless nights, let me tell you." Philber shuffled his papers. "From a social-anthropological point of view, I've looked at everything cultural you can imagine. I tracked family lines to determine the inbreeding coefficient, but we're no more inbred in Dennamore than any other American small town is. When Samantha invited me to become part of this group, other pieces of this puzzle started, if not to fall into place, then at least demand to be considered."

"You're driving me insane, Philber. Please, just tell us." Camilla's steely glance was familiar to Darian, who had seen her fair share of it during her teenage years.

"I'm getting to it," Philber said, and only the fact that he ran an index finger along the neckline of his T-shirt showed he was affected. "We've determined some things we consider facts. The technology cannot come from human beings who lived in the late 1700s. Things like the NIECs don't exist even today, to our best knowledge. The signs and symbols aren't like any writings any of us has ever seen before—yet the NIECs make it possible for us to read them quite effortlessly. The journal in Camilla's library is old, and the risk it might be a forgery is small to zero. The maps Samantha brought from the archive, where the tunnels and our access points are clearly marked, belong to the old archive. The fact that they're accurate speaks for itself.

"The ships, *Speeder One* and *Speeder Two*, are chock full of pieces of technology on par with the NIECs, such as these computers we're handling effortlessly while wearing the interfaces. All this, as unfathomable as it sounds, suggests that this is alien technology. We all agree this is the only logical explanation. Who they were, where they came from, how alike us they were—this we have no way of knowing. If we toy with the idea that they were all adults when they arrived here, and if they shared our estimated lifespan, the last of them ought to have passed away around 1840. This is a rough estimate."

"When did the census begin in these parts?" Raoul asked.

Samantha typed on her laptop. “The census started in 1790, but I haven’t seen any records for these parts earlier than 1812. Between us, I think Philber and I can figure some of these things out. Let’s exchange files later.”

Philber nodded and scribbled something on his papers. “Now to what my theory entails.” He sipped from a large mug. “It’s pretty obvious, when you think about it.”

Samantha slumped against the low backrest. “It is. We were onto it already when the NIEC did nothing for Brandon. We are their descendants.” Her voice trembled. “The NIECs recognize something in us, a genetic marker perhaps, that shows we are descendants of extraterrestrial beings.”

Darian knew in an instant, proof or no proof, that this was true. She looked between Samantha and Camilla on the screen, and the latter had clearly also begun to realize this truth. Darian cleared her throat. “More than two hundred and fifty years later, and God knows how many generations, it’s us. *We* are the aliens.”

CHAPTER SIXTEEN

Samantha placed her computer, the alien one, in her briefcase, but let her gaze linger on Darian. After Darian had voiced the likeliest explanation for everything, they had wrapped up the virtual meeting, needing to mull things over.

"I should go home and check on Gran," Darian said after having stowed her computer. She was obviously stressed. "I'm sure you have things to do."

"Nothing more important than this." Samantha wasn't sure how to read Darian right now. Sometimes it was so easy, as if they were of one mind, but now, she was afraid of overstepping.

Darian halted and let go of her backpack. "Really?"

"Really."

"Would you mind coming back to the house?"

"I'd love to." Samantha smiled, as she could read definite relief on Darian's face.

Stepping closer, Darian wrapped her arms around Samantha's neck. "Thank you. I don't know why, but I feel I ripped the bandage off everybody. I feel guilty and have no clue why."

"We're all in this. Nothing is gained from dodging the truth." Samantha had to stop talking to gasp for air, as being in Darian's arms made it hard to breathe. "And didn't you see how intrigued Carl looked. I think you made his entire year."

"He's a kid. He…I don't think he realizes what this could mean." Darian still didn't let go, and Samantha kept holding her close.

"Try not to worry about what isn't even on the horizon yet. Let's go back to your house and spend some time with Camilla and the guys. Perhaps we can read some more in the journal or whatever you feel like doing."

"You're amazing." Darian tipped her head back, her normally dark-brown eyes having switched to the amber hue again. "I can't imagine going through all this without you. I want you to know that."

Not sure where her impulse originated, Samantha bent and kissed Darian's cheek. Perhaps meant as an appreciative gesture, it ended up being slower…or longer. Darian hummed and turned her head as Samantha began to pull back, which meant their lips ended up just a breath apart. Unable to move, and not wanting to, Samantha felt Darian melt farther into her. Darian could feel dizzy, so she wrapped her arms closer around her. "Dar?"

"Yes."

"You all right?"

"Yes."

Pulling back enough to look into those amber eyes, Samantha sighed in relief. "Good."

Darian slid her hands up and cupped Samantha's cheeks. Holding her gently in place, she brushed her lips against Samantha's in a kiss that was so light, it felt like a breath. Yet it still had enough impact to make her head spin.

"I've wanted to kiss you for a while." Darian pulled back and lifted her backpack.

Samantha studied the woman who had changed her life in more ways than one. "I'm glad you did."

Darian's eyes widened and a smile formed. She hoisted the backpack. "Does that mean you'd welcome another attempt sometimes? I mean, I can do better."

Blushing, Samantha busied herself with her briefcase. "Better? Heaven help me," she muttered, but she had to return the smile when she turned back to Darian. "Ready?"

"I am. Not so sure about you though." Darian's smile grew to a wide grin.

"What do you mean?" Samantha blinked.

"Socks? Shoes? You're still barefoot."

Samantha rolled her eyes as she put down her briefcase and walked toward her bedroom. Behind her she heard Darian chuckle, a sound she'd never tire of.

The conversation with Camilla, Walker, and Brandon lasted an hour. They turned the facts over, and the theories even more so. Darian was relieved to see how calm Camilla became once they dived into the topics. She always worried about her grandmother, her only living relative who had been like a mother to her. It was all too easy to underestimate Camilla's strength because of her physical frailty.

Still wearing their NIECs, Darian and Samantha were walking down to the basement. Brandon had worked all day removing the last of the boards, freeing the rock wall behind them. Darian placed her hands in the spots on what she now knew was a computer console. The wall folded in on itself, and the opening looked exactly the same as it had in Philber's basement. "Walker's should be the same as well," Samantha said and peered down the stairs that had been revealed. "His exit is between yours and Philber's."

"We're the closest to the other end. Why don't we pop down to Philber's opening and get the hauler? I want to see where the tunnel ends and how it looks at the other end."

Samantha leaned against the rock, folding her arms over her chest. "I'm all for that, as long as the others are." She raised her right hand, palm toward Darian. "I know. I know. I'm the boss, but we need more people in the group to be aware that we're about to explore."

"All right. I'll go tell Walker and Gran. Philber's not going to brave those stairs again, that's for sure. Good thing you're not wearing any of your fancy suits. That'll do." Darian motioned to Samantha's leisure outfit. "I'll just grab us a couple of hoodies. It's cooler down there."

After letting Brandon know what they were up to, as Camilla and Walker had gone for a drive, Darian detoured to her room for the hoodies and her holster. Before she returned to the basement, Brandon showed up with a backpack.

"Water. Fruit. First-aid kit. Two-way radio." Brandon looked sternly at her. "You check in as much as you can—and be careful. Your grandmother will kill me if something happens to you."

"Gotcha." Impulsively, Darian rose on her toes and kissed his cheek. "We'll be back soon."

She rejoined Samantha and gave her one of the hoodies. "Brandon knows. He's on sentry duty, and he sent the essentials with us. Have your cell so we can both record and take pictures?"

"I do." Samantha patted her back pocket. She looked ridiculously pretty in the dark-gray hoodie, a color that Darian had never seen on the pastel-loving Samantha.

"Let's go then." Darian unclasped the holster after buckling it around her hips and then hoisted the backpack before taking the lead again.

As it was only the two of them, and they knew what to expect, it took them only a fraction of the time to descend the stairs. They walked to Philber's exit, where Samantha climbed into the driver's seat. Her elegant fingers flew over the controls as she started the hauler. Darian sat next to her, placing the backpack between her feet. She reported back to Brandon, who told her he'd forwarded the information to Philber and Raoul.

Samantha drove the hauler through the tunnel in the direction of the library. As the tunnel was built in a straight line between the lake and the center of Dennamore, it took only minutes to find a second elevator.

"This isn't the same as the other one." Darian stepped off the hauler as Samantha came to a stop. This is obviously not the end of the tunnel." Looking around the well-lit tunnel, Darian then turned to Samantha.

"I see what you mean. This part has an elevator console, but it's open on both ends." Placing her hands on her hips, Samantha turned a full three-sixty where she stood. "And I know it's impossible to see how far we've moved, but it doesn't feel as if we're quite at Town Hall yet."

Darian nodded. "That's what I thought. When I saw the console, I figured, already? Why don't we keep driving a bit? We'll pass this part when on our way back."

"Good point. Wouldn't want to ride up in the elevator and end up in someone's house."

"God forbid." Laughing, Darian climbed onto the seat again.

Samantha moved the controls again, and the hauler took off. After four minutes—Samantha checked—they saw the end of the tunnel but, at first, no computer console.

"What the hell?" This time Darian jumped off the hauler before Samantha had quite stopped.

"Hey. Are you trying to break your neck?" Samantha glared at her.

"Sorry. Just so baffled. Where's the console? The ridges by the walls?" Nothing looked like it had at the other end. Darian put on the backpack and made a quick shout-out to Brandon that all was well.

"Let's look." Samantha walked over to the wall and began to feel her way forward. "It might be concealed for some reason. Or perhaps they never got to finish this end."

Darian wasn't so sure. The tunnel looked as perfect and pristine as the other end, minus the elevator. She mimicked Samantha's search technique as she started with the opposite wall. After inching along the cold, smooth wall, when she was closing in on the right corner, she flinched as a small computer console lit up right in front of her. "Samantha. Here."

"You found some—oh, yes. That's it." Samantha hurried over. "It's an elevator console, only smaller."

"Will it ever stop being mind-boggling how we don't know these things one second and do know them the next?" Darian bent and felt along the tunnel floor. "I feel the thinnest of lines, as if someone pulled a pin through clay, if that makes sense."

"I understand." Samantha studied the console closely. "Can you determine if we're inside the elevator perimeters?"

"Hang on." Darian let her fingertip follow the hairline-thin indentation in what she surmised was a perfect square around their feet. "Yeah, I'd say so."

"Want to see where it leads?"

"Even if it's into the center of Town Hall?" Darian stood. "Granted, it's after hours by now, but still?"

"I'm ready to risk it." Samantha looked up at the ceiling. "I can't even see an opening, like at the other end. I can't fathom how this'll work."

"I'm game if you are." Darian placed her hand at the small of Samantha's back. "Just to be safe, keep close to me."

"All right." Samantha ran her fingers over the console, and with the same ease as the huge elevator at the other end of the tunnel had moved, this smaller one, about four square yards, ascended along the wall. "Let's hope we're not crushed against the ceiling, because I have no idea how to stop this."

Darian winced. She hadn't thought of that. As it turned out, their momentary onset of nerves was unfounded. The corner unfolded into itself as they neared the ceiling, much like the rock in the basement, and a hole the size of the elevator floor appeared. They moved through it with the same quiet ease, and lights came on within the bedrock as they ascended farther.

Darian still kept her hand protectively against Samantha's back. If they ran into someone about to lash out against the woman Darian knew by now she was falling for, they were going to have to go through her first. It wasn't a surprise to recognize this protective streak in her. After all, she was a cop, but she didn't usually react this fiercely.

The elevator slowed and came to a soft stop, much more gently than the elevator meant for the speeders. Four walls of bedrock now surrounded them. The next moment, one of the walls performed the now-familiar folding motion, and they cautiously walked through the opening. Darian made sure to keep one step ahead of Samantha.

They looked around, and Darian spotted familiar light sconces on the walls. "Holy crap…is this…?"

"Town Hall basement. We're at the end of the corridor. Over there's the door to the archives." Samantha pointed at the oak door.

Behind them, the elevator door closed. They both swiveled but couldn't do anything to stop it. To Darian's surprise, a small, illuminated console was located next to where they had exited. "We'll be able to use it to get back down. Good to know."

"It's amazing that it was there all along. I mean, all my life. And nobody knew until we put on the NIECs." Samantha turned to look at the panel. "Wait…look at the bottom of the panel. There's another elevator?"

Darian leaned in to look. "Where does that thing go? To the next floor? Why not ride up in the same elevator that took us to this floor? It doesn't make sense."

Samantha slid her fingers along the markings. Perpendicular to the elevator, the wall folded itself away from them. A light came on inside.

"Holy crap," Darian said. "The old archive. Wow."

Samantha peered inside. "Good to know we can always get in. And I'll be damned if I can understand why the interfaces can induce knowledge about how to operate technology, but not the memories of what the aliens did *with* said technology."

"I know. But now that we have access to this place outside office hours, so to speak, we're going to discover more."

Samantha closed the doorway to the archive. "All right. Should we move around and see if something else appears for the first time?"

"As long as you think we can get away with it. What about surveillance?"

"Only on the lobby floor and all windows. Because this building is constructed up against the foot of the mountain behind it, the town thought it was enough to have alarm systems protect those areas. And they were right, so far."

"You mean we can keep walking up the stairs and not encounter any cameras?" Darian shook her head. "Well, this isn't Los Angeles, that's for sure."

Samantha began walking. "Do you miss it?" She spoke casually, but Darian was so used to the cadence and tone of Samantha's voice already, she could tell her tone was for show.

"I did at first. Then I went to the library." Darian assumed a similar air, but the brilliant smile Samantha gave her suggested she had also understood.

"Must be a hell of a library." Samantha stopped by the stairs. "Still up for it?"

"Sure am. And besides, the library is impressive, but you should meet the head librarian."

Samantha's cheeks colored. "Hm."

"Okay. Let's go. Better stick to whispering from now on." Darian felt her gun to make sure it was ready, just in case, even if she hadn't had any reason to even look at it after she arrived in Dennamore. *Dwynna Major*. The words filled her brain as she started walking up the stairs. What was this place? It had to be another planet, but what had it been like? Why had their potential alien ancestors left? What was their mission—and why had their Elders decided to strand their crew on Earth? Had any of them revolted? Perhaps Bech'taia and Gai'usto's journal would tell them more about that situation. Or if they went through the ship's logs, they might find something.

"I wonder what they did with the *Velocity*," Darian whispered over her shoulder.

"What? Oh. The ship." Samantha spoke quietly. "Since her shuttles attach to her, can you imagine how big she must be? Where would they hide such a huge ship? I can't even begin to imagine."

Darian had to agree. "Yeah. If the mountains around us had been volcanos, that could have been it."

"It is an exciting idea though. We may find out if the speeders have any records of it. We should return to them tomorrow, if you're up to it."

"I am," Darian assured Samantha. "We're all a team, but you and I are the OG members. Well, maybe Philber too, a bit. He's not strong enough though, unless we find a way to get him back to his house without dragging him up the stairs."

"I know."

They passed the lobby area but remained on the stairs. Outside it was late afternoon, and it wasn't impossible for someone to pass the building and spot them. Darian kept walking upward, motioning for Samantha to hurry. On the next level, they relaxed some, and Darian pulled out a bottle of water for each of them. "Here. Drink some."

"Thanks." Samantha sipped from the bottle as she sat down on the stairs. "I don't know if it's the NIEC or the suspense, but I do get more tired than I ought to." She whispered the words and then drank some more water.

"Perhaps a bit of both." Darian murmured and put the cap back on hers. Tucking both bottles away in her backpack, she turned to look around. She hadn't been to this floor before, and it was as rustic as the rest, but with a thick red carpet and brass details on the windows.

"This the executive floor, I mean, for the council?" Darian counted the doors along the corridor. Eight on each side of the staircase.

"It is, and normally—"

Raised voices made Darian react instinctively. She pushed Samantha behind her and made her back up several steps toward the next flight of stairs.

"I'm telling you, something is going on!" a male voice roared from several doors down.

Samantha held on to Darian's shoulders as she placed her lips against her left ear. "That's Desmond Miller!"

CHAPTER SEVENTEEN

Desmond Miller's voice displayed a mix of frustration and anger, even through the filter of a massive oak door. Samantha nudged Darian gently. "We have to get closer."

"The way he sounds, he could rush out in anger any time." Darian shook her head. "And we can't be sure he's yelling about anything regarding us."

"I have an eerie feeling about that." Samantha peered around the corner. "We have to chance it."

Darian's jaws clenched visibly. "You stubborn woman."

"I know. The worst thing that can happen is for me to lose my job, but that entails a procedure that'll take a while. Not even the Elder Council's chairman can sack someone at my level without a certain procedure."

"All right." Darian sighed. "Hurry then." She bent her knees slightly and walked heel-to-toe in the way Samantha had seen cops and soldiers do on TV. It was clearly a thing. She did her best to mimic it and realized how much faster, and quieter, they moved this way.

When they reached the door to the room where Miller's voice originated from, Samantha pointed at the hinges. "Door opens outward. We might be able to hide behind it."

"Good point," Darian mouthed. They pressed against the wall, and now the voices were loud enough to permeate the massive door.

"Desmond, you're not making sense," a shrill female voice said. "Why would you think someone is illegally removing artifacts from the archive?"

"Don't be naive, Julia." Desmond snarled the words, and Samantha wondered what the inhabitants of Dennamore would think if they knew how vicious the man normally so cordial could sound. Julie had to be Julie Todd, the council secretary. "That old man, Phileas Beresford, has done it for years, only because the former chairman was his best buddy. I tried to revoke his privileges when I was voted in, but the older members of the council were clearly afraid of going up against him."

"Beresford is a renowned researcher, and our history is unique enough to be worth documenting," an older man's voice said. Samantha couldn't determine which one of the three old men that still sat on the council had just spoken. Obviously, it was someone who had Philber's back.

"That's not all," Desmond spat, as if the older man hadn't said a thing. "The woman who unfathomably got tenure as head librarian, Pike, has supplied him with original documents and artifacts, even taking them to his doorstep. We have no way of knowing if she has taken more than the lists say, and if she really returned every single document. I think an audit is called for."

"An audit? What do you mean?" Julie Todd asked. "Are you accusing Ms. Pike of embezzling money?"

"Of course not. She's being careless with our heritage, and trust me, we'll never be able to put Dennamore on the map if these people keep bringing up our history as a way to stop progress."

Samantha turned wide-eyed to Darian. "What does he mean? Progress?"

"I think Miller has plans that the rest of the town knows very little about," Darian whispered against Samantha's ear.

"We have very clear rules and regulations penned by the settlers and the first Elder Council, Desmond," another male voice said, and this time Samantha could tell it was Howard Pride. Pride was a staple in Dennamore and had been a member of the council for more than forty years. He had been suggested as chairman more than a few times but always declined, for reasons he never divulged. "I know you've had your heart set on exploiting the area around the lake and the large meadows north of us, but they're out of reach."

"Rules and regs are not laws," Desmond said, and it was obvious that he was feigning patience. Samantha could picture him tapping his foot under the table. "We can vote to disregard the old rules. They won't hold up in court either way."

"Don't be so sure," Julie now said, and it was evident even she, normally soft-spoken and mild-mannered, was getting angry. "Do you really think you're the first who has had their mind set on developing those areas through the years? I know you have a disdain for our history, but don't forget that Dennamore's inhabitants have always cherished it. We have a unique town, and the Lake Light Festival, for instance, could be destroyed if you fill the entire surrounding area with condos or vacation homes. The big meadows are equally as special to the people of Dennamore. We host all our big weekends there. Everything from seasonal markets to the Fourth of July and—"

"I think you forget yourself." Hissing, Desmond said, "Our finances depend too heavily on very short tourism events like the festivals and those markets. Dennamore needs tax revenues and more people moving here. Such moves will create more jobs, and also, we do need new blood."

"New blood? What the hell?" Darian breathed the words.

"That too is regulated in the Elder Council Rules and Regulations," Julie said. The woman was obviously going toe to toe with Desmond. "It's not easy for people who don't have a family connection to Dennamore to buy property here."

"Fuck the rules!" A loud bang made Samantha jump after Desmond obviously lost his temper.

"And you need to calm down," a male voice said. "We might be of a certain age, some of us, but we are well aware that your brother is one of the main contractors in our town, Miller. He is also the one who tends to underbid the smaller construction firms."

"What are you suggesting?" Snarling, Desmond sounded as if he was standing closer to the door.

"I'm suggesting that your input might be biased, whether you realize it or not," the man said calmly.

"Oh, he realizes it," Samantha muttered under her breath.

"We need to start implementing restrictions when it comes to our archives." Desmond changed tone, which seemed to take the other council members by surprise just as much as it did Samantha. "I've been down there a few times and seen some strange-looking items that make me wonder what witchcraft our ancestors were up to. If the Pike woman hadn't been so adamant about sorting everything and continuing to digitize it, I wouldn't be so concerned. But if we're going to have a chance for other people to see our town as a good alternative to other towns in the Adirondacks, we can't have them think the place is haunted or that we all stem from witches or warlocks."

"He's unhinged." Samantha clasped her forehead. "He's ready to sell out our common areas to make a buck and fill the pockets of his brother and himself."

"And he has no idea what the 'strange-looking items' are. He's in for a big surprise." Darian tugged at Samantha's hand. "Time to go. They're quieter. Perhaps they're wrapping up the meeting."

They took a couple of steps away from the door when Samantha heard, rather than saw, the doorknob move. She froze for a second as the door moved half an inch. "Shit!"

"Come here. The drapes." Darian reached for her.

Samantha stumbled as Darian pulled her behind the thick, royal-blue velvet drapes that hung on either side of the eight large windows. Lined with a blue silky material, they didn't let any light through. Samantha jumped up onto the deep window frame, pressing herself into the corner. Darian did the same next to her and pulled the drape far enough to the right to cover them. Their drape wasn't perfectly aligned with each twin, but if the Elder Council members were still annoyed at each other, surely they wouldn't pay any attention to uneven drapes?

The door squeaked faintly as it opened. Samantha placed her hand on Darian's thigh and squeezed. Immediately, Darian covered Samantha's hand with her own. "Just breathe," she whispered. "We're fine."

Samantha estimated that the council members were about two yards from them if they remained closer to the door and the opposite wall. Closing her eyes hard for a moment, she prayed the people on the other side of the drape would simply walk away. As it turned out, some of them did, but not all. Desmond, Julie, and Howard Pride stayed behind.

"Desmond, please be reasonable," Julie said, obviously trying to reason with the volatile chairman. "I can see benefits in expansion and development, and so can the others on the council. It's just that your approach to it, the way you're planning to do it…it will mean bad blood, and being a small town, so remote compared to the closest village, we're dependent on each other. You know as well as we do how we rely on each other when we get snowed in—and that happens almost every year."

"You're a bleeding-heart, sentimental woman. You cannot build a prosperous future in a town based on that sentiment," Desmond said, his tone cold.

Oh, no, he didn't. Samantha glanced at Darian, who gaped.

"That's uncalled for," Howard said, but Julie interrupted him, sounding furious.

"Don't say another word, *Chairman Miller*. For your own sake, don't say another word." There was a rustling sound.

"The hell, Julie? Are you bugging our meetings?" Desmond raised his voice.

"Don't be ridiculous," Howard said, and now the serene man growled. "Julie is the secretary of the council, which means she is in charge of keeping the records and protocols. Of course, she tapes the meetings."

"And you never know when it's going to be necessary to provide proof of what was said. I doubt that especially the female part of the population, and most men as well, will enjoy the fact that their elected chairman referred to a colleague as a bleeding heart and sentimental."

"I will not forget this." Desmond huffed. "I'm going to initiate an investigation of how our valuable old artifacts and documents are used. Something is up, no matter what you say, and once the investigation is underway, I'll make sure the access to the basement archives is restricted. *That* is within my jurisdiction, at least."

Darian squeezed Samantha's hand as they listened as first Desmond, Samantha guessed, and then the other two walked off. When it had been entirely quiet for a minute, Darian pulled the drape aside an inch. "We're alone," she whispered.

"Thank God." Samantha slid off the window frame and arched her back. "That was enlightening."

"He's barking up the wrong tree." Darian hoisted her backpack. "But he's onto something, and if we can't gain access to the library, it can be a real problem. I mean, we can get into the building, but if he changes the code to the lock to the archives, we still can't get in."

"We need to take as many scroll boxes as we can shove into your backpack. If we see anything else—map, document, or technology—we can carry it in one of the old baskets down there. I suppose we're living up to his assumptions by doing this, but we can't stop now."

"Agreed." Darian caressed Samantha's cheek briefly. "Let's go before anyone else shows up."

Samantha remained where she stood, her gaze stuck in Darian's. The ease with which Darian touched her made her relax, but part of her tensed up as if trying to decipher the emotions behind her reaction. She tried to tell herself she had no time for personal consideration, but that didn't work either. Darian's presence made this adventure, these discoveries into something more, something irresistible, and…right. Yes, that was it. Doing this, even risking her job, her reputation, and as they had no idea about any long-term effects of the NIECs, her life, felt *right* when she did it with Darian. If their theories were correct, they were both descendants of the extraterrestrials that had landed on earth around the time of the revolutionary war. If that fact played a part in how she felt, genetically speaking—no, that sounded too farfetched, unlike the theory about a genetic marker being required to use a NIEC.

They made their way down the stairs, relieved to find the lobby empty. The blinking red light by the entrance showed the alarm was set. Using the same caution while hurrying down to the basement, Samantha was still moving too fast. When they had five more steps to go, Darian stopped and caught Samantha before she tumbled into her. She placed her fingertips against Samantha's lips, shaking her head. And that was when Samantha heard footsteps approaching the staircase.

❖

Darian had her gun out, not taking any risk with Samantha's safety—or her own. As she peered around the corner, thinking she'd rather know who was approaching and then take action instead of going in blind, her knees nearly buckled.

"Walker," she said, forgetting to keep her voice low. Angry yet relieved, she re-holstered her sidearm.

Walker and Brandon were moving along the wall toward the stairs, the latter also carrying a weapon, a damn semi-automatic rifle. "You all right?" Brandon asked, his voice tight.

"Yes," Darian said, remembering to lower her voice. "What are you doing here—and armed?"

"Your grandmother sent us. She got worried when you didn't check in." Walker had relaxed now and snapped his holster closed. "When we saw you took the hauler, we hiked over to this end and managed to get the elevator back down. We were fairly sure we wouldn't need the weapons, but, just like you, Darian, we thought it prudent to bring them anyway."

"And then some," Samantha said, indicating Brandon's rifle.

"Actually, it's a good thing that you came," Darian said. "This might be our last chance to move artifacts from the old archive unobserved. We just heard the council talking about restricting access, or at least Desmond Miller did." She had motioned for them to follow her to the archive when a thought hit. "If you have your access card with you, Samantha?"

"Of course I do," Samantha said calmly, producing the card from her cell-phone wallet. "Allow me." She pulled out the card and punched in her pin. "You realize they'll know, if they think to check the logs. I can try blaming it on a glitch in the system since there'll be no record of me entering the building."

Darian sighed. It bothered her that Samantha's career was in jeopardy because of their explorations, but she couldn't see any other way to do this. After all, Samantha was just as mesmerized by their findings as she was.

Samantha guided the two men to the back of the archive, where she unlocked the door to the oldest area. Darian followed and took off her backpack as she made her way among the shelves.

It was interesting to see the reaction on Brandon's and Walker's faces when they looked at the shelves containing the remaining seventy scroll boxes. Four slanted shelves with enough space for nineteen boxes on each one.

"How many can we fit?" Samantha asked and perused Darian's backpack, plus the two larger backpacks the men carried. "I know Darian's takes five."

"I think at least eight in each of theirs," Darian said. "Let's take four from each side of the shelf. Not sure if that'll fool anyone, but worth a try."

"You pack the boxes. I'll just take a quick look around." Samantha moved in among the narrow shelves as Darian began pulling boxes and tucking them into Walker's backpack. Brandon did the same on the opposite side of the shelves. When they were done and Samantha still wasn't back, Darian risked calling out her name.

"Just a minute," Samantha replied from across the room.

"Where are you?" Frowning, Darian peered along the closest aisles.

"Four down to the left." Samantha sounded oddly absentminded.

Darian and Brandon walked over to the fourth aisle, and Walker took up the rear. Samantha was shining a small flashlight into the shelf unit and picking up what looked like small objects.

"What's that?" Darian unhooked her own flashlight. "Metal eggs?" She looked at the egg-shaped object about the size of a Ping-Pong ball in Samantha's hand. Gun-metal gray, it shimmered in an understated way where it sat in the beams of their two flashlights.

"Not really eggs," Samantha murmured and turned it over. The back of it was entirely flat but also adorned with symbols. "It says 'speaker three two.'" She motioned at the shelf. "And what do you know? Seventy-six of them."

"One each for the crew. Damn. Speaker?" Darian plucked another from the shelf and turned it over. "Speaker three one. Or speaker thirty-one? Can these be communicators of some sort?" Darian's vision blurred for a fraction of a second. "Yes, they are. They're numbered for the crew on different levels. The captain's number is one. Head pilot and navigator is number two." She blew at the shelf. "Wait. They're in order here. That means that this one is yours, Samantha. You're a navigator." Darian took the second from the bottom right on one of the narrow shelves. "Here."

Samantha placed the one she was holding back in its spot and accepted the one Darian gave her. She handed over her flashlight and pressed something on the back of the half-egg-shaped piece of metal, then pressed it against the lapel of her jacket. The speaker gave a quick whirring sound and seemed to fuse with the fabric. "As head of security, you have number three, Dar."

Darian repeated the maneuvers that Samantha had just performed, and the speaker melted halfway into her hoodie. "I'll be damned."

"How do they work?" Brandon asked.

"Let's spread out." Darian rounded two shelves. Then she closed her eyes after inhaling deeply. Running her fingertip down and then back up, lengthwise, along the speaker, she spoke quietly. "Darian to Samantha."

It only took a few moments until Darian heard Samantha say, "I hear you."

Returning to the others, Darian didn't explain but began filling her pockets with speakers. "We're taking as many as we can."

"Damn. Well, all right." Walker opened his jacket and displayed impressive inner pockets. I think I can fit half of them in here."

Between them, they managed to take forty of the communication devices. Samantha pulled out her phone. "We need to leave. Let's don't push our luck."

"All right. Everyone set to go?" Darian took the lead, making sure nobody had snuck up on them while they were busy. As they made their way back to the elevator, Darian wondered how long the range of these speakers was. She knew how to use them, but the information about the specs of the strangely shaped things was not yet downloaded into her brain.

"Camilla and I worked more on the journal and scrolls. She's waiting for us to return, as we learned a lot," Walker said.

"Why don't we stop for pizza and make it a working dinner?" Darian asked. "I'm starving."

"Sounds good to me." Samantha nodded as she reached out to the console and gave the command for the elevator to open.

"Pretty cool how you did that without even hesitating or looking." Darian stepped inside.

Samantha smiled broadly. "Cool. A little eerie still. But mainly cool, yes."

The elevator carried them down to the hauler, and Darian didn't mind Walker taking the driver's seat. She was content to sit next to Samantha. When Samantha grasped her hand, Darian lifted it to her lips without really thinking about it.

"I'm dusty," Samantha murmured.

"I don't care." Darian lowered their joined hands and half expected Samantha to pull hers back, but she didn't.

"Now we can communicate without anyone listening in." Samantha sounded pleased. "It makes me feel a little more secure."

"Same. All I want to know is, if I page you specifically, does that go out to all speakers in use?" Darian cleared her throat. "Just curious."

"Ah, I see. Well, yes, me too. Curious."

"We can run a test at the house later, how to go about it." Squeezing Samantha's hand, Darian trembled as Samantha readily reciprocated.

Samantha ran her thumb up and down the back of Darian's hand. "Agreed."

CHAPTER EIGHTEEN

The transcript of the scroll document was so densely packed with information, it took a while to digest it. Samantha found herself sitting on Darian's bed, propped up against several pillows, reading through Walker's translation into English. She knew he did all this for Camilla's sake, and for Brandon's, as nobody was ready to risk her health by allowing her to use a NIEC. It might be perfectly safe, but then again, it could cause damage they had no idea how to mitigate. Camilla was wise enough to heed Raoul's expert opinion, and the way she looked at Walker for working so hard to keep her in the loop with Brandon melted Samantha's heart. It also meant that whoever wanted could read through it all and let their brains rest from the NIECs.

"Listen to this," Samantha said, looking up at Darian. She lost track momentarily, as Darian came from the shower, looking so sensual with her dark hair still wet and combed back from her angular face. Samantha had borrowed the shower before and was now wearing one of Darian's old track suits, which was blissfully comfortable.

"Yes?" Darian stopped and raised her eyebrows.

"Eh. Yes. This part." Samantha cleared her throat and hoped she didn't look as flustered as she felt. "Once paired with operator, interface gains power from synaptic transmission process. Operator will give their brain relief from this process during regeneration. During emergencies, the interface can forego two sleep cycles. Any more than that is not advisable."

"Sleep cycles…" Darian climbed onto the bed and placed the alien computer on her lap. "If you count a human sleep cycle to be eight hours asleep, ideally, and sixteen hours awake, then two sleep cycles are day, night, day, night, day. Sixty-four hours, at the most. And considering that our DNA has been pretty mixed up with that of humans, if we still subscribe to that theory, and I do, we might be even less fit to wear it too long."

Samantha nodded. "I agree. I'm glad to be able to just not wear it for a bit." Sighing, she tipped her head back. "That's almost true. I do miss it when I take it off. Can it be addictive?"

Darian patted Samantha's thigh. "I feel the same sense, well, that something's missing, but that should lessen with time. Right now, there's a lot, a *lot*, we don't know, and that's why we feel like we're missing something, don't you think? I thought I'd pull up some of the stuff we wrote this morning and see how much my brain retained now that I'm not wearing it, but I want to finish what Walker and Gran figured out first."

"All right." Samantha returned her focus to the scroll. "Once the operator's function is established, the NIEC will engage and develop the individual's brain and synaptic responses. Over a short time, their ability to perform their duties will make them less dependent on the device until full autonomy is established."

"Holy crap." Darian slapped her hand over her mouth. "It'll actually infuse our brains with the knowledge we require? What if we can't tolerate it? We could be vegetables by next week!"

Samantha had to laugh. "I doubt that. I don't know why, but I do. If it were detrimental to our physiology, wouldn't it just ignore our attempt to connect it? Like it did with Brandon?"

"Yeah, I suppose." Darian sighed. "I always suspect brainwashing."

"Do you feel brainwashed…I mean, this far?"

"No. Well, a little. I'm not sure what to call it, but the yearning in itself, and this entire adventure…I can think of little else. I should be trying to find a job while I'm still here in Dennamore helping Gran. Why am I not even contemplating a visit to the police station and introducing myself? Or even asking Walker for a letter of introduction now that I know him? Instead, all I can think about is getting my ass into the chief of security's station on *Speeder One* and finding out if we can operate it. That, and—" Darian averted her eyes.

"And what?" Samantha leaned forward, trying to catch Darian's attention.

"That…and—" Darian hugged the computer to her chest. "Damn it. You have to realize my attraction to you is part of this? To be honest, it's the start of it all."

Samantha tried to figure out what Darian meant. "Am I part of your whole brainwashing theory?" That didn't sound encouraging.

"What? No!" Letting go of the thin, alien computer and pushing it aside, Darian rose onto her knees. "That's not it at all. Yes, I think about you, a *lot*. Believe me, I did that from the moment I knocked you over. Way before we attached the NIECs." Darian's eyes turned amber and then almost golden, reflecting the light from the nightstand table lamps. "Don't shoot me down here."

"What do you mean?" Samantha's heart was beating so fast, she could barely breathe.

"We haven't had time, or been comfortable enough perhaps, to talk about our preferences. Or anything private like that. For all I know, you're entirely straight, and I'm making a complete fool of myself."

Samantha refused to let Darian expose herself like this all alone. Just because Darian was tough and ambitious, she could still be hurt—and perhaps they were both a little extra raw from all the discoveries lately?

"All right. Listen to me." Samantha patted next to her on the bed. "Sit back down."

Darian shifted slowly and sat down, half facing Samantha as she rested her left arm along the pillows behind them.

"I'm not a very demonstrative person," Samantha said, choosing her words carefully. "I'm private, to a fault, according to the people I work with. Some consider me quite aloof. I know that. I have friends, but no one truly close. It's not that I don't want, or need, friendship. It's that my work has always mesmerized and fulfilled me, to a degree that only now is starting to make sense. It could be part of my yearning. Just a thought." She shrugged and let a finger follow the plaid pattern of the duvet cover.

Looking back up at Darian, she continued. "When you literally ran into me, a lot changed. We went down into the archives, and you turned out to live at Brynden 4, which was always a sort of magical myth for me. But it was more than that. Something clicked into place. I mean, I'm sure I'd have been interested and excited had Brandon or Camilla come for the blueprints, but they didn't. It was you—and, increasingly so, it has been you ever since." Samantha held her breath for a few moments, hoping Darian would understand. She was trembling so much on the inside, it was hard to think straight.

"In what way? I know we're friends. Loyal allies." Darian took Samantha's restless hand. "What I don't know, and I need to understand, is if there is even a remote chance that you might one day—"

Samantha pressed her lips to Darian's. The kiss was chaste in that she didn't try to deepen it, but it was also setting fire to every damn cell in her body. As if frozen in time, no, fused by fire in time, rather, she kept the connection going. When she pulled back, she did it in increments—letting go, returning to brush her lips across Darian's, letting go again, returning again. Eventually, she did allow for a few inches between them.

Darian looked dazed. "Mm. 'K. So one day, perhaps." She blinked slowly.

Samantha smiled, her lips swollen and hypersensitive. "Yes. One day." She omitted the "perhaps" and hoped that didn't escape Darian.

"Wow." Slumping sideway along the pillows, Darian sighed. "You have an interesting way of demonstrating your aloofness."

Chuckling, Samantha caressed Darian's cheek. "Don't I, though?"

They sat in silence, and then Samantha simply read the rest of the scroll's text. Oddly, she felt she already knew what it would say. A glance at Darian suggested that she too found the manual rather familiar.

Darian picked up the stack of notes that Camilla, Walker, and Brandon had worked on from different parts of the journal, and now Samantha made herself comfortable and ready to listen. This was much more interesting than the dry NIEC manual.

"They have written notes from both the alien language and the parts in English." Darian leaned against Samantha's shoulder. Not really thinking about it, Samantha placed her hand on Darian's left leg. She needed the connection.

"Here goes. This is from the fall of 1777. Bech'taia writes about it being one year since the ratification of the Declaration of Independence. She is fascinated by the politics of this world and frustrated that she can't study them closer. Gai'usto is more involved with the politics locally, as the crew has divided into two factions. About two-thirds of the seventy-six souls are fully prepared to live out their lives on Earth, while the last third wants to go home, or at least the option to."

Darian turned to a new page. "Bech'taia and Gai'usto belong to the third who don't want to burn their bridges, so to speak. In 1788, when they start building the town hall, the group led by…wow, *led by*, Bech'taia and Gai'usto manages to work underground, using the excavation tools they brought with them on the *Velocity.* They create the tunnel, the access points, and also work with the Elders to expand the lake by adjusting the influx of water using their superior technology. They manage to raise consensus regarding a law that proclaims the meadow planes sacred. Nobody can build there."

Samantha flinched. "Those rules go back that far? Why was that so important? I mean, yes, the water source, always crucial, but still? The meadows?"

"I know. Let's see what else it says." Darian kept reading. "They make it possible to hide the speeders, and when the Elders order the *Velocity* destroyed…they make it seem as if they did. Instead, they hide it."

Samantha gasps. "It can still be out there somehow? But where do you hide what I imagine is a huge spaceship? I know we toyed with the idea it might be around, I mean, at least parts of it, but if they hid it and it's in the same shape as the rest of the artifacts we've found…"

The implications make Darian tremble. "Yeah. It's mindboggling. More than that. It's freaking scary."

Samantha agreed. "Almost too much to think about."

Darian kept reading the summary. "They learned about how Bech'taia had four children during the next ten years. Dennamore prospered, and the families settled in as if they were earthborn and never came to this planet through the vastness of space.

"Later in the text, Gai'usto wrote how Bech'taia died in 1844, of an illness she contracted while visiting their oldest son in New York. The measles. The disease spread through Dennamore and took more than twenty of the original crew of the *Velocity*."

Darian wiped at her wet cheeks, and Samantha in turn had to swallow hard not to burst out crying. "They didn't have any antibodies for that type of thing. Amazing that they managed to save the rest of them, and the new generations."

"Yes." Hiccupping, Darian reached for a tissue and blew her nose. "I think I'm getting soft in my old age."

Samantha chuckled. "Me too."

After hiding her face against Samantha's neck for a few moments, Darian continued, her voice steadier again. "Gai'usto passed the journal on to his oldest daughter, Grace'Ann. She was married to an earthborn and had five children. Gai'usto died in 1858. Look, Gran's made a list from there on. I'm a direct descendent of them, Bech'taia and Gai'usto."

Samantha couldn't help but feel a pang of jealousy that Darian had all this proof, but it lasted only a second. She put her arm around Darian and hugged her. "This proves it. Wherever Dwynna Major is located, you are a descendent of the people who traveled to Earth, only God knows how far and surviving what dangers."

Tipping her head back, Darian looked at Samantha. "Just because we haven't found a journal outlining your ancestry—yet—doesn't mean you don't have a similar lineage. The NIEC proves it. If anyone could wear it, Brandon, that prime specimen of a man in his best years, would be it. And I know he's tried more than once, if nothing else than to help out Gran."

"Poor Brandon. I feel sorry for him, but I also think what we discover can be taught to anyone who's willing to put in the work to learn." Samantha reached for the last paper. "This is as far as they got today?"

"Yeah. Gran said there's about a third of the journal left. Some in the beginning, where they skipped some really dense alien text."

"Let me read from this then." Samantha didn't think she'd ever felt this safe, being tucked up against the headboard with Darian, reading from an unfathomably unique document. "Grace'Ann and her son, Marcus Wells, he was born in 1825, learned about the speeders from Gai'usto before he died. They in turn kept the secret, but so far, no more records of them appear in the journal. Perhaps in the pages Camilla and the guys have yet to translate."

"Think about what happened after the turn of the previous century," Darian said. "Wars. Depression. More wars."

"True." Samantha nodded. "That's actually a very credible assumption. And what were facts for the longest time can quickly turn to folklore and myths. Such as the fact that this journal sat on a shelf for quite some time without anyone paying it any attention."

"Not to mention how the archives were overlooked until you and Philber began going through them." Darian tapped her chin. "I wonder why Desmond Miller is so adamant about restricting the archive. It's not like he can know anything about what's there? Or can he?"

Samantha sighed and pushed her fingers through her tousled hair. "He's the chairman. Through his office he can have access to files we know nothing about. He might not know in great detail—I doubt he inherited a NIEC when he won the election—but he might have some knowledge. Enough to make him uneasy about Philber's research and my assisting him."

"That sounds plausible." Darian slammed a hand against the mattress. "Either way, the guy's bad news, if nothing else because he acts like a damn bully." Sitting up, she gently gripped Samantha's shoulders. "I think we need to work on the speeders tomorrow. If we can make them work, we'll be one step closer to finding out what happened to the *Velocity*. I can feel it."

No way could Samantha have denied Darian anything, even if she wanted to. "What if we cause complete chaos in that shuttle bay?" Samantha felt she ought to present some sort of objection.

"I'm not saying you should just plop down in the chair and hit the accelerator." Darian grinned. "We'll see how much knowledge the NIECs give you."

"Me? What do you mean?" Concerned now, Samantha sat up straight.

"You're the navigator. The pilot. We have no captain—yet—but you have me, Raoul, and Philber, if we can have him help us. Maybe Walker."

Samantha groaned. Of course. "Sounds like too small of a crew to me."

"Yes, if we were going on a mission in space. Absolutely. But to learn how to start it and perhaps take it for a spin at one point? We'll figure that out." Darian flung her arms around Samantha's neck. "And as your chief of security, if I feel it isn't safe, I'll be the first to pull the plug."

"I suggest we learn where said plug is located before we try anything at all," Samantha said dryly. "And I appreciate that you have my safety at heart."

Pulling back enough to meet Samantha's gaze, Darian had a softer expression. "I have a lot about you 'at heart,' and your safety is just the beginning."

"Dar." Samantha closed her eyes briefly. If Darian kept saying things like that, what little was left of Samantha's self-preservation would evaporate. She hugged Darian closer again, content just being safe there and then.

Apparently, tomorrow she would sit at the helm of a damn spaceship.

Chapter Nineteen

Speeder One sat as they'd left it. Darian wasn't sure why this was noteworthy. She hadn't expected the members of the Elder Council to have suddenly found their way down into the tunnel and sabotaged the vessel.

Standing under the stern, she looked up at its pointed fuselage. She had walked and inspected the surface from all angles, and it had dawned on her that the vessel didn't look pristine in the same way as the smaller artifacts they'd discovered. It had scratches, dents, and something looking like faint scorch marks. If those had occurred because of normal wear and tear, if that was the right expression, or if their ancestors had encountered dangers in space was still anyone's guess.

A gentle hand at the small of her back made Darian smile. She didn't have to turn her head to know who it was. "Samantha." Darian did turn then.

"Dar. I've seen you circle the ship several times. Are you worried about something in particular?"

"Not about the ship, not really. I'm worried about how we're going to get Camilla and Philber up and down the stairs."

"Either of the younger guys can easily carry Camilla. Even Carl." Samantha ran her hand in a small circle against Darian. "As for Philber, as long as he's careful, he'll be all right. Raoul won't let them do anything that risks their health."

"I know. I'm not super worried, but you know, it's Gran." Darian slid her fingertip up and down the half-egg-shaped speaker on her lapel. "Darian to Raoul. Progress?"

"Great minds think alike," Raoul said. "Carl and I were just going to check in. We're standing by the console of the elevator, and it looks the same as the one at your end, except for one thing. It has a maneuvering panel for speed. From what my NIEC sort of told me, it can be used from here, and from inside the speeder."

"Wow." Darian waved Walker and Brandon over. "Come listen to this. Go on, Raoul."

"Before we continue, I think we better give Carl a NIEC of his own. He's nagging a hole in my head." Raoul snorted. "All right. Here we go."

Darian debated whether they should have taken one of the haulers over to the other elevator, but she knew micromanaging every single step wouldn't work in the long run. "Talk to us, Raoul."

"Hang on. What the hell?" Raoul's voice rose half an octave. Darian could hear Carl say something but couldn't make out the words.

Samantha engaged her speaker. "Are you guys all right? Should we come over?"

"No, not at all. I mean, yes. We're fine. And no, you don't have to. It's just…it's just, this thing's moving sideways. Or not sideways, exactly. Diagonally?" More murmurs in the background. "Carl estimates at a ten-degree incline going north."

"So not straight up," Samantha said slowly. Walking over to where she'd placed her computer earlier, she tapped in a few commands. "Here's the map." She carried the computer over to Darian and Brandon. "Here's the elevator." She pointed at a small mark that Darian hadn't noticed before. It showed the exact location.

"North." Darian pulled her index finger along the thin, transparent screen. "This way. What's that area, up there?"

Samantha frowned. "Well, here's the lake. And if you imagine a line directly to the west—that's the meadows!" Using the speaker again, she gave Raoul the information. "You're not going to end up in anyone's kitchen. You're heading to the meadows. That's our best estimate, anyway."

"Yeah, but there's no hole in the ground up there where the elevator can just pop up. I guess we can speed up a little bit, or we'll be here all day," Raoul said.

"All right," Darian said. She trusted the levelheaded physician, but the fact that he had Carl with him made her nervous. As for the suggestion of Carl getting his own NIEC, she didn't want that, unless they brought Carl's parents on board with what was happening.

"Look!" Samantha had placed the computer on one of the hauler's seats and now bent closer and tapped at the controls. "I see them!"

Brandon and Darian hurried over. Staring at the map, whose markings of the tunnel had now taken on a glowing, magenta-colored hue, Darian saw how a tiny rectangle moved deceptively slowly upward. "I'll be damned. Darian to Raoul. We see your progress on the screen here. You've gone halfway already."

"Samantha here. The meadows are about eight miles away, which means you'll be there in less than ten minutes. You better slow down soon, unless the elevator is preprogrammed or something." Samantha opened another window on the screen. "I'm searching for any applicable protocols."

"Raoul here. No need. I managed to get the map onto the display. This is fantastic. I'll be sure to slow down if I need to. Don't worry." Raoul chuckled, and Darian thought she heard a bit of a nervousness in his mirth. "Carl is doing some interesting dance moves. This kid's not afraid of anything."

"Just make sure he's okay. Then he can do an Irish jig for all I care," Darian said.

Walker placed a hand on Samantha's shoulder. "Brandon and I'll head back to help the boys fetch Camilla and Philber once they return. Keep us posted. We'll wait by Camilla's access point unless you tell us differently."

"All right. Darian and I will enter *Speeder One* and go through the start sequence. We'll need a few practice-runs, I imagine." Samantha nodded briskly. "And by the way, no one gives Carl a NIEC without talking to me or Darian."

"Wouldn't dream of it." Walker quickly saluted them and joined Brandon at one of the haulers. As they drove off, Darian and Samantha walked up the ramp to the vessel.

"You nervous about this?" Darian shot Samantha a quick glance as they took their respective seats.

"Not as much as I should be." Samantha shrugged. "If you're asking me if I had nightmares last night of killing us all, then, yes. A bit apprehensive."

"Enough to call it quits?"

Samantha whipped her head toward Darian, her green eyes glittering. "No. Never. You?"

"Well, actually, I'm more worried that you might regret the kiss." Darian pulled at a lever on her armrest without even looking, but instead jumped when it turned out she'd deployed a harness. "Yikes. Here we buckle up automatically. Neat."

"Same answer. No. Never."

Darian's chest glowed with warmth, and she had to busy herself with the information that flooded her screen. She read through the sequences, but so far, she didn't need to do anything. "Looks like the security officer is also in charge of tactical and weapons. Cool."

"Don't get trigger-happy." Samantha had returned her focus to the much-larger screen at her disposal too. She sat front and center on the bridge, where a screen that was much wider than any of the rest showed everything a pilot needed to know. Behind her, a larger chair with a multitude of small screens, each on its own individual, adjustable stand that made it possible to position them at any angle, was meant for the captain.

"In retrospect," Darian said, "I'm surprised the scroll box didn't choose you as captain. You being our boss and all."

"Not sure why it happened this way, but I'm feeling increasingly comfortable, if that's even the right word, with my role as a pilot and navigator. Not the most logical choice, as that's not my usual area of expertise. Not like with you or Raoul. I wonder why Walker hasn't said if, and, or what the box chose for him."

"Can it be an age thing?" Darian answered her own question. "Perhaps not, since Philber learned of his new assignment. Anthropology. Not logical, but we'll figure it out with time."

They ran diagnostics as if it were second nature to both of them, learning the controls in minutes, sometimes seconds. They had started the last one when Raoul paged them.

"We've stopped." He sounded calm but definitely tense. "I'm going to let the elevator move very slowly the last few meters, all right?"

"All right," Samantha said. "Be careful." She pulled up the map on her big screen.

"We are," Raoul replied. "I have set the computer to record what happens. It should come up on yours."

Right then, a new window opened in the center of the navigational screen, and they saw Raoul and Carl stand as if braced for impact. Raoul used the console on the wall to move the elevator.

"All right. Full stop now. Opening the top." Raoul punched in commands and then directed the camera to what was happening above him and Carl. "My God, do you see this?"

Darian didn't even dare blink, afraid of missing something. "We do," she said huskily.

The elevator ceiling, which was really a part of the tunnel, folded back, while another layer shifted up and split in the middle, the halves separating. The sound it made wasn't as smooth or seamless as the elevator they had ridden up to the speeders, or in the town hall, for that matter. This maneuver by the diagonal elevator whined, growled, and gave popping sounds.

"What the hell's that?" Darian asked.

"It's the ground above. The dirt, roots, bushes shifting as the ceiling is moving," Raoul shouted, obviously trying to drown out the noise. "Imagine it as a double elevator door separating toward the sky, taking two hundred and fifty years of top layer with it. I'm glad it's getting late. Less likely for anyone to be out here."

The noise stopped so suddenly, Darian thought they might have lost audio. "Raoul?"

"Yeah. We're here. I wish we had a way to climb up and have a peek." He kept staring up toward the sky. "I can't hear anything. No voices shouting or anything that suggests we've disturbed anyone."

"Good. Well, see if you can close the darn thing again so nobody falls into the hole and breaks their neck." Samantha opened another channel on her speaker. "Samantha to Walker. We are a go. Boys are on their way back and will join you to fetch Camilla and Philber as we planned."

"Fantastic," Walker said. "Does this mean we're going flying?"

"Looks like it," Samantha said, and pressed her hand to her midsection. "Let us know when you're enroute."

"Will do."

"Raoul. Did you get it closed?" Darian asked as Samantha began running another diagnostic.

"It's an automatic function," Raoul replied. "As soon as I hit the settings for returning to the tunnel, it closed itself. We did get our fair share of debris, but that's to be expected, considering. We're returning to Walker and Brandon."

"Good. They're waiting for you. Darian out." Darian watched Samantha's fingers fly across the lines, dots, and symbols on the glass-like surface before her. "Like riding a bike, huh?"

"How can it feel as easy as driving my car to the library in the morning?" Samantha muttered while starting another set of diagnostics. "And why isn't anything on these ships corroded after all this time?"

"And are we all right in regular clothes, or should we put on uniforms?" Darian looked back at the storage facility in the far rear. "Another thing. I need the bathroom. I hope there is one. I'm not peeing in the space uniform. I refuse."

Samantha chuckled. "There is. Far back and to the left. Several, in fact."

"Where does the pee go?"

Samantha blinked slowly. "Um. Recycling."

Darian could feel her own NIEC catch up. "Ugh. Yeah. I sort of 'remember.'" She made quotation marks in the air and then hurried to the rear of the ship and used the recycling facility. On her way back, she stopped by the storage areas and pulled out eight uniforms. They all looked identical, even size-wise, which made her hope it was a one-size-fits-all kind of deal. She looked for boots or shoes, but after another glance at the uniforms, she realized they had built-in footwear.

"At least I don't have to stir some wood chips or something," she muttered as she came up the aisle again and was within earshot of Samantha.

"Excuse me?" Looking puzzled, Samantha turned around.

"As a kid, I went camping several times with my best friend and his family, and that experience involved that particular type of composting. For a kid around ten years old, it was disgusting. I prefer high-tech alien recycling."

Samantha laughed but then shifted her gaze to the uniforms. "Guess we better use them, though they look like their former users were all the same size."

Darian examined the fastening, which reminded her of Velcro, but it seemed to actually be a metal that fused together. As it turned out, all she had to do was pull at it. When she did, the uniform relaxed, and she could step into it without removing her jeans and T-shirt. The metal fused back together, and the uniform adjusted to Darian's size, even for her feet. "Cool." Darian moved her arms, and it felt as if the uniform had been tailor-made for her. "We better move the speakers to the outside of the uniform."

Samantha pulled on her uniform, reattached her speaker, and managed to look just as elegant as she did in her pastel suits. Darian watched in awe how what looked like pajama feet shrank around her shoes and hardened. Compared to the NIECS and everything else they'd found, this was probably not equally impressive, but to her it was visual and tangible in another way.

"You look good in uniform. I suspected that," Samantha said and nodded at Darian.

"You pictured me in uniform?" Darian grinned broadly. "Now, that makes my day."

Samantha guffawed. "We're about to try to launch a damn spaceship. That should be what makes your day."

"Completely takes second billing." Darian took Samantha's hand. "You're going to be at the helm. If you say we can't go, we won't. It's your call, Boss."

Her lips softening, Samantha regarded Darian quietly for a few moments with a stillness that wasn't like anything Darian had seen before. "Thank you."

"That's how it has to be."

"Walker to Samantha." Samantha's speaker made them both let go.

"Samantha here."

"We're almost at the elevator, ready to join you." Walker sounded calm, which reassured Darian, who was just about to ask about Camilla. "You all set?"

"We're set. Park the haulers at the back and then enter the ship." Samantha walked to the pilot seat while she gave her orders in such a natural way, Darian wondered if she noticed it herself.

"Yes, ma'am," Walker said, completely without irony.

"I'll begin the startup sequence." Samantha looked back over her shoulder. "Can you show them how to put on the uniforms?"

"Sure thing."

Raoul came through the hatch first, carrying a bright-eyed Camilla. He put her down gently, making sure she found her bearings.

"Darian. This…this is amazing." Camilla smiled broadly and hugged Darian. "Can you believe this has been here the entire time?"

"I can and I can't." Darian returned the embrace. "Let me help you with your uniform. I don't think we'll need any helmets, but the uniforms feel important." Holding it up before Camilla's slight frame, Darian thought of something. "I'm not sure it'll readjust to your size, as you're not wearing an interface, but at least you'll be protected."

"I'm sure it'll be fine either way." Camilla stepped into the uniform while holding onto the backrest of one of the crew chairs. "I suppose I'll just look like—oh!" The uniform acted with delay but then adjusted itself to fit snugly around Camilla's body. "Good Lord."

"I agree," Brandon said from behind. He looked in awe at the way his uniform fit him perfectly. "And I'm not even genetically compatible."

"This means our ancestors constructed these uniforms so just about anyone could use them. Cool." Carl grinned. "They look pretty chill."

"Chill?" Philber huffed. "I feel like I'm dressed in a baby-blue pajama." He looked down at himself. "I suppose they serve their purpose."

"Samantha's ready when you are." Darian motioned for them to take their seats. "Raoul, Philber, we need you up front, just in case. The rest of you, strap in—you'll find a sensor on your armrests." Darian turned and took her station to Samantha's left.

Raoul occupied the ops station on her right. "I know I've been chosen as a medical officer, which makes it rather amazing that I know what to do with this setup." He tapped a few symbols. "I suppose the entire crew required at least basic training in how to use the speeders."

That made sense. Darian engaged her harness sensor and felt herself being safely tucked into her seat. A quick glance at Samantha showed she was all set. Her face showed no onset of nerves, merely concentration.

"From what I see here, we are all secure and ready to launch," Samantha said. "We'll go slow, and I'm not about to take any foolhardy risks. I'll keep us low and hope the forests around the meadow hide us from view until we're farther into uninhabited areas, among the mountains." She paused. "The time is six thirty p.m."

"Sounds good, Boss," Raoul said. "Ops is ready."

"Tactical ready." Darian checked her readings. "I'll just keep my hands well away from the weapons' array."

"God," Samantha muttered, but then she smiled. "All right, my friends. This is it."

When the propulsion system hummed to life, Darian felt as if her heart fell from her chest and into her stomach. *Speeder One* vibrated, and she heard a clanking sound, which she suddenly knew was the landing struts folding into its belly.

They were hovering.

CHAPTER TWENTY

Samantha focused hard on the screen in front of her. It showed an outline *of Speeder One* and where it was located compared to its surroundings. Right now, it was hovering, and she needed it to move out to the elevator. In this case, the elevator was more of a hatch, since she would have the speeder hover while they rode it down.

"Nice and easy," Samantha murmured as she pushed a small bright-red dot to the left on the console. The speeder obediently glided in that direction, and Samantha was glad she had used caution when it came to the instruments. They were sensitive, and she couldn't risk slamming the vessel into the bedrock on the other side of the elevator.

"We're hovering above the elevator pad," Samantha said, realizing the others needed to know what was happening. "Raoul. Start the descent of the elevator."

"Got it," Raoul said and began tapping at his console. "Setting it to forty-percent speed."

"Good." Samantha switched one of the windows on the big screen to external vision. She saw them glide by along the bedrock to the left and how the shuttle-bay opening disappeared on the opposite side. It took them only two minutes to reach the tunnel floor. Finding the circular symbol that had a cross in the center, Samantha used two fingers and slowly turned the speeder, aiming for forty-five degrees. Adrenaline streamed through her veins, and she carried out the maneuver too fast, then overcompensated when she righted the speeder.

"You're doing fine." Darian's calm voice helped Samantha find her bearings, and she carefully made sure they were perfectly aligned in the direction of the tunnel.

"Everyone all right?" she asked.

"We're fine. Keep going," Philber answered. "Just don't hit anything."

"Funny," Samantha muttered.

"Be good, Philber, or she'll drop you off at your access point," Camilla said, sounding completely unfazed.

"I'm not going to try anything fancy," Samantha said. "There's an automatic setting for getting to the next elevator. No freehand type of flying in such cramped quarters." Nobody objected, and Samantha set the computerized navigation array to maneuver the speeder.

A sudden force she hadn't counted on pressed Samantha into the backrest. She involuntarily gripped the armrests and stared at the settings on the console and then over to the screen. The tunnel rushed by, and she was certain she'd screwed up the settings.

"We're going too fast!" Darian also held onto her seat. "Can you slow it down?"

"I can try." Samantha tapped the console, trying to disengage the automatic process. Nothing happened, and she was torn between panicking and having her NIEC override the emotional response. Drawing a few deep breaths, Samantha forced herself to let the NIEC do its thing. If she struggled against it, nausea and vertigo would be the result.

"Samantha! Look!" Darian pointed at a smaller screen next to Samantha's main screen. "That thing."

Samantha had managed to push back the onslaught of acute stress and knew what the gauge showed. "It's counting down." Relief flooded Samantha. "We should be all right. It's counting down the exact distance. I—I forgot."

"Are we slowing? Feels like it." Darian peered up at the main screen that wrapped around the entire bridge area. "See?"

"We are. We're almost there. I have no idea what speed we hit, but it'll take us there in less than three minutes." Preparing for the next maneuver, Samantha clenched and opened her hands a few times to loosen her joints. "Damn."

"That got the old juices going," Philber said, and it boggled Samantha's mind how he could sound so cheerful.

The speeder stopped right at the second elevator. Feeling more secure, Samantha guided it onto the pad, where it hovered steadily. "It's unfathomable that we're doing this," Samantha murmured. "Yet we aren't even close to hesitating."

"I know." Darian leaned forward and looked at Samantha and then over to Raoul. "You okay there, Doc?"

"Never better." Raoul flashed a bright smile Samantha had rarely seen from the normally quite serious man.

"Then let's start up the elevator here. Ops, you're in charge again."

Raoul performed the procedure. "This elevator is faster. According to my console, the speeder will adjust, and sensors on its belly will keep it aligned."

"I see it too," Samantha said and let her gaze double-check all the readings. The NIEC had infused her mind with so much knowledge, it was remarkable that it hadn't exploded by now. In passing, she wondered how much she might retain once they returned, and she disengaged it. "Commence elevator sequence."

"Here we go," Raoul said.

Samantha had thought the flight through the tunnel was fast, but now it felt as if the speeder burrowed into the bedrock at lightning speed. She couldn't see anything but a blur on the screen showing the external cameras…no, sensors. Double-checking the smaller screen that she'd forgotten earlier, she saw it count down at a much faster pace. It was daunting to imagine what might happen to them if the speeder slammed into the bedrock at the end of this part of the tunnel at this speed. All they could do now was trust their ancestors' technology.

"Thirty seconds," Raoul said. "Twenty-five. Twenty." As he counted down, Samantha readied herself for what would be required of her when they reached the hatch to the meadows.

"Slowing down," Darian said after Raoul counted twelve seconds.

Speeder One stopped softly about two yards from the end of the tunnel.

"Damn, this thing is incredible." This time it was Camilla's voice from behind. "If only I were a little younger."

"At least we get to take part in it," Walker said.

Samantha jerked as something hit the speeder from above. "Tell me that's just dirt, Raoul."

"It is. Adjusting sensors to show topside."

Soon the screen showed the hatch opening above them. More dirt and debris fell, but no big boulders that risked damaging their ship. When the hatch was fully open, Samantha realized it was her time to prove that her NIEC hadn't made a mistake. "Hold on. I have the controls now." She shot Darian a quick glance.

Darian gave her a thumbs-up. "Go for it."

Samantha let her instincts take over, set on not second-guessing herself and what needed to happen. They had traveled sideways through this tunnel, and she saw the hatch was aligned the same way. Carefully, but with entirely steady hands, she let *Speeder One* rise. The visible layers of sediment began to switch from bedrock, to clay, to dirt, and then to roots. As soon as the sensors reached ground level, the rays from the setting sun flooded the ship via the main screen.

"Adjusting settings," Darian said. "Let's not blind our pilot."

Samantha agreed. She was busy maneuvering the speeder through the opening and keeping it from rising too far off the ground, well aware of how important it was to fly below both civilian and military radars. As soon as they were completely through the hatch, it closed underneath them. She hoped the ship had a record of the exact location for their return.

"Heading northwest toward the mountains. I don't think we should push our luck this first time," Samantha said as she pulled up the preset course she'd practiced during their diagnostic dry runs. "Unless we run into trouble, we'll take more flights."

"Agreed," a chorus of voices said from behind.

Samantha smiled as she slid her fingers into a pattern on her console surface. The speeder turned where it hovered and took off due northwest. They had the sun slightly from the side, and the screen showed how they passed along the meadows. Before them stretched the vast forests that clad these parts of the Adirondack mountains. In the distance, Samantha could make out the road that led farther into the mountains and then west. Only one road ran into her hometown, and this was the continuation of it, heading out. It made her town vulnerable in many ways, but perhaps the extraterrestrials had also considered this location easier to defend—and control?

Setting the distance to the ground to twelve feet, she thought of a smooth roller-coaster ride as the speeder kept this setting while they crossed valleys and forests. Samantha was itching to let the vessel soar, shoot straight out toward orbit and get close to the celestial bodies out there. Something pulled her, no, *beckoned* her. How could the Elders among the crew that landed here decide for every single soul on their ship that they were to remain on this, for them, alien planet?

Was this the origin of the yearning? Had the descendants of the crew from Dwynna Major inherited their ancestors' longing for home?

"Time to turn back," Samantha said quietly. "I could go on forever, but the risk is too great."

Darian nodded. "I could keep going too. This…it feels right, doesn't it?"

Samantha was about to agree when Raoul slapped his forehead. "Not sure if my NIEC is slow on the uptake or I am. I have a setting that will make it a lot easier, and safer, to return to the meadows."

Samantha blinked. "What?"

"None of us has understood that we can use stealth mode, and I assume, as a doctor, it was a need-to-know thing for me. Once we have a true ops officer, these things will go smoother." Raoul stared at them. "Permission to engage it?" He was clearly very serious.

"By all means." Ready to try to mitigate any trouble, Samantha squared her shoulders.

"And we're supposed to be invisible," Raoul said after dragging both index fingers along his console. He raised his hands, palms up. "Hard to know if it's working."

"Only one way to find out," Darian said and pointed to the screen. "There's the lake. Set the sensors on the belly to film the surface as we pass it."

"Brilliant," Raoul called out. "If there's no reflection, we are invisible."

"And if someone's there?" Camilla asked.

"Who'd believe them even if they saw us?" Darian said.

Samantha hesitated but decided to risk it. "I think we can do it. I'll do a sweep first above the trees. If tons of cars are in the parking lot, we'll abort."

"Good thinking," Darian said.

After circling the dense woods around the lake, they passed the parking lot at enough distance to spot cars, but to Samantha's relief, only one occupied it. Two people were getting into it, and she steered away toward the water. "Ready with the sensors?"

"Yes." Raoul was tapping his screen. "You're good to go."

"Keep looking at the water. I'll be busy flying." Samantha meant to go low, perhaps ten feet. Letting the speeder down as soon as she cleared the trees, she flew it across the lake at a slower speed than before.

"Nothing. Apart from causing some waves, no reflection of the speeder!" Darian raised her hands in the air. "Amazing! Wow!"

"Wait. Go around. I thought I saw something just after you passed it." Raoul adjusted something. "Try to go even slower."

"All right?" Frowning, Samantha came about, her hands certain now as she used the controls. "Here we go again."

"Oh, my God!" Darian said, making Samantha take her eyes off her readings and look at the screens. "That has never happened like that. It has to be us. It has to be!"

Samantha stared at the surface of the lake and didn't see any reflection of them, just like Darian had said before. Instead, she saw the lake lights, brighter than ever before.

❖

Darian looked over the readings while Samantha took them back to the meadows, replayed them several times, and made sure she had copied them over to their computers. She still had problems understanding what had just happened. The lights had been bright, tinted green and yellow, and the rippling water *Speeder One* had created had made the lake look alive with something…alien.

"Fuck," Darian said as a thought began to gain traction in her brain.

"What's wrong?" Samantha asked, focused only on the instruments on her screen.

"Let me just try to figure out what I'm thinking." Darian pulled up texts on her console. She logged in and began searching security folders she hadn't accessed before and kept looking for any sign that she might be right. It was one thing to guess, another to bring the theory to the others with some sort of proof.

"All right." Samantha slid her fingertips back and forth on her console. "We're here. I'm cancelling stealth mode."

Darian knew she could keep reading once they'd gotten *Speeder One* safely into the tunnel. She needed to be ready to assist Samantha if they ran into problems. "You are right on path, according to the sensors."

"Agreed," Raoul said. "Reduce speed a little more than recommended. We need to be sure the hatch doors don't get stuck."

"Point taken," Samantha said. "Reducing speed."

"It's almost dark. We were gone longer than we anticipated." Darian looked at the screen showing the outer sensor videos. "The lights are on in Dennamore. Going to be pitch-black soon."

"I can still get us in. Sensors don't care about what kind of light we travel in." Samantha gave Darian a gentle smile. "I wouldn't dare just use the screens anyway."

"Smart." Darian watched the doors in the ground open. "Raoul? Can you see if they're locked in place?"

"Not yet. Give it a moment." He drummed his fingertips on the armrests. "There. All set."

"Going in." Samantha sounded tense, but her fingers moved in a slow, soft kind of a ballet, turning the speeder around ninety degrees. Hovering above the opening in the ground, she began their descent, and then the automatic process commenced. "Thank God." Exhaling, Samantha extended a hand to Darian. "We're inside, and now we know we can trust the instruments to take us back to the shuttle bay."

"You were amazing." Darian grinned. "Nobody could've guessed you usually drive a little blue sedan." She turned her head and looked back at the others. "Are you okay there in the rear?" She spotted tears on Camilla's cheeks. "Gran?" About to detach her harness and rush over to her grandmother, she stopped in midmotion when Camilla held up her hand, palm toward Darian.

"I'm fine. More than fine. Imagine that I would live long enough to be a part of something like this." She leaned her head against Walker's shoulder. "And more than that. To experience it with you, and with this one." She patted Walker's chest. "Unbelievable."

"Hey, what are we? Yesterday's newspaper?" Philber huffed, but his eyes were radiant where he sat next to Carl.

"Carl?" Darian asked.

"If you don't give me a NIEC, I'm going to be really, really mad," Carl said, and it was obvious he was only half joking.

"That's up to Samantha at this point," Darian said, "and if we can find a way to bring your parents in on this…what?"

Samantha had squeezed her hand hard. "You said you were thinking about something, and even if it isn't what struck me as we flew back from the lake, I bet it is similar." She glanced back at Carl. "If you can be patient a little longer, I might find a way to figure this out. What do you say?"

Blushing a hot pink, Carl nodded. "Sure. Of course, Ms. Pike… Samantha."

Darian's stomach clenched when she heard the decisiveness in Samantha's voice. Something had dawned on both of them, and if it was by any means related, they were going to have more than one discussion about it.

❖

Two hours later, which had included getting the speeder back to the shuttle bay, putting the uniforms back, downloading all the information they'd gathered into their computers, and driving back in two haulers, all eight of them sat in Camilla's parlor, curtains pulled. The ones wearing NIECs had placed them safely in their boxes.

They had eaten a dinner that Brandon had prepared ahead of time, and Darian had noticed their appetites had varied from zero—Samantha—to voracious—Carl. Now they held on to their beverage of choice, and Darian was grateful that Brandon had suggested a cup of hot chocolate to Samantha. Darian was sipping a glass of red wine, and so was Camilla. The men, predictably, had opted for beer, except Carl, who gladly downed another Coke.

"Should I start?" Samantha turned to Darian. "Or…?"

"Yes, please do." Darian sipped her wine, wondering if Samantha had the same thoughts she did. She shifted until she sat toward Samantha and pulled her legs up. She wanted to be able to see Samantha's expression as she talked. Something reverberated in the depths of her stomach, and she was more nervous than she'd ever been.

"To be honest," Samantha said, "I had this thought already when we flew among the mountains. After the lake lights went on, it hit me even harder. We can't do it like this." She looked at each of them, one by one. Carl seemed about to object, but a gentle tap on his shoulder from Brandon settled him down again.

Samantha waited a few beats and then continued. "What I mean is, this is not our secret to keep. We can't do this on our own because it isn't right. We have so many direct descendants from the original settlers living in this town, people who never left here, like Walker and Carl, and people who returned because something pulled them, like Camilla. Even some like Darian, who never lived here but still are affected by the yearning. These ships, artifacts, and information belong to them as well. Perhaps it took us, this particular constellation of people in this room, to figure out that something about this town is remarkable. After all, people have lived here for many years, and not one has been curious enough to start browsing the oldest archives, not until Philber and me. We might not have gone any further than writing papers about the peculiarities if Darian hadn't knocked me off my feet that day. She brought me to Brynden 4. And she…" Samantha cleared her throat as she looked over at Darian. "To me, you are the catalyst in all this."

"Likewise." Darian didn't trust her voice to manage more than one word.

"What are you saying, Samantha?" Camilla asked. "That we take it to the Elder Council?"

"Not just that. We have to inform the town in a way that shows them we're not just a bunch of fools making up fairy tales. If we inform the Elder Council first…I'm not sure that's a good idea. I don't trust Miller. He's planning to line his own pockets, I fear. He won't want the town to know that these amazing things exist."

"What about the feds? Air force? Government in general? Won't they take these things from us? I mean, from Dennamore?" Carl asked.

"Oh, they'll want to, when they eventually find out." Philber chuckled. "I'd like to see them try. Unless any of them possess the right DNA, they won't be able to use any of the artifacts, let alone fly the speeders."

Carl looked relieved.

"You're right." Walker stood and walked behind Camilla. "After we make sure we have the rest of the scroll boxes and speakers secured, we let everyone know. How we'll go about it… we'll figure it out."

Samantha looked relieved. "History should never be proprietary, but some people disagree. I realize we take a great risk, but as I see it, we do that either way." Touching Darian's knee briefly, she said, "Now you. Does what I said tie into your thoughts?"

"Sort of, in the sense that it emphasizes that it's not ours to keep or hide." Darian gripped Samantha's hand.

"We're all trying to wrap our minds around the lake lights switching on as we passed. After all, they go on the same time every year, and several of us were there together this year to see it happen. It was my first time seeing them, and I was mesmerized. Now when they went on, I think it was because of the speeder."

"Yes, but why would that be?" Camilla asked.

"The speeder must be connected with something. I was able to search the database for information while Samantha flew us back to the meadows, and even if what I did find is only circumstantial…it makes me certain that I'm right."

Samantha sat up straight. "Dar? Are you saying…?"

Darian could see that Samantha had figured it out. "Our ancestors were ordered to bury their ship. That's what Bech'taia wrote in her journal. Not sink. *Bury*. But I think they actually did sink it. And I believe we'll find proof when we go through more documents and the rest of the journal."

"What are you saying, sweetheart?" Camilla looked stunned as she fumbled for Walker's hand. He put his arm around her and stroked her upper arm.

"The lake. That's where the ones who still hoped to go home one day hid their ship." Darian caught Samantha's gaze and saw tears cling to her lashes. "The lake lights. They come from the *Velocity*."

EPILOGUE

Desmond Miller regarded his perfectly organized desk, admiring especially his collection of pens. It was a hobby of his, an expensive hobby, to collect the latest editions of new, exclusive pens. Signing contracts with a pen that cost more than most made in a month showed the world that he valued himself and his mission in life. Hell, his most expensive pen cost more than a year's salary.

Walking out into the corridor and over to the window, he let his gaze roam the center of Dennamore, his little kingdom. Being elected chairman of the Elder Council had been a life-long dream come true. From this window, he could see all the way to the meadows in the distance.

Desmond was about to go back to his desk when something caught his eyes. Something over by the meadows. It looked like…a helicopter? No. Too big, surely. He blinked several times to see better, and it was gone.

Resting his forehead against the window, he darted his gaze back and forth as he tried to see the object again. Nothing. Frowning, he returned to his desk. It could have been a bird, but much closer, of course, so it looked bigger. Surely that was it.

Grabbing his favorite among the pens, Desmond turned it over between his fingers until he calmed down. A bird. Naturally.

Nothing to get worked up about.

About the Author

Gun Brooke, author of more than twenty-five novels, resides in Sweden, surrounded by a loving family and two affectionate dogs. When she isn't writing her novels for Bold Strokes Books, she works on her art, and crafts, whenever possible—certain that practice pays off. Gun loves creating cover art for her own books and others using digital art software.

Web site: http://www.gbrooke-fiction.com
Facebook: http://www.facebook.com/gunbach
Twitter: http://twitter.com/redheadgrrl1960

Books Available from Bold Strokes Books

Flight SQA016 by Amanda Radley. Fastidious airline passenger Olivia Lewis is used to things being a certain way. When her routine is changed by a new, attractive member of the staff, sparks fly. (978-1-63679-045-9)

Home Is Where the Heart Is by Jenny Frame. Can Archie make the countryside her home and give Ash the fairytale romance she desires? Or will the countryside and small village life all be too much for her? (978-1-63555-922-4)

Moving Forward by PJ Trebelhorn. The last person Shelby Ryan expects to be attracted to is Iris Calhoun, the sister of the man who killed her wife four years and three thousand miles ago. (978-1-63555-953-8)

Poison Pen by Jean Copeland. Debut author Kendra Blake is finally living her best life until a nasty book review and exposed secrets threaten her promising new romance with aspiring journalist Alison Chatterley. (978-1-63555-849-4)

Seasons for Change by KC Richardson. Love, laughter, and trust develop for Shawn and Morgan throughout the changing seasons of Lake Tahoe. (978-1-63555-882-1)

Summer Lovin' by Julie Cannon. Three different women, three exotic locations, one unforgettable summer. What do you think will happen? (978-1-63555-920-0)

Unbridled by D. Jackson Leigh. A visit to a local stable turns into more than riding lessons between a novel writer and an equestrian with a taste for power play. (978-1-63555-847-0)

VIP by Jackie D. In a town where relationships are forged and shattered by perception, sometimes even love can't change who you really are. (978-1-63555-908-8)

Yearning by Gun Brooke. The sleepy town of Dennamore has an irresistible pull on those who've moved away. The mystery Darian Tennen and Samantha Pike uncover will change them forever, but the love they find along the way just might be the key to saving themselves. (978-1-63555-757-2)

A Turn of Fate by Ronica Black. Will Nev and Kinsley finally face their painful past and relent to their powerful, forbidden attraction? Or will facing their past be too much to fight through? (978-1-63555-930-9)

Desires After Dark by MJ Williamz. When her human lover falls deathly ill, Alex, a vampire, must decide which is worse, letting her go or condemning her to everlasting life. (978-1-63555-940-8)

Her Consigliere by Carsen Taite. FBI agent Royal Scott swore an oath to uphold the law, and criminal defense attorney Siobhan Collins pledged her loyalty to the only family she's ever known, but will their love be stronger than the bonds they've vowed to others, or will their competing allegiances tear them apart? (978-1-63555-924-8)

In Our Words: Queer Stories from Black, Indigenous, and People of Color Writers. Stories Selected by Anne Shade and Edited by Victoria Villaseñor. Comprising both the renowned and emerging voices of Black, Indigenous, and People of Color authors, this thoughtfully curated collection of short stories explores the intersection of racial and queer identity. (978-1-63555-936-1)

Measure of Devotion by CF Frizzell. Disguised as her late twin brother, Catherine Samson enters the Civil War to defend the Constitution as a Union soldier, never expecting her life to be altered by a Gettysburg farmer's daughter. (978-1-63555-951-4)

Not Guilty by Brit Ryder. Claire Weaver and Emery Pearson's day jobs clash, even as their desire for each other burns, and a discreet sex-only arrangement is the only option. (978-1-63555-896-8)

Opposites Attract: Butch/Femme Romances by Meghan O'Brien, Aurora Rey, Angie Williams. Sometimes opposites really do attract. Fall in love with these butch/femme romance novellas. (978-1-63555-784-8)

Swift Vengeance by Jean Copeland, Jackie D, Erin Zak. A journalist becomes the subject of her own investigation when sudden strange, violent visions summon her to a summer retreat and into the arms of a killer's possible next victim. (978-1-63555-880-7)

Under Her Influence by Amanda Radley. On their path to #truelove, will Beth and Jemma discover that reality is even better than illusion? (978-1-63555-963-7)

Wasteland by Kristin Keppler & Allisa Bahney. Danielle Clark is fighting against the National Armed Forces and finds peace as a scavenger, until the NAF general's daughter, Katelyn Turner, shows up on her doorstep and brings the fight right back to her. (978-1-63555-935-4)

When in Doubt by VK Powell. Police officer Jeri Wylder thinks she committed a crime in the line of duty but can't remember, until details emerge pointing to a cover-up by those close to her. (978-1-63555-955-2)

A Woman to Treasure by Ali Vali. An ancient scroll isn't the only treasure Levi Montbard finds as she starts her hunt for the truth—all she has to do is prove to Yasmine Hassani that there's more to her than an adventurous soul. (978-1-63555-890-6)

Before. After. Always. by Morgan Lee Miller. Still reeling from her tragic past, Eliza Walsh has sworn off taking risks, until Blake Navarro turns her world right-side up, making her question if falling in love again is worth it. (978-1-63555-845-6)

Bet the Farm by Fiona Riley. Lauren Calloway's luxury real estate sale of the century comes to a screeching halt when dairy farm heiress, and one-night stand, Thea Boudreaux calls her bluff. (978-1-63555-731-2)

Cowgirl by Nance Sparks. The last thing Aren expects is to fall for Carol. Sharing her home is one thing, but sharing her heart means sharing the demons in her past and risking everything to keep Carol safe. (978-1-63555-877-7)

Give In to Me by Elle Spencer. Gabriela Talbot never expected to sleep with her favorite author—certainly not after the scathing review she'd given Whitney Ainsworth's latest book. (978-1-63555-910-1)

Hidden Dreams by Shelley Thrasher. A lethal virus and its resulting vision send Texan Barbara Allan and her lovely guide, Dara, on a journey up Cambodia's Mekong River in search of Barbara's mother's mystifying past. (978-1-63555-856-2)

In the Spotlight by Lesley Davis. For actresses Cole Calder and Eris Whyte, their chance at love runs out fast when a fan's adoration turns to obsession. (978-1-63555-926-2)

Origins by Jen Jensen. Jamis Bachman is pulled into a dangerous mystery that becomes personal when she learns the truth of her origins as a ghost hunter. (978-1-63555-837-1)

Pursuit: A Victorian Entertainment by Felice Picano. An intelligent, handsome, ruthlessly ambitious young man who rose from the slums to become the right-hand man of the Lord Exchequer of England will stop at nothing as he pursues his Lord's vanished wife across Continental Europe. (978-1-63555-870-8)

Unrivaled by Radclyffe. Zoey Cohen will never accept second place in matters of the heart, even when her rival is a career, and Declan Black has nothing left to give of herself or her heart. (978-1-63679-013-8)

A Fae Tale by Genevieve McCluer. Dovana comes to terms with her changing feelings for her lifelong best friend and fae, Roze. (978-1-63555-918-7)

Accidental Desperados by Lee Lynch. Life is clobbering Berry, Jaudon, and their long romance. The arrival of directionless baby dyke MJ doesn't help. Can they find their passion again—and keep it? (978-1-63555-482-3)

Always Believe by Aimée. Greyson Walsden is pursuing ordination as an Anglican priest. Angela Arlingham doesn't believe in God. Do they follow their vocation or their hearts? (978-1-63555-912-5)

Best of the Wrong Reasons by Sander Santiago. For Fin Ness and Orion Starr, it takes a funeral to remind them that love is worth living for. (978-1-63555-867-8)

Courage by Jesse J. Thoma. No matter how often Natasha Parsons and Tommy Finch clash on the job, an undeniable attraction simmers just beneath the surface. Can they find the courage to change so love has room to grow? (978-1-63555-802-9)

I Am Chris by R Kent. There's one saving grace to losing everything and moving away. Nobody knows her as Chrissy Taylor. Now Chris can live who he truly is. (978-1-63555-904-0)

The Princess and the Odium by Sam Ledel. Jastyn and Princess Aurelia return to Venostes and join their families in a battle against the dark force to take back their homeland for a chance at a better tomorrow. (978-1-63555-894-4)

The Queen Has a Cold by Jane Kolven. What happens when the heir to the throne isn't a prince or a princess? (978-1-63555-878-4)

The Secret Poet by Georgia Beers. Agreeing to help her brother woo Zoe Blake seemed like a good idea to Morgan Thompson at first…until she realizes she's actually wooing Zoe for herself… (978-1-63555-858-6)

You Again by Aurora Rey. For high school sweethearts Kate Cormier and Sutton Guidry, the second chance might be the only one that matters. (978-1-63555-791-6)

Coming to Life on South High by Lee Patton. Twenty-one-year-old gay virgin Gabe Rafferty's first adult decade unfolds as an unpredictable journey into sex, love, and livelihood. (978-1-63555-906-4)

Love's Falling Star by B.D. Grayson. For country music megastar Lochlan Paige, can love conquer her fear of losing the one thing she's worked so hard to protect? (978-1-63555-873-9)

Love's Truth by C.A. Popovich. Can Lynette and Barb make love work when unhealed wounds of betrayed trust and a secret could change everything? (978-1-63555-755-8)

Next Exit Home by Dena Blake. Home may be where the heart is, but for Harper Sims and Addison Foster, is the journey back worth the pain? (978-1-63555-727-5)

Not Broken by Lyn Hemphill. Falling in love is hard enough—even more so for Rose who's carrying her ex's baby. (978-1-63555-869-2)

The Noble and the Nightingale by Barbara Ann Wright. Two women on opposite sides of empires at war risk all for a chance at love. (978-1-63555-812-8)

What a Tangled Web by Melissa Brayden. Clementine Monroe has the chance to buy the café she's managed for years, but Madison LeGrange swoops in and buys it first. Now Clementine is forced to work for the enemy and ignore her former crush. (978-1-63555-749-7)

Lightning Source UK Ltd.
Milton Keynes UK
UKHW011003040122
396596UK00002B/652

9 781635 557572